Rattlesnakes Strike Twice

EA Mayes

Dark Sun Press

Chapter One

M inoa found her old buddy's house where the gummy asphalt succumbed to parched earth. A few dirt brown stucco houses clustered like survivors of a desert expedition. Beyond, a late summer evening mellowed a panorama of rangeland backed by mesas backed by mountain ranges.

Only a couple vehicles hunkered in front so there'd be no crowd of mourners to hide in. Her hand clutched the key in the ignition, her foot moved to rest on the old truck's clutch pedal, fantasizing escape, but some vestige of propriety clocked in. So she checked her image in the rearview mirror and forced steps up the walkway.

The front door swung open revealing Dreema's mom, Georgia, on the threshold, grabbing the door frame, trembling like a dust devil threatened to whoosh her into space. Her gray eyes looked sun-blinded.

"Hi Georgia, I'm Minoa."

"Come on in. Glad you could come."

Georgia started to turn around, paused and looked back at her.

"Minoa?" She blinked several times. "My goodness, all the way from ... where were you? Tha-anks for coming."

She shuffled through an entry hall toward an illuminated room. Minoa followed, entering a living room furnished in fake leopard skin and gold shag. Vases of flowers blocked a huge flat screen. A sliding glass door in the back house wall framed a two-tone vista: two-thirds sky turning aquamarine, one third beige desert.

In the center of the room a man and a woman stood looking awkward. It took her a couple brain-clunks to recognize the man as Dreema's younger brother, all grown up now. She'd ignored his existence when he was a skinny kid with knotty elbows and glasses slipping down his nose. Now he wore a blazer and tie and sported a spotty mustache. Georgia disappeared through a cantilevered door.

"Bobby," Minoa said, extending her hand. "I'm so very sorry."

"Minoa, thanks for coming. They call me Berry now."

He shook her hand as if weary, then his hand went so limp it slid from her grasp. He moved to a table with bottles, cans and chips and fiddled. The woman wore a beaded headband over a mane of strawberry blonde hair, silver and turquoise earrings dangling to her shoulders. She clutched Minoa's hand between her two, staring with huge cornflower blue eyes.

"I'm Inanna. Dreema spoke of you."

"She did?"

"Dreema participated in a group I lead. She was there on the night of her death. I never imagined it would be the last time."

Minoa nodded.

"It's awful."

"She often spoke of you."

"Of me?"

"She envied you. You went out into the world and achieved so much."

"Right. Look, we lost touch over the years. I was in New York and then Ecuador."

"She told me about your anthropological studies and your travels among the indigenous people of South America. It sounds fascinating."

"I did my fieldwork in Ecuador. I didn't know Dreema was interested."

"I certainly am. Tell me, did you observe native people going into trance?"

"Well, I was, in part, trying to determine how traditional shamanic practices have changed since pacification. I was working with the Huaorani near Yasuni National Park."

"They use ayahuasca, don't they?"

"Uh, yeah."

"Did you try it?"

"I'm not sure this is the moment ..."

To escape Inanna's stare she gazed out the sliding glass door at a backyard pockmarked by little pools of shadow thrown by the sinking sun, maybe prairie dog burrows. Surely not rattler holes. A Chinese elm at the property line, leaves laced with insect borings, caught the last rays of the day. She turned back to the room where failing light bled the leopard skin print.

"Do you know how Dreema died? Was she ill?"

"The manner of her death is archaic." Inanna flipped a curtain of hair over her shoulder. "Fatally struck by a serpent while lying in bed."

"What? A rattlesnake bit her in bed? How could that happen?"

"Apparently she slept with the sliding glass door open."

"Why didn't they give her anti-venom? People rarely die of rattler bite anymore."

"She was dead when they found her."

"*Dios mío*, how tragic."

"Death can be a door of liberation to a tortured soul."

Minoa's flesh plumped with a burst of angry blood.

"What are you talking about?" She noticed her voice ring too loud and tamped it down. "Dreema was only thirty-six. She had a child, a husband."

"Ex-husband. She was divorcing Amilcar. I only referred to her depression. Incarnation is temporary for all of us."

"I suppose."

To avoid more conversation she moved to the sliding glass door and pressed her cheek against it. Beyond the strip of scabrous yards, beyond the hills crumbling where the terrain rose, lay a plain she remembered from the last time she saw Dreema. She'd come back to New Mexico for her dad's funeral, then met up with Dreema and her new boyfriend, Amilcar. Nothing else to do until her return flight, nobody else she wanted to see.

They'd driven in his double cab pickup out across the desert south of town making small talk, gossip about people they'd known in high school. The pickup bushwhacked across bunch grass desert and dry bed arroyos to crawl up a hillside and perch on a bluff. Dreema spread a cloth on a rock and set out supermarket containers of fried chicken, potato salad, neon-frosted cake. She'd asked, a piece of cake poised on a fork in front of her mouth, if Minoa would move back to Santa Fe? A laugh, a quip, something to avoid answering. Then a lull.

Afterward Amilcar had handed Minoa a pistol. She'd fired, staggering from the jolt to her arm and shoulder as puffs of dust arose on the distant mesa side. Dreema had laughed saying a woman who travels alone should know how to defend herself. Then Amilcar took sips from a tall can of beer, surveying the surrounding desert through eye slits. Suddenly, he raised the pistol and fired, blasting rock chips off a nearby boulder. Dreema screamed. Minoa jumped.

"Why are you firing so close?"

"Rattler."

In the direction of fire she saw a small rattlesnake lying on a low rock, its head now blasted to smithereens leaving a reddish stain that would be mistaken for iron ore within a day.

"Oooh, I hate them."

Dreema had wrapped her arms around her ribs with a shiver.

An anguished cry gushed out of the slatted doors where Georgia had disappeared. Berry lurched. Minoa and Inanna spun around to stare.

"This house was your idea."

Georgia's voice bounced from word to word like a rock ricocheting down a slope.

"I got her a fantastic deal. How was I supposed to know some rattler would get in?" A deep voice.

"We should have made the house safer. Why didn't we ..."

"What in the hell was she doing leaving her door open?"

"She trusted ...."

"She trusted drug pushers and soothsayers. Like that New Age cult leader. She turned away from Jesus for that witchcraft."

"It wasn't witchcraft. Anyway, she threw Amilcar out. What more could she do?" Sobs.

Berry hurried to the doors, disappeared inside.

"She's been going downhill ever since Loren left. Now you got to come on home."

"Dad, Mom, please."

"She was trying to ... to find a life for herself."

A pan clattered to the floor, grunts mixed with a strangled cry.

"No!" Berry's voice.

Minoa froze in ready pose, tempted to run over but unsure, perplexed by Inanna's relaxed posture.

"The family is traumatized but the pain must be surrendered to the plenum where all healing occurs."

"The plenum?"

"The womb of our mother, the goddess. She is rising once again after millennia of suppression." She handed Minoa a card fished from a fringed leather pouch. "I'll be going now. Come visit the Tuesday group sometime. I'm sure you'll find it helpful."

She strode to the front door, skirts swishing around tanned ankles, one ringed by a silver and turquoise anklet. Minoa glanced at the card. 'Women Rising' said the heading followed by some address in Pojoaque. Sounds of clinking china and splashing water emerged from the kitchen. Glancing around she saw nobody and was about to make an escape when Georgia stumbled out the kitchen door.

"Oh, Minoa, I'm sorry we left you alone. I'm so ... distracted."

She passed a limp hand across her forehead where permed locks of graying frizz clung to damp skin.

"Why don't you sit down?"

Minoa gestured at a chair and Georgia tumbled sideways into it. Minoa froze. Was she collapsing? But Georgia rooted around in the chair and sorted herself into the posture of a leaking rag doll.

"Can I get you something?"

"No, I'm alright, I just ..."

She buried her face in her hands as silent sobs shook her body. Minoa's gut clenched. She forced a few ragged breaths between pursed lips, scoured the empty room. Found no answers. Felt like a blithering fool for all her self-centered complaining. Finally patted Georgia's bony shoulder blade.

"I understand this is horrible. Is there anything at all I could do? Should I come by tomorrow afternoon? I could run errands, clean up, whatever you need."

Georgia nodded without looking up, continuing the soundless jerking movements that caused her shiny polyester blouse to ripple as if touched by a breeze.

Something moved on the periphery of Minoa's vision. She jumped and turned to face a little girl in footed pajamas standing in the entrance to a darkened hallway. Thick chestnut hair fell from her head like a mop. From beneath overgrown bangs she glared at Minoa as if she had caused this incomprehensible life disruption.

"Aracely?"

No response. When she took a few steps into the living room, Minoa saw that one of her irises fractured on the rim into a tiny starburst, almost as if she'd seen something so awful it ruptured the cornea. Shifting her focus to Georgia the girl's face convulsed as she squeezed out a wail that wouldn't stop, pitch rising and rising.

"Mommy!" she screamed, "I want Mommy!"

As Minoa approached the wail sharpened to an ear-piercing shriek. She backed away making pacifying gestures. Georgia rose and plodded over to the girl, lifted her onto her hip and carried her over to look out the sliding glass door.

"There, there."

She smoothed the child's hair over and over. Outside, the lowering sun darkened multiple receding layers of mesas and mountains to an inky plum. The girl laid her head on Georgia's shoulder, occasional sobs whipping her tiny body. A squeezed down conversation between Berry and his dad in the kitchen textured background noises. Suddenly a crack on the front door rent the stuffy air.

"Shall I get it?"

When there was no reply, Minoa headed to the entry. As she grasped the doorknob and pulled, a twilight gust blew into the house spewing dust and bits of paper into the air. A slender man with dark wavy hair and bad skin stood on the threshold, one hand held out in front as if to stop the door from shutting in his face.

"I've come for my daughter."

Minoa hesitated, unsure what to say.

"Amilcar? Just a moment."

"You? You're here?"

He pushed the door wider and strode past her into the living room. Minoa followed. Georgia was standing in front of the sliding glass door, arms clasped around Aracely, staring wide-eyed.

"Brereton!"

"I don't want no trouble. But I'm her dad and her mom's dead. She's got to come with me."

"You're not supposed to be here. There's a protection order. Brereton, please."

"Protection order don't work when somebody's dead."

Brereton Sr. stepped out of the kitchen. He paused, muscular arms crossed over a belly barely softer than the steely abdomen Minoa remembered from high school.

"What are you doing here? You're not welcome here."

"I'm taking my daughter. I can get her things later."

Amilcar walked toward Georgia, reaching his arms out. Berry strode over and positioned himself between him and his mother.

"Hold it right there. You need a judge's order to transfer custody."

"You can work on that. For now, I'm her closest relative."

He moved around Berry but ran into his uplifted arm.

"I said you need legal papers to take custody."

"Nobody takes my daughter away from me."

Amilcar grabbed Berry's arm by the wrist and wrenched it down. Brereton Sr. took a step forward.

"Hey, hey, there's no call for that kind of behavior."

As Berry regained his balance, he cocked the other arm back and launched a fist into Amilcar's jaw. Amilcar whirled around folding at the waist like a dropped marionette. When he stood up and turned back to face a panting Berry bouncing on the balls of his feet, he held a hunting knife, tip aimed at Berry. Everyone stared.

"No, please," whined Georgia.

"Now wait just a minute."

Brereton took another step forward, hands in front.

"Stay out of the way, old man."

Amilcar carved a circle in the air with the knife, then took another step towards Berry. Berry seemed to thin out in real time, his spine curving backward to evade the gut cut he imagined coming, arms floating up, hands trembling like quaking aspen leaves. His face stretched longways in an expression of terror tugging at incredulity.

"Stop!"

Georgia's exclamation taffy-twisted into a moan. Brereton took another step, waving an index finger like a school principal cautioning the school bad boy.

"You drop that knife right now."

Minoa thought she saw Amilcar's lips curve up at the corners. Was he enjoying this bullying performance or would he knife his ex-brother-in-law? She scanned the room to see if something lay within reach that she could throw at him but saw nothing. After a breathless moment Georgia stepped in front of Berry and held Aracely out.

"Take her. You're her father. Just don't hurt anyone."

"Mom, don't," Berry said, but didn't move.

Amilcar took the girl into one arm. She whimpered but wrapped her arms around his shoulders. Georgia's hands tumbled to her sides. Brereton dropped his wagging index finger.

"You had no call to interrupt my daughter's wake. I'll report this to police."

"Just remember: you're gonna have to ask me for permission to see Aracely."

Amilcar spun around and strode out the front door, leaving it open. For a moment no one moved. Then Georgia doubled over and stumbled down the hallway. Berry called out 'Mom!' and ran after her as Brereton backed out of sight into the kitchen. Minoa dashed to the front door in time to see Amilcar's silver pickup flash out of sight. She paused there with a trembling hand on the doorknob, glancing back and forth between the vacated road end and a square of illuminated living space at the end of the entry hall.

"Berry? Georgia?"

No response. She pulled the door shut and headed down the driveway.

***

At Lucky Coyote Casino that night Minoa mixed drinks and popped the lids off beer bottles in a whirl, nauseated by the swirling scene, the memory of her evening at Dreema's wake like a rancid after-taste. Toward midnight she had a moment to prop her elbows on the bar and observe the casino floor: gamblers cackling and hooting with over-amped gestures like this was the night they'd finally reverse all the years of sour luck, hallucinating a moment of beating the system as if they wouldn't wake tomorrow to the same old grinding routine.

Her thoughts wound their way back to the wake. She told herself it didn't matter if Amilcar kidnapped Aracely or Dreema died young of snakebite. Because what's done is done and it doesn't matter if you spend all day wishing it turned out different. Still, some spunky seven-year-old part of herself stomped her foot and said it wasn't fair.

She knew poisonous snakes. She'd spent several years living on dirt floors in a rainforest with some of the most dangerous snakes on the face of the globe. The fer-de-lance loved human dwellings and could float on water and reach branches twenty feet above ground. It was a notorious grouch and its bite caused amputations or death in most anybody who wasn't near anti-venom. Then there were all the viper cousins, eyelash, pit, the bushmaster. And boas and anacondas, hanging out of trees, waiting in rivers. She'd lived in fear in the *Oriente*, ever conscious she was eight hours in canoe and six in bus from the nearest clinic.

Yet back in Santa Fe Dreema leaves the sliding glass door open one night and ends up dead of rattlesnake venom. Dreema who never left town, who sashayed from one local bad luck encounter to another. Who'd already suffered a loss that made your thorax ache to think about it. Now this? Made you fear the maliciousness of fate. Or the malevolence of local spirits. She'd fled New Mexico to escape those screaming *La Lloronas* that dragged off locals to their death. Now they'd killed her old high school buddy.

A server put up an order at the end of the bar. Minoa went back to work on the assembly line of dream concoctions, placing olives and lime slices and miniature parasols to prettify those bubbly potions meant to distract the gamblers from their losses.

A couple hours after midnight the casino emptied. She scrubbed the bar for closing and headed down the highway to Brent's estate north of downtown Santa Fe and her one room rented guesthouse. Shut out billions of stars, trillions of grains of sand and who knew how many rattlesnakes, curled up under an alpaca wool blanket and for once slept through the night.

Chapter Two

M inoa pulled a hand off the steering wheel to punch the call receive button on the phone tossed onto the seat. The distraction almost made her crash into a monster pickup truck zooming out of a car wash to swerve all the way across Cerrillos Road, flinging a rainbow spray of drops that evaporated before it hit the asphalt. She braked hard, screamed a curse in Spanish out the open window. Ireni's clear voice spouting out of the cell speaker over the traffic sounds brought her back.

"What's going on?"

"Hey, Reni. Near fatality but I'm okay. Can you talk?"

"Bomb makers are at lunch. I'm taking a walk around Los Alamos on my break so talk away."

"An old friend of mine died. Dreema Adkins. A rattlesnake bit her in her own bedroom. Think of the improbability, Reni."

"Shocking. Don't tell me you're treating this as some sort of black swan event?"

"Who would ever imagine such a thing could happen? The probability must be infinitesimal. Way beyond bad luck."

"A single death by rattlesnake strike is random and unpredictable. But anyone living in New Mexico faces a higher probability of getting bit by a rattler than the national rate. Probably close to your chance of getting killed by a drunk driver and more than getting struck by lightning."

"She left a young daughter. She was screaming for her mom. It was heartbreaking."

"That's awful. I'm sorry about your old friend."

"I'm going out to help her mom. She's destroyed."

"Understandable. But be careful. You don't want to get bit by a rattler like her."

"Of course I won't. If it was a black swan event, it won't happen again for a long time. Maybe never."

"I don't know about that. Strange stuff happens in New Mexico. Remember that black bear that crashed through some woman's living room window up north?"

"And ate her?"

"The drought produces food scarcity up and down the food chain. Poor bear was starving."

"That's crazy. The thing is, if anybody deserved to die of snakebite, it's me."

"Weird way of putting it."

"I spent years in a snake-infested rainforest."

"We had plenty of cobras and vipers in the Thai highlands, Min."

"Yeah, but you were a child there with doting parents while I tramped all over the rainforest with native people who knew what they were doing. Problem was I didn't."

"So you feel guilty that a snake didn't bite you? Min, what the hell."

"I just feel sorry I forgot about Dreema. She helped me survive my teenage traumas."

"It's easy to lose contact when you move around."

"I guess I thought I'd never come home. Anyway, I'll help with the packing at Dreema's place. Not much else I can do."

"Good idea. Avoid idle hands and all that."

"Have fun with your day of bomb making."

"Hah hah. I'm just a gofer for all these nuclear weapons scientists at the lab so I bear no moral responsibility for the destruction their toys may cause, right?"

"You're absolved, Reni."

She survived the congestion where Cerrillos met Airport Road and picked up speed heading south. Spotted Tierra Feliz out on the plateau west of the interstate, an outpost of criss-crossed asphalt strips on naked desert. After passing the sales office she ticked past rows of fake adobe houses to the end of Dreema's street.

As she stepped out, her gaze met that of a woman on the other side of the street supervising tots clambering over climbing toys scattered across the yard. A hint of friendliness in the eyes encouraged Minoa to cross over.

"You are sister of the woman who die?"

The woman furrowed her brow so much the ponytail of black hair on the top of her head stood up straighter.

"In a way."

"It is terrible. She so young and beautiful. I am sorry."

"Did you know her well?"

"No. I have three kids and I babysit." She spread her hands to indicate the little ones. "But we talk about problems with houses. She making group to fight the company to fix it."

"Neighbors here are demanding remediation of their homes?"

The woman nodded.

"Do all the houses have problems?"

"Oh, *sí*. The floor, the roof, the windows — *todo*."

"Have snakes entered any other houses?"

"We got in the garage." She pronounced this last word with 'hey' at the end. "Four time this summer. I scared the kids get bit."

"That's frightening."

"But the *pobre señora* have worse—in her 'bat-room.' I think lucky the little girl not kill, but now the *mamá*!"

Minoa had to think this over.

"Are you saying the snake that killed Dreema went into the bathroom first and then into the bedroom where it bit her?"

"No, no, before, *antes*. The little girl find big snake like this" — she joined her fingertips to make a large circle — "when she go to the bathroom. 'Mommy, snake!' she yell. Otherwise she dead. That's why the lady making group. We all scared we find snakes in our houses."

"That's ... unbelievable."

"Miguelito, *párate*!"

A chubby little boy started after a ball that rolled into the street and she ran after him. Minoa waved and headed for Dreema's house. She rang the bell three times. Gave her time to wonder if getting involved in the world she'd fled was a wise idea. She was turning to leave when the door swung open. Georgia blinked as if emerging from a cave.

"I'm sorry if I woke you. Should I come back later?"

Georgia shook her head, shuffled back to the living room, sat down, stared up at Minoa like an obedient school child.

"What can I do to help?"

A lightning spasm convulsed her face as if to say, 'You can't help. Nobody can.' She glanced at the entry as if expecting someone to arrive. Looked back at Minoa. The pupils of her eyes were huge, filling the iris.

"We have to move out, I mean, I have to."

"Where will you go?"

"I ... I'll have to go back to my husband."

Now she turned to stare out the sliding glass door on the back of the house. Seconds ticked by.

"I should have protected her."

Her voice was so low Minoa struggled to hear.

"Look, Georgia, I understand there are problems with these houses and a snake even got in once before. Maybe there's a hole in the foundation or a nest of snakes in the crawl space. But Dreema's death was an accident. No one could know a rattlesnake would bite her in bed."

"I never protected her like a mother should. I was always too scared. I'm just a scared old woman."

She hit a fist on her thigh, then dropped the hand to dangle near the floor. A little moan escaped. Minoa scanned the room, sucked a breath.

"After something horrific happens, we think we could have avoided it if only we'd paid attention or done something differently. Everybody feels that way."

"Her dream ... was to be free ... Maybe now she is."

Georgia's head fell like a gavel to her chest.

"Let me get you something to drink."

Minoa hurried to the kitchen. Filling a glass at the tap she noticed a bottle of prescription Diazepam on the counter. Counted the pills. Eight missing, not enough to kill even if Georgia had swallowed them all at once. She walked out, handed her the glass. Georgia's face drooped, all emotion wiped away, her voice monotone.

"Could you pack some toys and clothes for Aracely? Maybe you could take it to Amilcar's house? Berry shouldn't go."

"Of course. You just relax. I'll take care of everything."

She headed down the hallway. In Aracely's bedroom she found a princess motif suitcase and filled it with neatly folded pastel clothes, adding a few toys and a purple pig with pink satin ribbon sitting on the pillow, fuzzy fibers rubbed off in spots. When she carried the bag out and placed it by the front door, Georgia lay on the sofa asleep.

Passing back down the hall she spied a bathroom on her left and paused to try to imagine a rattlesnake coiled up beside the toilet hissing at little Aracely. Her mind balked.

n Dreema's bedroom sunshine from a sliding glass door bleached everything except a black bedstead. She walked across the matted carpet trying to imagine a rattlesnake beside the bed. Her mind went along this time. She saw Dreema asleep as a rattler slithered over the door runners seeking warmth on a chilly night. Maybe Dreema dropped an arm over the side of the bed startling the snake which struck by self-protective instinct. Then Dreema jumped up, screaming in pain and shock, calling for help.

Stop. That visualization didn't work. Inanna said she died in bed. But anyone bit by a rattlesnake would scream for help or call 911. Maybe the snake bit her over and over so the poison immobilized her? No, she'd heard that once a rattler was milked, subsequent bites contained no venom. Rattlesnake venom didn't produce a coma and it didn't kill in a few seconds like those east Indian asps in Sherlock Holmes stories. So why would she have lain there in agony as her arm swelled to the point of ripping the skin, waiting alone to die?

What difference did it make? It was too late to do anything now. She opened the top drawer of a chest and found a shoe box of photos. Despite telling herself she shouldn't, she sat on the edge of the bed and began to thumb through them.

The first few showed Georgia holding Aracely before one of those indoor merry-go-rounds they have at shopping malls. Then several of Dreema's dad, Brereton Sr., the child on his back as he crawled on all fours, riding on his shoulders, hanging upside down, her ankles in his hands.

She kept shuffling through. Came to shots of family members grouped around a Christmas tree. In one Berry stood with his arm around some young woman, cute and petite, not statuesque and striking like Dreema. The whirl back through time continued to a snapshot of Dreema in cutoffs and halter top, a baby in her arms, Amilcar's arm around her shoulders.

Minoa's swirl of curiosity faltered under a sensation like a rock sinking in her belly. She gazed out the sliding glass door on the back wall of the bedroom, remembering. If she'd stayed in town would her camera roll contain happy family get-togethers like these? No, it'd be a roll of sad-faced selfies. Her mom gone, her dad ... well, impaired and herself alone. With willpower she shut down that mortifying fantasy.

Rifled through more photos pausing at another of Dreema, barely out of her teens, long hair, dowdy shift. Next to her a towheaded toddler boy. On the child's other side stood a muscly fellow, knuckled hands dangling, crew cut above a receding hairline. That was the lost child, the one her first ex- kidnapped.

Minoa stared as if she could time-travel back and do something to stop that life-shattering event from happening. She'd been in New York, heard about it but didn't even break stride in her life of books and classes and thinking, thinking, thinking to comfort her old buddy. Oh well. They'd already distanced by then so what did it matter? Plenty of people lost their moms, right? The little boy wouldn't even remember Dreema. He'd never know she died of a rattler's bite.

Paged through more snapshots while telling herself to get to work. Near the bottom of the pile she came to a shot of Dreema and her in their senior high prom dresses, arms around each other's waists, hair teased up into strange lumps on their heads. A wave of heat rolled up her face. They'd been like sisters in those days. She glanced out the sliding glass door for visual escape. It was open a few inches leaving swamp-cooled air to pour out a sagging screen.

She moved over to slide the door shut and froze, listening. After a moment she heard it again. Not a car backfiring, not a leftover firecracker. Some teenager shooting jackrabbits out in the desert? She opened the screen and stepped outside, pulling the glass door shut behind her.

Instantly heat enveloped her evaporating the film of air-conditioned chill off her skin. As she listened individual noises punctured a vast silence: the slamming of a car door down the street, the distant rumbling of a semi-truck passing on the interstate. She tiptoed past two fraying lawn chairs to where the moribund lawn surrendered to pebbled dirt. Then she heard it again: rifle fire for sure. Was there a shooting range out beyond the hills? More likely some laid-off gun enthusiast with a case of beer cans and too much time to kill.

She walked out of the yard leaving the straggly row of houses behind. Avoiding cactus spines by habit, she moved toward a juniper-dotted slope ahead, dwarfed by the overarching bowl of turquoise. A few more shots rang out as she walked, not frequent enough for target practice or drunken hijinks. Her squinting eyes scoured the landscape of low hills crested by rock ledges, naked land folded by dry bed arroyos, lunar against a cardboard backdrop of flat-topped mesas and teal cordilleras.

At the crest of a hill she ducked behind a boulder before peeking over the other side. There lay another glittery slope trailing down to another arroyo. She caught sight of two figures near a monster SUV parked far down the arroyo just before it buckled out of sight. One had a rifle tucked into his shoulder while the other moved some pole along the ground. Prospectors, she wondered? Another rifle shot rang out. Why was that guy firing into the air? If only she had binoculars.

She made a run for a juniper farther down the arroyo edge. Now a rocky outcrop blocked her view. Hunched over she scurried to a cluster of rabbit brush within shooting range of the SUV and crouched behind. Parting the branches she saw the figure with a pole, sporting a ten-gallon Stetson, lift something from the ground, something long and wriggly — a snake. Spotted a good-sized rattle at the tip of the tail. The figure dropped the snake into a container in the back of the SUV.

What the hell? Had snake-trapping become a business? Legal or black market? Either way, why would a snake-trapper want to draw attention to his activities by having someone stand by and fire off rifle shots at the cloudless sky?

The trapper and the rifleman climbed into the vehicle, drove up the riverbed coming closer to her inadequate blind. Stopped about twenty yards down. She waited, squatting on the balls of her feet, thighs burning, as the trapper scouted up and down the banks of the arroyo while the rifleman stood by the car. His arms, she now saw, crawled with tattoos.

The trapper paused to peer under an overhang at the lip of the arroyo. The brim of the Stetson blocked Minoa's view of his face and his view of her. When he looked up she saw with a start that it was a woman, face fringed by gray wisps, scored with its own topography of eroded channels. She stiffened, unable to invent a credible excuse to explain her presence. But the trapper woman turned without betraying awareness of her and headed back to the SUV. As soon as the pair climbed in and continued up the arroyo, the SUV's fat tires spitting sand, Minoa sprinted up the hill and slid behind a boulder.

Times had gone to hell while she was away, she thought as her breathing calmed. Senior citizens reduced to poaching Diamondbacks to survive. Laid off construction workers blowing their last paycheck at the casino. How was she supposed to reinvent herself in this rattlesnake-infested dust bowl? She stood and started striding back across the corrugated terrain, swinging her arms in a calming rhythm, lulled by the sauna temperatures of a late summer afternoon.

Suddenly a man stepped in front of her. A lopsided smile creased his unshaven face under an incongruous derby hat. A tattered overcoat hung to his shins. He reached out a scabby arm, closed fingers around her forearm. Instinctively she jerked her arm away. But within a fraction of a second, and without a thought, her old judo training kicked in and she shoved him with the other hand while hooking a foot around his calf and snapping back.

As he clattered onto the rocky ground, she took off running like an antelope, toes barely touching the ground. Sprinted all the way back to slam into the sliding glass door on Dreema's bedroom. Jerking the handle open she jumped inside, slammed it shut and peered through the glass to see if she'd been followed. Nothing ... no one ...

She paused in the cool gloom to think. *Ouchi gari*, major inner reaping throw. Not a perfect execution but it had erupted out of long distant memory and taken control of her body without conscious effort. During those years after her mom left, she'd spent afternoons after school at the judo dojo slamming people into the mat, or getting slammed, burning off rage and depression. Then she'd left for Columbia U. and forgotten all about it. Made her wonder what other memories would escape the dungeon where she'd locked them when she left New Mexico.

One thing was clear: the solitary soul-cleansing desert of her childhood now harbored animal traffickers, homeless mental patients and who knew what else. No clue who would pay for freshly caught rattlesnakes. Maybe the shots fired into the air scared snakes out of their holes? Ridiculous. She gave up pondering and started packing.

Chapter Three

Puttering along a dirt track south of Abiquiu, Minoa scanned the plateaus for Amilcar's place, peeved she'd trusted Georgia to describe the route. According to Georgia it was 'just outside Abiquiu,' but she'd been driving on dirt roads through open desert long enough to run out of songs she knew by heart. Below, the land splayed into finger mesas stretching to the Chama River valley. Above, scrubland rose to crumble at the foot of a volcanic plug blazing orange in the light of a sinking sun.

Topping an incline she tipped down toward another sandy riverbed, this one wider than the others she'd spun across on balding discount tires she couldn't afford to replace. Started down, pumping the brakes. Once on the arroyo bottom the tires sank deeper with each revolution until around the midpoint they spun. She gunned the motor, went nowhere.

Stepped out to take a look. Sand reached the bottom of the painted yellow wheel rims. She kicked at it. Soft as pudding, a quicksand combination of rock dust and silt. She climbed back in and revved the engine, tried rocking back and forth, finally just slammed the gas pedal to the floor and spit a curtain of sand out the back end. Paused with hands gripping the steering wheel so hard it hurt, breathing in short angry spurts. When she stepped out again the truck was dug in up to the frame.

She stomped her foot and yelled a curse into an immense dome of sky. The cry fizzled into deafening silence. There was no use looking in the back of the truck — she knew she wasn't carrying tools. She turned a full circle scanning the landscape and spied only one dwelling, so far away it was the size of her thumbnail.

Gazing blankly out across the clustered mesas above the Chama River Valley to the peaks of the Sangre de Cristos stretched along the eastern horizon, a chilling awareness of her situation seeped into her flesh. She estimated how many miles she'd driven from the highway. Then she thought over Georgia's description of where Amilcar lived. Either way she faced a long evening walk through remote country with the temperature in free fall. After a few minutes blasting hot air puffs into refrigerating air, she slipped on a flannel shirt, pocketed her cell, shouldered the princess motif suitcase and continued on foot.

As she walked the sun sank behind ridges leaving a twinkle of gold trailed by apricot radiance. A blanket of chilly air muffled the scorched landscape, penetrating the thin material of her clothes. She swung her arms higher, flexing fingers closed, open, closed, open. Squinting to follow the track, she belted out a popular song she remembered from the long bus rides to Quito, "*Quiero comprarle a la vida, cinco centavitos de felicidad.*" Five cents worth of happiness, went the song, was more than she could afford these days. Regardless, the last thing she needed was to run into a mountain lion on its twilight hunt.

The track passed arroyos and hillocks, curving past a crumbling adobe hut, straw-speckled walls melted to thigh level and a door frame standing empty, darkly drawn against the fading western glow. Peering into the purple evening she had to admit she couldn't see the track anymore. She stopped, dropped the suitcase, rubbed her arms, took stock. Realized that even if she did find Amilcar's place there might be nobody home. Should she call for help? She glanced at her phone. No service.

As her breaths shriveled, the yipping of coyotes sliced the air. Coyotes didn't usually attack people but the sound stiffened the hair on her icy skin. Then there was an answering cry — a dog. That meant either a house nearby or wild dogs in the area, meaning two bad alternatives: face a pack of half-starved feral mongrels or some Shepherd mix watchdog, the kind of mean-spirited cur barking from every property in northern New Mexico. She hoisted the suitcase and trudged up another slope.

A couple arroyos later, in a hollow amidst cottonwoods, she spotted a flat-roofed adobe with a pickup parked in front alongside some shadowy humps, maybe auto bodies. Listened hard for a dog but heard nothing. It would have smelled her by now if it was outside.

An illuminated window cast a fuzzy glow across the house front. The door was a massive hand-carved piece with the head of an Aztec warrior as a door knocker. She raised the warrior's head to knock but stopped in midair. From inside came the sound of yelling. A man's angry voice but she couldn't make out any words. Then the sound of a child crying, a girl's voice. She cocked her head, listening. Another cannonade of words thudded against the door. Backtracking a few paces she placed the suitcase in the pickup's bed. Then she sidled around the corner of the house to another window and peeked inside.

The ceiling sagged, the walls curved, traditional adobe slumped over the course of a century. A velveteen portrait of Elvis graced one wall; on another hung a bloody depiction of the crucifixion. Aracely appeared against a glowing TV screen. She looked scared. In the threshold of a hallway stood a young woman with curled tendrils hanging to her waist. Amilcar moved into Minoa's view, his back to her, jabbing his finger at the child.

Chemicals of outrage surged into Minoa's bloodstream. She positioned her cell up against the glass, daring him to act. When he cocked his arm and the hand flew out to Aracely's cheek, the camera flashed. Aracely reeled as Amilcar spun around, eyes spitting. Minoa jerked her phone from the glass and took off flying on toes with eyes. She was sliding into the first arroyo when she heard the front door open and Amilcar cry out.

"¿Qué diablos haces aquí? Cabrón!"

Crouching, she listened over the bellowing of her breathing to footsteps, pebbles skipping down a slope, a click — a rifle cock? She huddled there, quivering. The bastard. Stealing Aracely at knifepoint and then hitting her. No wonder Dreema had sought a protection order against him. The guy was violent and mean. Would he shoot her? Shootings for trespassing were pretty common in northern New Mexico; even if he shot her he might walk. What was her plan if he came upstream to where she was hiding? Run or give herself up?

She strained her ears, following the direction of his steps. First they approached, then retreated. Maybe he was going back to the house. She glanced up at the stars, countless glittering pinpricks, and thanked them. But then the steps approached again from the other side of the house. He was circling the house, probably planning to widen each circuit in a spiral to search his entire property. In the next revolution or two he would reach the place where she crouched. The raspy steps diminished again but she didn't move. Should she run up the arroyo into unknown country or head back to the truck?

Before she could decide what to do, the steps grew louder again. No time to run now so she froze. A cone of light from a flashlight passed about twenty feet on the other side of the salt cedar where she hunkered, sweeping back and forth across the ground. He muttered a string of curses as he walked. On the next lap he would walk right up this arroyo. She had fifteen seconds to move while he passed behind the house. Upstream or downstream? Into the outlands or back to a vehicle that didn't drive? Every runoff channel cutting these plateaus looked like every other, even in daylight. She'd wander lost in those uplands till dawn, maybe catch hypothermia and die. But if she headed back to the entry track, he'd likely find her. Could she lock herself inside the truck for protection?

The instant his footsteps dulled she took off running down the arroyo praying not to trip over rocks strewn along the stream bed. Sensed the track leading out of the arroyo more than saw it, starting up a slope just as the door of Amilcar's house banged open followed by a cascade of hoarse barks. He'd let the dog out.

She hesitated as the noise of her heart pumping filled the cavernous night sky. The sequence of barks stretched up to one side, probably following her scent to the arroyo where she'd hidden. It would come down the arroyo and find her in a moment. Could she beat it to the truck? She took off sprinting down the track. As she raced, pulses of excited yips followed her in an accelerating crescendo until, after a pile-up of galloping footfalls the beast leaped on her, knocking her to the ground. She snapped into a ball, then staggered up, the dog snapping at her back. As she stretched a leg for a stride the dog caught hold of her shirt tail and jerked backwards.

"*Buen chico!*" she heard from a distance.

Squirming around she brought her fist down on the dog's nose several times until it let go. Then shot up, mind fixed on an image of the stranded truck, trying to calculate how far down the track she'd left it. But the beast was on her again, leaping, twisting its body to slam paws onto her chest, slavering teeth clacking at her face.

She pushed its jaws away, driving her knee into the dog's chest to throw it off. Within a few strides the dog jumped her from behind, raking teeth down the back of her head, biting hair. She spun around, arms swinging, and flung the dog off sending a good combing's worth of hair with it. It bounded at her again. This time she had a foot up. Shot out her leg to launch it through space. At the instant she started running she heard a squeal followed by urgent whimpers. The dog must have landed on a cactus.

She had reached the crest of a rise and spotted the shadowy hulk of the truck ahead when she heard Amilcar call out.

"*Ay*, Rocky! *Qué te hizo*? I'm gonna kill you, son of a bitch!"

When the threat hit her eardrums she spun left and, without a thought, abandoned the track, sprinting into the desert, flying through darkness over a prickly carpet of cactus and yucca. She hardly felt the ground, it seemed she bicycled her legs while floating through zero gravity right into starry blackness. Time vanished in a whoosh of panicked flight. She only stopped when her lungs threatened to rip. Pausing with hands on knees she sucked air, exhaling blasts. As her breathing calmed, awareness of interstellar silence seeped in. She poked sensory tentacles into the night. Heard nothing. Maybe he had retreated into the house with the dog? Or was he out in the desert tracking her, gun cocked, hunting knife at hand? Her eyes bored holes into a universe of shadow, imagining his face appearing.

Suddenly a fusillade of shots rang out. Was he taking out his ire on some desert creature? God forbid he shot the dog to avoid the vet bill for extracting a load of cactus spines. She strained to hear. After a time she heard a faint thud that could have been the house door slamming shut or it could have been her imagination.

She checked her cell: still no reception. Would she have to wait out here all night until she could get her bearings at dawn to hike out? Icy air gnawed her arms through the flannel shirt. No food, no water, no jacket. How was she going to fight off hypothermia?

If she headed back to the truck she might miss the track and continue on to lose herself in the finger plateaus she'd observed when she drove up from Abiquiu. But staying here doing jumping jacks till dawn was out. She toe-touched her way along until a silver arc of moon peeked over the eastern horizon spilling lavender light across the landscape, brushing the air with cactus flower perfume. The moon dusting defined the track when she came upon it. Reaching the truck it seemed to have sunk in deeper. She walked around kicking each tire. They were all flat. Now she understood the shots. A lava river of rage bubbled up, throwing red sparks across her grayed field of vision.

For a moment she considered striding back to his house and throwing a rock through his truck windshield. That insane idea drowned in a wave of helplessness that drove her temperature back to near freezing. She was miles out of Abiquiu on a chilly desert night without cell service with a truck she couldn't drive even if pulled out of the sand. She walked around it again, imagining the amateur blue paint job, the single speed windshield wipers, the gear shifter that rattled at high speeds. Was it even worth hauling out and fixing? Maybe she should leave it here to clog Amilcar's entry road. Damn, if only she could make him pay.

A memory flashed across her mind, squatting by the side of a turgid *café con leche* river as a Huaorani man hacked at a stick, recounting in disjunctive phrases, bizarrely discontinuous to her foreign ears, how his father was speared to death in a revenge killing. As the stick looked more and more like a spear, he expressed longing to kill his father's killer, frustrated by his understanding that the Huaorani were now subject to the *policia nacional*. Revenge seemed sweet but that cycle of endless violence had led the Huaorani to have the highest homicide rate on the face of the earth. She unclenched her fists and took deep breaths, willing herself to let anger go.

After a moment she took off walking down the track that would lead to a road that wound through the village of Abiquiu and ended up at the highway. The rhythm of her steps calmed chaotic brain waves, stilling her mind as she moved over a black velvet landscape beneath a glittery crystal globe. The new moon smiled down trying to cheer her with a sense of the triviality of human affairs. But her feelings, like the landscape she stumbled across, remained mired in gloom.

She finally made it out. After a couple uncomfortable hours sitting in a blue-lit bar at the Abiquiu crossroads, squeezing bar napkins soaked in beer over her canine-scraped forearm, an effort to sterilize, and fighting off a pathetic series of drunken attempts to 'buy her a drink,' she located a tow truck driver willing to rescue her car at that hour for the tidy sum of $450. That represented a couple week's tips at Lucky Coyote. Still, she told herself, she was lucky the bullets had landed in synthetic rubber, not flesh.

Chapter Four

Heat with the force of a commercial dryer shoved Minoa's torso against a rough stucco wall. Rough but pleasant ...

"Hey, Min."

The sound pierced the hot air layer coating her face, jostled an eardrum. She levered open the eyelids, barely. Perceived Ireni's blonde hair and pale blue button down glowing around the edges. Sat up straight, blinking into a stampede of sunlight.

"Did I fall asleep?"

"Don't worry about it."

Ireni moved to sit beside her on a plank hammered onto two-by-fours that served as the customer waiting area in front of Romero Tire Shop on Espanola's main drag.

"You should have called Carter or me to pick you up last night instead of pulling an all-nighter hiking out of the Abiquiu badlands."

"I copped a few hours sleep in the truck waiting for Sammy's to open. Anyway, I figured you'd get lost trying to find me. And there's no reception up there."

"You can insult me if you want but Carter's the queen of search and rescue."

"She would have lectured me on the stupidity of heading into the backcountry with no food, no gear, no warm clothes. She'd say I'm lucky a cougar didn't get me."

"She probably would. She's our in-house ethics and survival coach."

Minoa rubbed her eyes and stood up.

"I'm so sorry, Reni, for this trouble. I get paid next Friday and then I can reimburse everything."

"Quiet, Min. Tires are essential. Anyway, you're doing me a favor letting me play the Good Samaritan. Lets me compensate for spending my days helping scientists create weapons of mass murder. And I can wield it for self-defense next time Carter attacks me for my complicity with the war machine."

"Carter is tough love incarnate. Still, she holds herself to the same standards."

"She does."

They both stared out across Riverside Drive at a string of sunburned small businesses. From the bays behind them came clinking sounds, overlaid on the patter of Española's morning traffic. Minoa stretched her arms.

"I can't believe that scumbag Amilcar. He added over six hundred dollars to my stressed budget with that tire shooting spree."

"Will you go to the police?"

"What good would that do? He shot at a car on his land after a peeping tom terrified his family. They might arrest me instead."

"Maybe your deceased friend's mom should cover the tires and towing?"

"She's worse off than I am."

"Okay. Just stay clear of him from now on, will you? He's unbalanced."

"I draw the line at child abuse. He's going to pay for that."

Ireni arched her brows, bleached white in the sunshine.

"Don't lose focus on your own plans. Text me later."

She walked to her dented red Fiat, backed out and took off heading for her job at the lab in Los Alamos.

"My plans? As if."

As Minoa stared across the road, blinking away tears from light crashing in every direction, fighting a rolling cloud of sleepiness, her eyelids slid shut. In the groggy darkness that followed a rattlesnake slithered lickety-split across her mind's eye. A jolt of electricity shot up her backbone popping open her eyelids and rigidifying her legs. Just as quickly the rattler vision slithered back into her unconscious. She stood there in front of the tire shop ratcheting her brain back into the daytime world. Was that snake from a memory? Would Dreema's strange death make Minoa recall scary snake encounters from her high desert childhood? Or cause her to develop a rattler phobia?

Sammy stuck his head out the door and said her truck was ready. She wiped the snake image from her mental slate, spotted her blue truck parked beside the shop and headed over.

***

Sitting at a stoplight on Paseo de Peralta, Santa Fe's seventeenth century beltway, she googled the Child Abuse Hotline. At the next light she dialed. Summarized what she'd seen, highlighted the fact that she had a photo and provided contact information. The operator said they'd send the report to the investigations department.

"Can I follow the progress of the investigation?"

"Only if you're a family member."

She hung up feeling dissatisfied. At the courthouse a clerk in the domestic violence office explained which forms to fill out to request a protection order on behalf of Aracely against her father.

"Are you a relative of the child?"

"Not exactly."

"Physician, teacher, therapist?"

Minoa shook her head.

The clerk gave her a questioning glance.

"Family members and professionals are the ones that usually file these cases."

"I'm picking up the forms for the grandmother."

The clerk nodded. Minoa wondered if she'd have to sedate Georgia with another overdose of valium to oblige her to appear for the hearing. The court papers only needed Georgia's signature. Helpful Minoa could fill out the rest. But in no possible universe was she giving up. Aracely needed protection and Amilcar needed a good shaking.

On the south side of town she made a stop to print out the photo. It was shadowy but well-timed, clearly a photo of a man walloping a terrified child. Amilcar's face wasn't visible but Aracely's was. She printed a second copy for backup.

Chapter Five

When no one answered the doorbell, Minoa beat on the door. In ten seconds it swung open. Berry stared at her.

"Sorry. I thought Georgia might be asleep."

He frowned, backed up without a word. She followed him into the living room where he stared out the sliding glass door, back to her, arms crossed tight.

"I didn't mean to interrupt but Georgia sent me out to Amilcar's place with Aracely's things."

Berry looked over his shoulder, shifted sideways.

"Oh, sure. The thing is, I've got to get back to Oklahoma City and my mom ..."

"Amilcar shot out my tires. All of them."

He swung around to face her.

"What the hell?"

"It took me a few hours to walk out. And it cost me a lot of money."

"That bastard. Why did Dreemer have to hook up with such a lowlife before she went and died on us?"

His face squeezed. Georgia came padding out of the hallway.

"Did you see Aracely? Did you tell her hi from Grandma?"

"I saw her but ..."

"That sonuvabitch shot at her, Mom."

Georgia slapped a hand over her heart like she was going into cardiac arrest.

"Did he mistake you for a burglar?"

"I'm gonna drive out there right now and nail that criminal."

"No, Berry, you mustn't."

Berry turned and stomped down the hallway. As her hand dropped Georgia looked at Minoa, an expression bobbing within her irises of a non-swimmer tossed into the water. Then a film slid over the eyes.

"I'll get you a cup of coffee."

She disappeared into the kitchen. Minoa stood in the center of the living room, gripping the legal papers in one hand, eyes ticking back and forth. Finally she walked into the kitchen. Georgia was measuring teaspoons of black granules into two cups. She poured water out of a teapot on the stove, then headed out to a dining table carrying the two cups, calling over her shoulder, "Could you bring the milk?"

Minoa fired a breath, grabbed a carton of skim milk and followed Georgia out to the table. Waited till she'd poured and stirred.

"I'm afraid I saw something disturbing when I went to Amilcar's place."

"I'm sorry he shot at you. He's very ... protective."

"He slapped Aracely."

She shot up heading for the kitchen.

"I forgot the sugar..." trailed behind her.

Minoa sat there watching dust particles spiral in currents from AC vents wondering if she would be here trying to manipulate Georgia to file for a protection order against Amilcar if he hadn't shot out her tires.

'The tires are irrelevant,' she told herself. 'We've got to protect Aracely.'

After more minutes staring at the slatted door to the kitchen, she concluded Georgia needed rescuing. She was halfway to standing when Georgia shuffled back in and collapsed into her chair. She'd forgotten the sugar. Minoa impaled her with her gaze as Georgia squirmed.

"Oh shoot. I forgot ..."

She placed hands on the table to push herself up.

"Georgia, sit down. He's hitting her."

Georgia paused with knees bent.

"Did she misbehave?"

"Georgia, it's child abuse."

Minoa set the legal papers on the table. The photo stayed in her bag. Georgia slumped back into the chair.

"This is a petition for a protection order against domestic violence. They'll take her away from him, at least for a while, and he'll have to take parenting classes or go to therapy or something. You should call the state hotline to report child abuse. I called, but they should get a call from a family member."

Georgia shrank back from the papers.

"But what would happen to Aracely? Where would she live?"

"Maybe they'd give you custody, at least until Amilcar improves his behavior."

Her fingers kneaded the tablecloth.

"I have no money and I haven't worked since I was twenty-seven years old."

"Could Mr. Adkins help?"

"It's better he doesn't find out about this. I don't know what he'd do."

"Wouldn't you rather have her with you than in that household getting hit?"

"It's terrible, but with her mother gone ... Maybe you could talk to Amilcar?"

"I don't intend to speak to him until we meet in court. I suppose if you won't file I could pursue this on my own but it will be harder."

Georgia flinched, turning to stare out the glass door at the withered yard and unforgiving desert. The complexities of the situation mired Minoa's benevolent impulses, sucking her gaze down down to stare at the oilcloth table linen that burst with flowers native to some other continent ... until a surge of defiance bounced her out of the chair. She paced the room from the giant TV screen to the table, back and forth, then stopped.

"Georgia, there are ways to get money. Lots of other women have faced difficult economic situations and found a path."

Georgia turned her gray eyes up to her, lashes quaking.

"They have?"

Minoa grimaced, ransacked her brain for inspiration, paced a few more laps across the room.

"I've got it. Why don't you file a civil suit against the developer for complicity in Dreema's death, you know, negligent construction or something?"

"A lawsuit?"

"I bet he's shaking in his boots up there in that Wild West office of his, worrying that you'll do exactly that."

"Did he have something to do with ...?"

"You know there was another snake in the house beforehand. Either the house was built on top of a snake pit or the construction is substandard or both. Sounds like other Tierra Feliz homeowners have problems with the construction as well."

Now Georgia's eyes consumed her face like a starving beggar contemplating a banquet.

"Listen, these days nobody dies without somebody being blamed. Just call a personal injury lawyer. They'll take it from there and they don't charge unless you win."

"Could you write down the number?"

"You'll need to talk to a few lawyers."

"Could you do that?"

Minoa walked over to the sliding glass door and stared out. The sun was flagellating the face of the desert as if it hadn't done the same a million million times before. When she turned around, Georgia hadn't budged; she probably hadn't blinked in five minutes.

"I'll look into the lawsuit angle and let you know."

"Thank you."

Her over-stretched eyes sagged as she placed her hands on her knees and levered herself to standing. She muttered something and stumbled down the hallway. She might have been going to the bathroom.

'God forbid there's another rattler in there,' Minoa told herself, repressing the urge to run down the hall and check.

She needed air that wasn't iced and splashed with gloom. She pulled open the sliding glass door, stepped outside. At first she heard nothing, saw nothing move as if time were on pause. After a moment she perceived a scratching sound. Looked both ways. A neighbor was raking something. She put on her 'great weather we're having' smile and walked over to the next backyard where a spindly-limbed stubble-haired geezer was raking a bed of rocks.

"Good afternoon. That looks like hot work."

The old fellow squinted at her as if she'd emerged from a hovering spaceship.

"I'm a friend of the family," she explained to alkalize his vitriolic stare. "Have you had any problems with rattlesnakes this year?"

"Snakes ain't gonna go where they're not invited."

She contemplated this statement.

"Do you mean ...?"

"Take care of your own and you won't get no unwelcome intruders."

"So you've had luck keeping rattlesnakes out of your property?"

"T'aint luck."

"I'm sure you heard of your neighbor's death by snakebite."

"Anybody sleep with their door open ought to have their brains flushed out with vinegar."

She tried and failed to picture this.

"Isn't it unlikely a reptile would enter a human dwelling? Surely they have some fear of people?"

"Let me put it this way: if a female don't shut the bedroom door at night you got to wonder."

The old man was staring at her with eyes almost buried by reddened folds of skin.

"Wonder what? If a venomous snake will slither in and kill her? Is that what you mean?"

"You can take it anyway you like."

"I take it as disrespectful to the dead."

"Respect got to be earned."

"Psssst!"

Someone was trying to catch the old fellow's attention from within the house. He swiveled his head around, swirling neck skin like drapes.

"What do you want, woman?"

"Herb, come in here."

The old guy shuffled to the back door of the house, propped his rake against the wall and disappeared inside. Minoa exhaled air that still felt hot on the way out. In the old boy's mind Dreema had committed a sin by sleeping with her door open, akin to walking around without underpants. What a neighbor. She could imagine how lovely it might feel on a warm summer evening to throw open the door to your gypsum-walled shag-carpeted fiberglass-insulated box and lie in bed uncovered, a sage-scented breath of desert air caressing your legs, lulled by a symphony of crickets accented by the distant yipping of coyotes running the ridge tops. On the other hand, the grouchy neighbor was still alive while Dreema had been forced to walk the trail to the spirit world where a giant Anaconda awaited, according to Minoa's Huaorani informants. Even death promised no escape from snakes.

Georgia was in the kitchen cutting up asparagus with an empty Rice-A-Roni box to one side and a pot puffing on the stove.

"The petition for a restraining order against Amilcar — do you want to submit it?"

She set it on the counter beside the cutting board. Georgia nodded. A tear splashed onto the asparagus chunks.

"I'm sorry I'm so ..."

A sob escaped though she slapped her fist over her mouth. Minoa gazed at the blanched skin and limp hair, recalling her own mother's wavy auburn mane and freckled complexion. Her mom would have been unflinching if somebody hit her granddaughter. She would have driven to court, obtained a judge's signature and gone straight out to Amilcar's place to serve the order.

'Shutup,' she told herself. 'She left when you were eleven years old. What do you know?'

When she glanced back at Georgia she noticed her inching downward, curving over the countertop as if about to collapse. She threw arms around her waist to catch her. Georgia patted Minoa's forearms as she choked back sobs. Minoa stood there, hyper-aware of Georgia's pudding-like abdominal flesh beneath her clasped arms, jiggling with each sob, afraid to release the embrace lest she ooze down to the linoleum floor. Finally, Georgia shifted and Minoa released her grasp. After a moment pretending nothing had happened, she scooped up the papers and headed out.

Chapter Six

A blue-black veil of rain dripped down the far side of the sun-starched sky. As Minoa strode down the drive a woman with a bubble of stiffened orange hair scurried out of the grouchy neighbor's house and stopped at the property line, teetering.

"I'm sorry about your friend," she called out. "Please don't take offense at Herb's manner of speaking. He's testy with younger people."

"Don't worry about it."

As Minoa approached, the woman rocked back off the balls of her feet.

"I blame her family. There were lots of people around. Why didn't anybody help?"

"Are you referring to her mother?"

"Well, her mom was right there in the house, but between you and me, she may not have been in a condition to help, if you know what I mean."

The woman winked, making one side of her face pleat like an accordion skirt.

"Her father came by. And that ex-husband of hers — he's the kind that might have put a bullet through her head, if you give him half a chance — even he was here. So how could somebody die like that in a house with people traipsing in and out at all hours? I feel so sorry for the poor thing."

Minoa stared as the echo of Georgia's grief dissolved in the sunlight allowing her mind to gear up.

"You mean all those people were here in the house the night she died?"

"Not all at once, of course. They don't like each other, that's obvious. But I saw them all." She dropped her truculent chin, assuming a demure posture. "It's summer, you know. Herb and I spend a lot of time working in the yard and the way these houses butt up against each other it's impossible not to notice."

"So much coming and going would have disturbed anyone. But are you sure Dreema's husband came here? I thought she had a protection order against him."

"That's what she screamed at him. They had a tremendous fight. Everybody at the end of the street must have heard it."

"What did he want?"

"He came for his things. Backed his truck up to the garage, opened the garage door and went right in. She should have had a padlock on it. An ounce of prevention, you know. She came out and started yelling at him. 'You can't be here! I'll call the police!' and things like that. He let loose with a stream of Spanish and English. I couldn't get the Spanish but the English was enough to figure out what kind of language he favors, if you get my meaning."

She shook her head, still scandalized. Not a hair on her head budged.

"Did the police come?"

"By that time he was gone with a freezer, a load of electronics, and some other big boxes. The coppers must have been on coffee break when she called."

"But it was much later that she was bitten by a snake, wasn't it?"

"Must have been. But there was more comings and goings over there, enough to make you do cartwheels. I was in bed when I heard crunching on the gravel. I was afraid the ex- come back with a gun. You hear about that kind of thing every day of the week on the news, you know, 'Man Murders Ex-Wife after Break-Up'. Why, a woman I used to work with over at Albertson's lost her daughter to an ex-, some hot-headed Mexican, probably a drug trafficker."

"Someone walked across your yard?"

"Passed right outside the bedroom window. Woke me up. I panicked, thought maybe a couple of them juvenile delinquent gang bangers was about to break in. But I didn't want to wake Herb until I was sure it wasn't just a drunk teenager or something. Herb's trigger happy with trespassers. So I sneaked over to the window and peeked out."

"Could you tell who it was?"

"I wish I could say. By the time I got to the window he'd gone around back of her house."

"So it could have been a stray dog?"

"Oh, no, this creature was two-footed. Afraid I'd hear a shot and find out the next day she'd been murdered in cold blood. But look what happened. A rattler got her instead. You just never know, do you?"

"No, you don't. Did you see him when he came back?"

"I hardly slept a wink. Seemed like every time I drifted off there'd be something going on over there. I'll be glad when we've seen the last of that family. Oh, excuse me. I didn't mean I want them all to die or anything, just find another place to live."

"Have you had any snakes on your property?"

"Herb blows their heads off before I get a look. He had himself a snakeskin belt made out of one of them. I bet it scares the others away." She chuckled.

"What about problems with the construction of your house? My deceased friend thought there were code violations in these homes."

"I heard about that group she organized, meeting at night in secret like commie agitators. That kind of activity just drives down property values. Our house is solid as a bank. She probably didn't keep up with repairs. You got to be vigilant to protect your investment."

"No holes in the wall or floors then?"

"Got to spray for spiders every month. No pets and no kids, that's the key."

Smiling, she shook an index finger as Minoa headed for her truck.

Chapter Seven

The rain had moved in fast, covering half the sky with wine-black clouds flashing internal lightning. Driving up Camino de Destino she pondered the curious facts surrounding Dreema's death. Another rattlesnake in the house before? A fight with her violent ex- earlier the same night she died? A neighbor's belief that someone walked around the back of the house late at night? Rattlesnake poachers in the desert behind her house? Did any of that tip an unusual death out of the realm of improbable tragic accident into something more sinister? Or was it just more weird New Mexico stuff she'd better get used to?

At the neighborhood entrance she spotted the developer's fake Wild West sheriff's office and a memory flashed. A family car trip along the old Route 66 through Indian country. They'd stopped at a trading post outside Gallup with a fake western town, a sheriff's office like this one, a saloon, a couple cement teepees. Her dad had bought her one of those kitschy rattlesnake toys, a jointed wooden snake body with a button that pushed a forked tongue out of the mouth. She scurried around poking her mom and dad until he sent her onto the porch with some quarters. Plunking the coins in a slot for a pony ride, she'd ridden the bucking horse facing a snarling stuffed mountain lion until she threw up. When her parents saw the mess they started arguing. She couldn't remember any words, just the high scary tone of the voices and a feeling of crushing shame. Finally her dad drove off in a dry drunk rage. Minoa and her mom had to catch a Greyhound bus home.

She pushed delete on the memory and pulled into the rutted lot in front of the subdivision developer's office. What could the developer think about two rattlesnake intrusions into one of the houses he built? Did he care? She slid out of the truck and entered the office. The interior resembled a large house trailer furnished in saddle blanket print with stylized paintings of Native American women in traditional dress hung on wooden panels that bowed out from the wall. On a glass-topped table sat an architect's model of the planned develop-ment, a dream of a fake adobe village, streets and cul-de-sacs covering the arid hills like some invasive vine species. Looked like the handful of streets currently scratched into the desert floor represented only the seed of a magnificent civilizing vision. The man leaning back in an executive chair, iron hair fleeing a craggy face, wearing a bureaucrat's pinstripe shirt with a salesman's flashy tie, leaped up.

"Good afternoon. Welcome to Tierra Feliz. How did you hear about our development?"

"A friend of mine lived here."

He launched into a description of the amenities the community would offer, bike and walking trails, a swimming pool, basketball court, playground, dog run and group picnic shelter, waving his hands above the model as if conjuring this vision out of rarefied high altitude air.

When he paused she said, "I've heard there are a lot of rattlesnakes here."

His magician's hands dropped to his sides.

"This is pristine nature. It's a vibrant ecosystem with all kinds of wildlife. Just wait till you see the cottontails and prairie dogs. They're real crowd pleasers. I assure you any snake issues have been remediated through our reptile elimination program."

"Reptile elimination? Did you set traps or something?"

"My assistant, Felipe, is in charge. It's a comprehensive elimination program."

"Didn't a woman just die of snakebite here?"

"Uh, I don't think the cause of death has been determined. She was probably on drugs."

"On drugs? What makes you say that? Are there problems here with drug trafficking?"

"No worries on that score. Tierra Feliz attracts hard-working happy families. An ideal place to raise children. Just like the name says, a land of happiness."

"Didn't that snake come right into her house?"

"Look miss, if you leave the door of your home wide open all night, even in Beverly Hills, undesirable elements may come in."

"But wasn't there another snake in her house before that?"

"Where did you hear that?"

"It was in the news report I read."

"I didn't see that. There was no coverage."

"Have there been any complaints about construction?"

"Why in the world would there be complaints?"

"All the permits and inspections in order? No pending violations? No investigations by county authorities?"

Now the developer squinted his sun-faded amber eyes at her.

"Are you with that group of troublemakers?"

"I might like to see a model home. But I'd have to be assured that you've made all necessary repairs to keep reptiles out. I'm morbidly afraid of snakes."

He kept squinting as he handed her a brochure.

"The first house on your left is a model, open to the public. Here are the floor plan options."

"Thanks awfully."

She hurried out, aware of his skeptical stare following. Outside, a refurbished classic pickup truck painted bright turquoise, sporting extra large tires with silver rims, pulled up in front of the office. A young man with tattoos up and down his arms got out. As he walked to the office, she glanced into the cab. A carved wooden cross dangled from the rearview mirror on a beaded string, a rifle sat in a rack on the back window. She climbed into her truck and headed for the highway.

Pausing at the intersection with the frontage road she put in a call to 888-GOT-HURT, put the phone on speaker and positioned it in front of the funky indicator dials on the dash, each accumulating seeped dirt in tiny sand dunes behind the glass cover. She recalled the number from one of those billboards of personal injury lawyers lining the freeway in Albuquerque. The image lingered: a mammoth photo of a well-shaven middle-aged male, eyebrows furrowed, lips flat, index finger jabbing at the phrase: "Hurt on the Job? Chet Morrison Has Got Your Back!" Followed by the most important words: "Free Consultation - No Fee Until You Win." A receptionist answered, screened her and, when she realized she was calling about a wrongful death case, transferred her to the man himself. He cleared his throat in a dramatic manner.

"Hello, Mrs. Adkins. Please let me express my deepest sympathies. I understand you'd like to pursue a civil suit regarding the death of your loved one."

Minoa explained she was calling on behalf of the mother of the deceased. When she got to the part about the cause of death Morrison grunted.

"Rattlesnake?"

"We believe the developer used substandard construction and that's why snakes got in more than once."

"She was snake bitten on two separate occasions?"

"No, I mean they encountered rattlesnakes in the house twice. The first time a rattlesnake appeared in the bathroom and Ms. Adkins' granddaughter barely escaped snakebite. The second time a rattler came into her daughter's bedroom in the middle of the night. She was struck and died before help could arrive."

Minoa waited for a response but there was none. She heard him breathing into the receiver. Did he think this was a hoax? Was he going to hang up? She rushed on.

"Other residents of the subdivision have problems with their houses as well. Construction problems, structural defects, probably code violations. Surely the developer bears some responsibility for selling houses that allow venomous snakes to get in, doesn't he?"

"It's possible. At any rate it's worth exploring. Why don't you make an appointment with my receptionist for Mrs. Adkins and we'll discuss the case in greater detail. Once again my most heartfelt sympathies."

He transferred her to the receptionist and Minoa took the first available slot. Halfway up Cerrillos Road she stopped by the Cultural Renaissance Cafe for a double mate. While waiting for her cup-to-go she scanned the flyers tacked to a community events bulletin board. A familiar phrase caught her eye.

Women Rising — Experience the Return of the Divine Feminine

Tap ancient traditions of female empowerment to achieve your dreams in the 21st century. Group workshop Tuesday evenings at 7:30. 45113 County Road 117 off Camino de Rincon in Pojoaque. Contact Inanna @shamanwoman, facebook.com/womenrising.

That must be the group Inanna had mentioned at the wake, the one Dreema attended on the last night of her life. She noted the time and place. It wouldn't hurt to document Dreema's movements on the night she died as background for a civil suit against the developer.

Chapter Eight

The whitewashed walls of Pojoaque Pueblo Church reflected dazzling sunlight, superimposing a scintillating image of the church on her vision that dissolved as she drove on. Past the pueblo the road branched into a skein of washboard lanes, stretches of baked dirt hyphenated every so often by the shade of a cluster of cottonwoods. Scanning flat-topped adobes in big messy yards, she couldn't see a single house number. Finally located Inanna's place by a 'for sale' style sign that said Women Rising. She rolled down a steep dirt drive cut through with channels from the last big rain into a small lot filled with cars and parked.

The property was a collage of utopian visions. A solar greenhouse clung to one side of an aging adobe, a homemade solar water heater sat on the flat roof near a rusty wood stove pipe. Wind chimes and hummingbird feeders hung from *vigas*, a dreamcatcher dangled behind the glass of a window, a teepee stood off to the side. Rows of corn peeked out from behind.

As the front door was ajar Minoa walked in. Voices drew her down a hallway past the greenhouse, verdant with twining vines, tropical leaves, purple centered star flowers — not the usual cherry tomatoes and green chile. She emerged into a large addition on the back with floor-to-ceiling windows framing a burnt orange setting sun.

Women's whispered conversations ruffled the air as they leaned this way and that off meditation cushions. In front of the bank of windows stood an art nouveau altar carved of grotesquely gnarled wood. Minoa hiked her jeans, sat cross-legged and watched the western sky smolder. Finally Inanna walked in through a side door, spotted Minoa and approached.

"I knew you'd come."

She walked away before Minoa could respond, calling out "Let us begin the purification."

The women followed her out a door into the back of the property. Beyond the rows of corn and vegetables the tops of cottonwood trees formed a bumpy green carpet. In the distance, audible beneath the murmur of voices, a stream tinkled. They milled toward a cattle watering tank with a handmade solar panel propped to the side and started doffing their clothes onto a bench. Approaching Minoa saw steam rising from the surface of the tank. A toe stuck into the water came out scarlet, but after a few minutes trembling naked in twilight air she submerged herself.

At first the water burned like fire, but soon an affectionate warmth seeped into her flesh. She leaned her head against the rim of the tank and watched the first stars winking. Someone placed a ceramic goblet of wine in her hand. Before long her limbs floated limp like pork shreds in a pot of overcooked *posole*. The water steamed in an eternal present, currents caused by shifting bodies caressing her. The chatter mingled with crickets coaxing her to relax, to stop trying to understand. She gave in and floated in a watery revery.

Suddenly one woman with frosted waves twisted into a clasp on the top of her head scooped water into her hands, poured it over her head and called out, "I let go of jealousy of younger women."

"Here, here," said the others, lifting their glasses to toast.

Another woman, ping-pong ball cheeks and curly black hair, splashed water on her face saying, "I let go of my obsession with cellulite," followed by cheers and toasts.

Now they took turns yelling out vows to let go of this and that, from the man who hadn't called in two weeks to the need to pass the bar exam.

A blonde boney woman next to Minoa said, "I let go of the feeling I should get married to be successful."

More clicked glasses, then a moment of quiet when several women glanced at Minoa.

Finally she spit out, "I let go of my old dreams."

Glasses clinked and everyone returned to sipping wine and soaking. Night squeezed out the sapphire glow edging the horizon.

When she climbed out of the tub black spots popped before her eyes and she staggered, but she was feeling better than she'd felt in days. A chronic sensation of struggle, as if life were an endless rocky ascent, had drained out of her muscles leaving barely the muscle tension necessary to stand. She almost giggled.

Back in the shrine room they watched Inanna light candles in niches around the room. Then she set a match to a bundle of sage on a platter and they took turns waving smoke over themselves. A gray-haired woman with round wire rims, the old-fashioned stereotype of a librarian, handed Minoa a shiny robe in a butterfly print. Minoa frowned but gave in, covering her jeans and 'Save the Rainforest' tee shirt, loosing a cloud of rose oil scent from the fabric.

The platter of smoking sage left on the altar released a spectral trail of smoke. Inanna picked up a guitar and began to sing some modal tune about temples and descents into the underworld. Some of the women joined in on the chorus, others swayed side to side on their pillows. Then she grabbed an ornamental dagger off the altar and waved it around while chanting gibberish. Without warning she aimed the point of the dagger at her hand and made a cut on the tip of her left middle finger. With an ululating cry she rubbed the finger on her forehead between the brows, leaving a scarlet oval. Minoa glanced around the room to see how the others were taking this. Several sat with their hands in mudras and eyes closed, others gazed transfixed.

"Sisters of the earth," Inanna cried.

"We are sisters," the women intoned.

"Brave sisters who venture into darkness to retrieve what was lost, the sacred feminine, stomped out of our bodies that were tortured and raped and burned for the pleasure of the priests of male power, our spirits beaten into submission."

"Sisters return."

"We beat our drums to travel in dreamtime, we crawl with the sacred snake, Basmu, so that we may take flight to discover our future."

"Sisters sleep to awaken."

"We dare to marry spirit and flesh, we retrieve our bodies from the meathook of male barbarism, we infuse ourselves with the energy of the mother, dancing to create a new world out of the destruction patriarchy has wrought."

"Sisters dance for life."

Inanna picked up a native style drum and beat it rhythmically, chanting more phrases about 'sisters' while dancing around the room. One by one they all fell into line behind her.

Minoa scooted into a corner. The chanting circle went round and round and round for so long she grew bored and wondered when this would end. Suddenly one woman let out a wail, twirled like a top and spun into the center of the room, staggering from side to side like a closing time drunk. Hands on knees she groaned, sputtered, fell to the floor, kicking her legs, arms flinging. For a moment Minoa feared she was having a seizure. After consideration she visually reviewed the writhing figure for the biological markers of trance. No twitching, no loss of control of facial musculature, no rapid eye movements, maybe altered breathing. As for insensitivity to pain she'd have to poke her to find out.

For a moment she was back in the Huaorani village watching Minkayani blow huge quantities of green goo up his nose and then fall to the ground, twitching all over, groaning. Minkayani's eyes would roll up in his head, drool oozing out of his mouth and nose, facial musculature torqued. At some point he would mumble a song that went on and on. Hours later when he came to, if she'd brought him enough *cumbia* CD's from the open air market in Quito for his solar-charged portable radio/CD player, he would tell her what the jaguar sons had shown him. Or maybe he made it all up to keep the CD's coming. The CD's enhanced his status with the other men so Minoa was useful to him.

Another woman stumbled out of the circle, keening and beating her arms like a flightless bird. Then a petite blonde took a few steps forward, fell over, curled into a ball and began to sob. Someone knelt beside her patting her back; the rest continued their circular dirge.

All those years studying shamanism in exotic locales, Minoa thought, and now she was witness to a trance party right here in her hometown, a wannabe trance party unless those plants in the greenhouse were helping. She sneered at this simulation of possession trance, then told herself to chill. Why shouldn't these social workers, bureaucrats and restaurant managers try to experience a bit of the altered states of consciousness tribal peoples accessed? Might make their nine-to-five existences more bearable. And who was she to criticize? Former anthropology adjunct with some publications in obscure journals. What good had reading a million ethnographic monographs done her? Left her splat dab in the middle of the world she'd fled years ago, alone, underemployed, drinking too much with no idea what to do next.

At some point she noticed Inanna was not in the room. A few minutes later one of the women slipped out the back door. After a little while another went out. Finally only two others were left in the shrine room

"What's going on?" she said.

No one responded so she headed outside. The Milky Way was rich and thick but failed to illuminate the rough ground. She walked away from the back of the house testing each step, holding arms out in front like a zombie. Where had they all gone? Was the idea to stumble into the *bosque* to commune with nature spirits or seek some sort of backyard vision quest? She stubbed her toe on a rock and tripped, crashing into a fence post wrapped with barbed wire. Rubbed her arm until the pain faded, then continued, sliding her feet across the ground. Sensing raspy leaves against her forearm she shuffled down a corn row, fingertips brushing the stalks. Something scurried through the corn up ahead. She paused but now heard only the distant hum of the highway.

Leaving the corn rows behind she toe-touched through chilly blackness until a hand hit bark. She hugged a tree trunk, then sidled past tripping over a root. Ahead she caught sight of a yellow light flickering between the vertical black lines of tree trunks. Moving toward it she heard voices. She prayed she hadn't stumbled into a neighbor's property where locals were running a meth lab or dividing up the take from a run of house burglaries.

Palming from one trunk to another she navigated to where she could see the dwelling. It was a tiny adobe the size of a suburban kitchen. Candlelight wavered through one small window. Against the dim amber glow a row of silhouettes stretched like paper doll shadows. She tiptoed into the dissipating light and fell into line behind the others. No one spoke.

After a time, that could have been five minutes or could have been fifty, the door opened and a young woman with loads of curly hair stumbled out of the house clutching something to her chest. Behind her came another. It was Marion the Librarian as Minoa had dubbed her. She invited the person at the front of the line to enter. Noticing Minoa she reached into her pocket and handed her a scrap of paper and a pencil, then turned around.

"Wha- what's this for?" Minoa squeezed out.

"Your question." Marion re-entered the little building and shut the door.

Minoa pondered for a moment and wrote down: 'Why was Dreema bitten by a rattlesnake?' She settled down to wait.

Each of the women in line had their turn inside. By the time the woman in front of her disappeared into the tiny house a scimitar of moon had appeared in the east, but among the trees it didn't shed enough light to make a difference. Finally the door opened and that woman came out. She kept her eyes on the ground as she stepped into the night and disappeared. Marion appeared in the doorway and beckoned to Minoa. She went in. The door shut behind her.

The room swirled with perfumed smoke, rippling in candlelight. In the middle sat a figure on a stool: Inanna. The stool looked to be above floor level and for a moment Minoa thought it was hovering in midair. Was this the trick initiates came one by one to see — levitation? She blinked and stared. Now she saw that the stool was on a platform, perhaps to raise this oracle woman above the impure earth.

Marion reached out her hand and Minoa placed the piece of paper in it. She read out loud: "Why was Dreema bitten by a rattlesnake?"

Inanna swayed side to side, let out a wail and almost tipped off her stool. Marion rushed in to steady her. Inanna groaned, head lolling around on neck muscles like over-stretched rubber bands. She twitched all over, as if pesky gnats were biting her. A sob coagulated in her throat, she gasped for breath.

Minoa stared to keep from losing her balance. The wisps of smoke floating to the ceiling made the walls quiver. That smell nauseated her, made her intestines feel sloppy. She longed to lie down, to sleep. The blackness under the platform where Inanna sat drew her eyes. It was darker than a sky without stars yet permeable, inviting, as if it were a tunnel, as if she could see all the way through to another time and place.

She slid in and started falling, a tumble that became a panicked whoosh through blindness, then slowed when she caught sight of a circle of sky and aimed for it, a thrill of ecstasy surging to her mind as she realized she could control this loss of gravity, she could fly. Somewhere in the tunnel the identity named Minoa fell aside like a cast-off shell. She aimed for the azure opening, gliding out into a world of lemony sunbeams crashing into rust-colored rocks, flying weightless over tabletop mesas like interlocking puzzle pieces, until she spotted a pueblo below and zoomed closer.

A little girl sat on the dirt playing with a stick and a bead bracelet, throwing the bracelet into the air over and over, trying to catch it on the stick. She swooped closer, drawn by the girl's innocent laughter, her bubbling life energy. Touching down she sensed dirt under her toes while her head still floated. In between a sensation of shared innocence blossomed. She had decided she would stay here and never leave when she noticed, on the plain brown earth, a patterned line undulating, triangular head aiming straight for the little girl who played with her toy, unaware.

Her body twanged like a struck metal bar.

"Watch out!"

She heard the scream though unsure where it came from. As the girl jumped the snake struck, sinking its fangs into her chest. The girl flopped backwards, landed in corpse pose, a drop of blood leaking from the corner of her mouth.

"The oracle has spoken," said Marion.

Minoa blinked hard, noticed a hand on her arm, perceived the walls of the hut, flickering in candlelight. Gathered her sense of who she was, where she was. Inanna sat still, her great orbs fixed on nothing.

"What did she say?"

"The oracle has spoken."

"What did she say?"

Marion tugged her toward the door. Minoa flung her arm free and lurched toward Inanna who stretched out an arm to stop her, suspending her in midair with a hand on her belly. She rocked on the hand, waving her arms, and then rolled off and across the platform to stop with her head and shoulders hanging over the edge, staring into a pit. At the bottom a rolling wave of movement. Then a furious rattling broke out. The sound puckered the skin all over her body.

Now Marion hauled her to her feet and led her to the door. As she pushed Minoa into the night she stuffed a piece of paper into her hand that Minoa absently slid into a jeans pocket. She stumbled through darkness, bracing her hands on a tree trunk to get her breath and her bearings. She felt like throwing up but the sensation passed.

Somehow she found her way back to the house. Tossing the butterfly print robe into the shrine room she spied several women, one asleep, the others sitting with eyes shut. She walked around the house to her truck, slid into the seat and sat there, hands gripping the wheel, mind flipping and flopping like a hooked fish, trying to find her way back to a world that made sense. After a moment, she picked up her cell off the passenger seat and stepped out. Went to the back of each vehicle, snapping a photo of the license plate.

As she started up the hardened dirt drive the wheels spun, recovering traction at the top to kick her down the unlit road before the puny headlights could catch up. No street lights out here and most houses didn't bother with exterior lighting. Trying to recall the route, she turned one way and another, only able to see a short section of corrugated dirt ahead framed in the headlights.

Abruptly the front end of the truck tipped down and she slammed on the brakes. Over the hum of the motor she perceived the lazy rippling of water. She must be teetering on the bank of an irrigation ditch. Leaning into the brake pedal she froze there, afraid to move her foot. Finally jerked the gear shift into reverse, jumped her foot onto the accelerator, gunned the motor and leaped backwards. Reorienting the front end of the truck to where she judged the road to be, she squinted into the yellow light cones ahead where dust swirled, thinking.

This was the route Dreema drove on the night she died. Or did she drive it? The coincidence was too great, dying of rattler bite on the same night she attended a gathering where a rattlesnake was present. When Dreema left Inanna's place was she already snake bitten? Maybe she became disoriented in the oracle chamber, like Minoa, and fell into the snake pit. The effort to retrieve her would have caused that massive rattler to strike over and over. Then would they have called an ambulance or hauled her to a hospital? Neither. Inanna must have realized she would be held responsible for the actions of her venomous pet in her silly New Age ritual. Maybe she and Marion agreed to conceal the incident. Inanna might have convinced Dreema some herbal remedy would save her but instead fed her tranquilizers. Then they drove her home. After helping Dreema into bed, she left the sliding glass door open to make it appear the bite had occurred at home. She must have known Dreema wouldn't survive.

What an outlandish speculation. She squeezed the steering wheel and gunned the motor, ordering her mind to curtail this crazy train of thought. Rolling along at parking lot speed, eyes glued to the sandy lip on the edge of the road, jumping when cottonwood branches telescoped across her path like wraith arms reaching for her, another thought popped up. Maybe Dreema was already dead when they drove her home. Maybe Inanna had used her as a ritual victim in one of her trumped up archaic ceremonies. Was that the real reason Inanna kept a dangerous snake on her property in Pojoaque? Was goddess-worshipping Inanna so deranged that she carried out human sacrifice in her New Age possession trance parties? Could she be Dreema's cult murderer?

She swerved at a jog in the road she couldn't see until she was about to drive into a fence, jerking the steering wheel left and right. As she came out of the turn, she told herself to get a grip. Human sacrifice by rattler bite? Sounded like something out of a B-grade horror movie. Still, the idea that Dreema had contact with rattlesnakes twice in separate places on the night she died pushed probability to the brink of the impossible.

And hadn't Dreema's neighbor mentioned hearing footsteps around the back of the house that night? Dreema might have told Inanna about the rattler in the bathroom so she knew no one would question another apparent rattlesnake intrusion. The convenient fact that Dreema's house had been invaded by a rattlesnake in a neighborhood with a weird snake trapping program gave Inanna cover. Was this line of thought insane? Maybe, maybe not. Bottom line: the hypothesis of a freak accidental death by rattlesnake bite no longer seemed certain.

She refocused on the shadow stripes drawn by light beams angled low across a washboard road. Guessing at the turns she persevered until the glow of lights from Pojoaque's strip of stores along the highway appeared on the horizon to guide her back.

Chapter Nine

She woke jumping to her feet. As she blinked away sleep, the bland morning percolated into her senses defining her surroundings: a floor of reddish brown tiles, a fallen city of books on the desktop, speckled formica countertops, walls the color of old bones. She inhaled, telling herself to relax. Outside, the crusty desert braced for another day of solar beatings. A snake dream. That's what woke her up and left slithery things lingering on the periphery of her vision. Inanna's goddess gathering must have spooked her dream mind. Last night it had seemed evil but now, with unfiltered sunlight sterilizing everything, she realized it was just another New Mexican fringe cult in a place known as a haven for everything from hippie communes to gun-toting yogi ashrams to desert monasteries cloaked in perpetual silence.

The logical explanation for Dreema's death was shoddy construction by a real estate developer who put profit over safety. Simple. Anyway, Georgia had an appointment today with a civil lawyer in Albuquerque. Should she have agreed to drive her? Georgia was leaning on her as if she were the daughter she'd lost. Too late to back out now. She put a container of water in the microwave, grabbed a towel off the floor and headed into the bathroom.

***

Georgia sat still as a post as they headed down I-25 to Albuquerque, staring out the windshield past a hairline crack that split the glass into schizoid halves. She'd never been a big talker, so nothing new there. Minoa passed the time viewing the colossal landscape, a play of enormous grassland wafers pierced by escarpments like the teeth of some chthonic monster chewing its way out of the underworld. When they hit the Bernalillo exit north of the city Georgia finally spoke.

"Will this lawyer investigate to find out what happened to Dreema? I mean, how that snake got into the house?"

"I imagine the construction of homes at Tierra Feliz will be relevant. And they'll surely want to review the documents relating to her death. Was there an autopsy?"

"Yes. They won't try to say he ... he murdered her, will they?"

Georgia flinched, tucking her chin back into a couple folds of neck skin as if preparing for a slap.

"He? Do you mean the subdivision developer?"

Georgia glanced at her, nodded.

"I believe a civil suit would allege that the developer's negligence contributed to Dreema's death, not that he murdered her."

No response. Hard to tell what was driving her. Georgia presented as full of dread but unable to name what she feared or do anything to avoid it. Maybe she was battling her own sense of guilt, like the neighbor lady suggested, for allowing her daughter to die in the same house where she slept sedated.

Squinting through sunglasses Minoa located the building: the only multi-story office building amidst a chain of cheap boxes lining the interstate. They followed a mound of teased black hair down a hallway. The young woman paused and turned her face to them, candy red lips directing them into a conference room. Plastered walls painted earth tone on the lower half, a massive carved wooden table and Navajo rugs on the walls lent the room an aura of Spanish territorial nobility. Georgia curled up in an armchair. Minoa paced the bank of windows framing the Sandia Mountains, the jagged pinkish cliffs washed sparkly gray in the sunshine.

Soon a paralegal with blond bob and office-miss blazer breezed in and noted their answers to a series of questions on a clipboard, cocking one eyebrow when Minoa said the cause of death was rattlesnake venom. After another wait, during which Georgia murmured maybe they should just go, Chet Morrison strode in. His face was more lined than the billboard image but his navy suit and crimson tie were crisp and expensive. Georgia offered a limp hand to Morrison without leaving the safety of her contraction. Morrison grasped Minoa's hand with the reassuring grip of a surgeon.

"You're the sister of the deceased?"

"A family friend."

He glanced at Georgia.

"Her mother."

Georgia peeked up, then dropped her head back down.

"I'm assuming there is no spouse?"

"Dreema Adkins, the woman who died, was in the process of getting a divorce when she passed away."

Morrison addressed Georgia even though she continued to hide behind her knees.

"I'm deeply sorry for your daughter's death. I understand you're interested in a wrongful death suit against the developer of the subdivision where she lived."

Georgia's facial muscles squeezed like she bit a lime, so Minoa explained how Dreema died in bed of snakebite.

"I've never heard of wrongful death litigation over snakebite. You'd have to prove that someone had a duty to protect the victim from rattlesnakes and failed to do so."

"But didn't the subdivision developer have a legal responsibility to make sure the houses he sold were of sound construction? Lots of people in the development have problems with their houses. They even formed a protest group to force the developer to make repairs. This was the second time a rattler got into her house."

"The second time?"

Morrison's brow arched into a forehead bumping a suspiciously youthful crop of dark hair. Minoa nodded. He leaned forward.

"I see two issues here. Did the developer use shoddy materials or improper construction methods? This could provide a basis for a suit alleging breach of contract. The other option would be breach of a duty to care. But off the top of my head I can't imagine how we could prove that the developer had a duty of care to protect her from getting bit by a rattlesnake."

"But if a structural defect provided a gateway for a lethal creature to get in?"

"It would be hard to establish that causal link. Have you seen any holes in walls or floors, gaps between panels, or some other obvious result of improper construction?"

"I don't live there. Maybe Georgia?"

They both turned to look at Georgia, causing a startled look to appear on her face.

"We were terrified after Aracely found a snake in the bathroom. Dreema took photos so she could show them to the developer."

"Do you have the photos?"

"They must be on her phone."

"May I see the autopsy report?"

Georgia handed him a document which he scanned with practiced eyes.

"It says here she died around three in the morning. Is it known when she went to bed?"

Georgia brought a tissue to her nose.

"I was asleep, but she usually came home from those meetings at midnight or later."

"How did she die of snakebite so quickly? Doesn't it usually take hours? Why didn't they administer anti-venom?"

"The coroner said Dreema couldn't call out."

Georgia snapped shut like a pocket knife and coughed out some sobs. Morrison read out loud.

"Neurotoxic venom leading to blindness, paralysis and inhibition of respiration. Interesting." He pulled out a phone and searched. "Neurotoxic venom is rare in our region. Bad luck, I suppose."

"Bad luck?"

Minoa squinted at him.

"Did the decedent file written complaints either with the developer or the city?"

Georgia nodded her head within her cave of femurs.

"She filed complaints with the developer and she was going to file a complaint with the city, but then she died."

He stood and paced back and forth in front of the picture windows facing the mountains. After a moment he paused and turned to face them.

"Here's my preliminary opinion. If a rattlesnake entered the house previously, if she complained to the subdivision developer, if others have similar problems, then it's possible you have a case. But another way to approach this might be through a class action suit alleging construction defects throughout the neighborhood. We could organize

legal action on behalf of a group of homeowners with the potential
for a huge judgment. Imagine it as a structural failure analogous to
what occurs when a building collapses in an earthquake zone. This
just happened to be a rattlesnake zone."

He smiled at his *jeu de mot*.

"But a class action suit would mean a smaller payout for the Adkins
family, wouldn't it?"

"No matter what kind of action we decide to file, the untimely
loss of a young mother is compelling for a jury. And if we add in rattlesnakes — everybody hates them. The emotional persuasion factor
will be tremendous. The award could set records."

"Can we get this moving right away?"

"I'll have my paralegals do some research."

He passed his open hand from one side of the bank of windows to
the other like a director on set.

"This case has promise, real promise. We could set a precedent for
the entire rattlesnake-ridden Southwest." Now he shepherded them
to the door. "My condolences again. You'll hear from my assistant in
a few days."

Outside the building Minoa whistled a breath, blowing out the
scents of expensive cologne and room deodorizer.

"Do you think he blames me?" said Georgia as she clambered into
her seat.

"What? The question is whether he can prove the developer responsible for that rattler getting in."

"Will the developer go to jail for a long time if the lawyer proves he
killed her?"

"Murder is a criminal charge. You're consulting Morrison about a
civil suit."

Georgia stared out the window, lips glued together. Minoa wondered how much of the interview she'd comprehended. She couldn't think of another thing to say so she drove back onto the interstate heading north to Santa Fe.

***

Back at her guesthouse she changed into rhinestone-studded jeans and a slinky top for work — not her style but she'd found that a flashy look increased the tips. Before leaving she took a moment to google 'rattlesnakes neurotoxin'. At the University of Arizona's Poison and Drug Center website she found a relevant article:

Toxicologists have noted a disturbing trend in rattlesnake attacks over the last few years: The death rate among victims in southwestern states has skyrocketed. An increasing number of patients admitted to emergency rooms display neurotoxic symptoms which become life-threatening within an hour or less of being bitten. One species, the Mojave Rattlesnake, found in western Arizona and southern California, is known to produce neurotoxic venom called Mojave Type A toxin. Researchers believe the venom of other species is becoming more neurotoxic. This could be due to the shyness of Mojave rattlers which helps them avoid potentially fatal encounters with humans giving them a competitive advantage. Or it could accompany hybridization of species.

Unlike the more common hemotoxic bite, which produces severe swelling and bruising at the bite location, the neurotoxic bite may produce little effect on the local area. This can lead to dangerous delays in seeking treatment. Soon victims experience swelling of the mouth and throat, making it difficult or impossible to breathe. At the same time they are assailed by extreme weakness, even paralysis, as well as nausea and diarrhea, so that their capacity to seek aid quickly disappears. Shortly thereafter the victim becomes lightheaded, collapses and goes into shock. Hemotoxic components of the venom may simultaneously produce internal bleeding and organ failure. Without immediate emergency medical treatment survival is unlikely.

Neurotoxic super-rattlers that could kill you in under an hour. So Dreema didn't die quickly because she'd taken drugs at Inanna's gathering or swiped some of her mother's valium dulling her ability to seek help. Instead, she was paralyzed by neurotoxic venom from a snake whose normal range was over five hundred miles away. Was Basmu, Inanna's ceremonial rattler, a Mojave? If so, it would increase circumstantial evidence against her. Or maybe neurotoxic venom already occurred among hybridized New Mexican Diamondbacks. If not, how did a Mojave or Mojave hybrid from California or southern Arizona show up in Tierra Feliz?

Against her will Minoa imagined that fatal after-midnight. A chill breeze blew in off the back of the desert through the open glass door. Dreema was exhausted. She'd fought with her ex-, then spent the evening at Inanna's goddess gathering. Back in her bedroom it'd been too much trouble to slip on the ruffled baby doll pajamas that showed off her long legs. Besides, what difference did it make? She was sleeping alone. She might have wondered when that would change or maybe she took a deep breath of violet night air, blew it out with a sigh and thanked her not-so-lucky stars there was no one around to paw her or yell at her or give her a black eye.

She crawled between the sheets naked, enjoying the schoolgirl sensuality of plain cotton fabric against her skin, listening to the desert noises unobscured in this far-flung satellite of town. Had she posed a question to the oracle at Inanna's gathering? She must have asked about her future, must have wondered how she could escape the low-paid purgatory of dental offices, what might be her future career, something that merited the word 'career' rather than 'job'?

Of course she wouldn't have asked 'will I marry again?' After two failed marriages — one still ripping itself apart, the other a story for a novel, the weight-lifting ex-marine who knocked her around for a few years and then drove off one day with their two-year-old son — at this point she only wanted to hang on like steel to the child left to her and try to figure out if a woman really could live her life without a man.

It was so late and she was so tired and Aracely would jump up bright and early in the morning, so she let herself drift into a deep hibernation, so lost to the outside world that an arm slipped over the side of the bed and dangled. When the bite came it probably woke her but the bite area didn't hurt much and she was sleepy so she told herself it was probably a red ant bite — they had taken possession of the patio in back — or maybe a spider bite, but she hadn't seen any black widows around so not to worry.

She drifted back to sleep until she woke again to find her throat so swollen she couldn't breathe or call out. When she tried to rise to go to her mom for help she couldn't control her limbs. She collapsed back onto the bed and lay there, paralyzed, sucking breaths, terrified out of her wits until ...

Minoa gagged and drew a curtain across the theater of her imagination. Grabbed her keys and headed out to the truck, recalling, as she tripped across the channels carved by summer thundershowers, all the times she'd encountered a rattlesnake growing up in high desert country. There was that youngster coiled up in a corner of the utility shed when she'd gone out after school to collect her hula hoop, the fat diamondback catching summer shade on the underside of a log she jumped over out hiking with her Girl Scout troop, another under the car in the carport rattling when she peered under looking for a roller skate. Countless stretched out bodies smashed on the highways and other rattlers, more than she could count, sunning on flat rocks, coiled on open dirt, rattling in bushes. But never one inside a house.

Every time she heard that unmistakable dry shaker sound, like grains of sand agitated inside a speaker, something in the base of her brain poured shivers of archaic fear and awe down her spine. And there was that characteristic smell tainted with musk and decay and skin that slithered across unspeakable things. Still, rattlesnakes were a fact of life in the southwest and her attitude had always been blasé. Yet if she'd thought a rattler's bite could kill you in an hour would she have roamed the mesas and arroyos of her childhood home as if it were her birthright?

She cranked up the truck and sped away.

Chapter Ten

When she arrived at Lucky Coyote Casino the bar was half-full. Scott had things under control, jiggling an ice shaker with one hand while pouring a dollop of kahlua with the other.

"The sinners have been missing their saint."

He flashed a bleached smile as Minoa dumped a bucket of ice in the bar sink and checked a fridge for beer brands that needed restocking.

"I took a couple days off. A friend of mine died."

"Wow, monumental bummer!"

She glanced at his angular profile, dewy with perspiration under a prow of yellow hair. The muscles above the neck of his shirt and below the sleeves bulged and relaxed, bulged and relaxed, as he worked.

One of the waitresses handed her an order for mango strawberry margaritas and she began throwing the ingredients into a blender. As soon as she set up the pinkish tubs at the end of the counter there was another order for a Corona and a Charro Negro—date night for a Mexican couple. She saw them cooing and grinning in a booth on the far side of the seating area. Then a tray full of drafts. She watched the server carry them to a boisterous group of young men in gray work clothes, laughing as if the casino were a comedy club.

Beyond stretched the casino floor where people zombie-stared at slots, squinted at the blackjack dealers, froze as the roulette wheel spun. A waitress plopped down a challenging order with a Singapore Sling, a Bloody Maria and a Ramos Gin Fizz. Minoa scanned the customers in the bar. Who in the world ordered a Ramos Gin Fizz? Normally she would say they were out of the ingredients but she was anxious to stay busy. So she found some eggs and cream in a fridge, asked Scott if he knew where the vanilla was and decided to substitute a splash of orange juice for the orange flower water the recipe specified. She measured the ingredients into a shaker while staring out at the gamblers, so intent on their games, repeating over and over the same wager with chance they'd been losing all their lives.

"I am not my job," she whispered over and over.

Added crushed ice and shook. Finally strained the mixture into a tall glass and topped with a squirt of soda water to froth the creamy liquid. She surveyed the result. Definitely her finest creation of the night. As soon as it went out she folded her arms on the counter and laid her forehead on the back of her hand. Was this what a million years of education had led her to?

A friendly whack on the shoulder blades brought her back to reality.

"Still got you beat, huh?"

She turned her head to look at Scott.

"Your friend. How'd she die?"

"Snakebite."

He whistled.

"That's ugly. Why couldn't they save her with anti-venom?"

"She died too soon. The venom was neurotoxic."

"Neurotoxic?"

Glancing out at the bar she caught sight of a familiar silhouette: large bones, heavy jowls, a wave of silvering hair. Brereton Adkins Sr. was walking beside one of the managers. She murmured a description of neurotoxic and hemotoxic venom while watching the two men move around the casino. They disappeared and Minoa whipped up a flagon of Kachina Martinis — a local concoction that added a rim of chile jam and a prickly pear garnish instead of an olive to the traditional cocktail — for a group of menopausal carousers giggling at a table like schoolgirls.

A few minutes later there he was, sitting in a booth in the corner, sipping a highball. She observed him lean over the divider and shake hands with a fellow in the next booth but the overture didn't go anywhere. He returned to sipping his drink, a pale yellow liquid on the rocks, probably scotch, staring at other customers, his eyes drawn briefly by each attractive woman who passed. After a moment she pulled off her bar apron and asked Scott to cover for her.

Once they were sitting face-to-face she wondered if he had even noticed her at Dreema's wake. Would he remember her as Dreema's teenage 'partner in crime,' as they'd called themselves, as the girl he'd forbidden his daughter to see because she was a 'bad influence'?

"It was heart-breaking to hear about Dreema. I'm so sorry."

He clenched his glass harder, looked down at the tabletop.

"You recognize me, don't you?"

He met her gaze.

"I know who you are. I thought you left town."

"I did ... I'm just back here for a little while."

"Long enough to be employed?"

"It's temporary, like I said. Are you looking for a job here?"

"Me?"

He snorted and took a sip from his drink, rolling the tumbler to make the translucent golden liquid swirl.

"We've got a contract for service and maintenance of the casino equipment. I'm a rep for a company that sells and services gambling equipment."

"Oh, really. Do you work with other casinos as well?"

"Yep, we have Hollywood and Route 66. And we're working on a deal with the Apaches up at Dulce. We'd like to get Tewake if they move ahead with plans for a new casino complex. Economy could put a yellow flag on that one though."

"How interesting."

He finished the scotch, probably a double, and waved for another. She checked his eyes — steady, controlled.

"I'm sorry I lost touch with Dreema."

"She got herself into a heap of trouble since you left town."

"You mean the divorce?"

"Divorce, court battles, wacko lesbian groups, drugs, you name it. When you live like that things are going to go wrong."

"I thought her first husband abandoned her and kidnapped their son."

"She never understood him. He was a vet." He gave her a hard stare over the top of his drink. "War is tough. She just wanted him to take her out dancing all the time."

Minoa had to force her eyes away from the vortex of golden fluid swirling round and round his tumbler as he tilted it side to side.

"Did you kill the first snake she found in her house?"

The waitress deposited his new drink on the table, definitely a double. He wrapped thick fingers around the glass and squinted at her.

"Look, that house was a hell of a deal. How was I supposed to know rattlers could get in?"

"Of course you couldn't. It's the developer's responsibility."

"The developer sent his man down to kill the first one. That's about all he could do."

"He could have checked for holes in the walls or floor."

"The house was built and sold. He wasn't in charge of maintenance."

"But what if there were defects in the construction? I've never heard of a house where rattlesnakes invaded on two separate occasions, have you?"

"I saw the house when it was under construction. Framing and foundation looked okay. Those illegal Mexicans they hire to do construction probably screwed up. What do they care if a citizen gets killed? Just means more room for them to move in."

She stood up.

"I have to get back to work."

"After a rattler near struck little Aracely, why in damnation did she leave her door open all night? Damned irresponsible."

He bunched a fist in midair, then swung it to the table like a hammer. Minoa paused, flushing with a confused mixture of compassion and distaste.

"She couldn't foresee this. Nobody could. Anyway, are you sure she left the door open? Maybe someone opened it after they found her."

"How should I know?"

His cheeks bulged red as he glanced around the bar.

"I'm so sorry I mentioned this painful subject. Please forgive me and accept my deepest sympathies."

His expression softened.

"Dreema always talked real good about you."

"We were ... we were close."

He broke off eye contact, tipped his glass, rapped the table with the bottom edge.

"Damn rattlers ought to be exterminated. Just use crop dusters to spread poison across the desert and get rid of 'em all."

"I understand why you hate them but they're part of nature."

She took a step to leave.

"Those crazy Indians worship 'em like false gods."

She turned back around.

"Gods?"

"Some of those pueblos keep a giant rattler out in a cave somewhere and they feed it and ask it questions and leave little presents for it. Devil worship, if you ask me."

"They must view them as sacred."

"Damn crazy fools! Serpents are the source of all evil."

Minoa clenched her lips.

"I have to go."

She headed back to the bar.

"Dreema never should'a..."

She kept walking leaving his words to sink under the surface of casino chatter, clinking glasses, clattering chips. Tying on her bar apron she started popping the lids off a tray of beer bottles, cleaving a lime slice onto the mouth of each. Dreema had complained about her dad's views but, unlike Minoa, she never tried to escape, to become somebody else. Maybe she accepted what fate had served up? Until a rattler stole half her life away. Showed what acceptance got you. No way would Minoa suck up whatever bad deal chance tossed her. She'd fight for something better, fight to the death if necessary.

After handing the tray of beers to a server she poured Maraschino cherry juice and a hefty shot of rum into a cocktail glass for a Shirley Temple Havana. Handing it to the server she noticed Brereton stand up. He was looking toward the escalator that led down to the casino from the hotel's main concourse. Following his line of sight she spied

Georgia walking toward him, unrecognizable in a black cocktail dress and heels, hair tightly curled, lips shimmery bubblegum. She took a seat across from him and he waved for more drinks. Minoa had to grasp the edge of the bar to keep from dashing over there and shouting, 'Don't go back, Georgia. We'll find money somehow.'

The deepening hour led to brooding on memories. Did she have an advantage over Dreema because her own mom left town and never came back providing an example of how to say no, how to put yourself first? Or did Georgia's mom keep the family together prioritizing emotional stability for Dreema and Berry over her prospects in life? Neither of those stories made much sense at this point. But what did? Not the Huaorani playacting fractured ceremonies they no longer believed in. Not people in the casino gambling their paychecks away while laughing like they just won the lottery. Nothing in this world made much sense, certainly not her situation. Oh, shut up, she told herself, and get back to work.

Georgia and Brereton chatted for a few moments and then mercifully left the bar. Minoa worked like a factory, vowing to make it to closing without another lull.

Chapter Eleven

"**S**he's a trespasser! She's a peeping tom!" Amilcar's index finger stabbed at the air in Minoa's direction. "She trespassed and spied on me. And she took photos without permission. Now she's tricking my ex-wife's mother, taking advantage of her grief, trying to make her blame me. Believe me, I'm sorry Dreema died. But it's not my fault."

The words echoed in the courtroom at the First Judicial District Court in downtown Santa Fe, public benches emptied for this emergency preliminary hearing on Georgia's request for a protection order on behalf of her granddaughter.

"No screaming, Mr. Burgos. I'll find you in contempt of court if you don't control yourself."

The silver-haired judge frowned at him. Minoa sat tight beside Georgia at the petitioner's counsel table praying Georgia would do the same. The photo lay on the judge's bench showing a male, arm in mid-swing, hand heading toward the face of a terrified Aracely. It was a pity you couldn't see the man's face but Minoa's testimony substantiated the time and place and Amilcar hadn't tried to deny that she was at his house when the photo was taken. Instead, he'd railed about her trespassing.

"Now is there anything else you'd like to tell me before I rule on the emergency petition for a protection order and temporary custody?"

"Yeah. That *sapa* is saying I'm a bad father. But what about my ex-wife's family? Why aren't you putting them on trial? They're worse than I am."

"What are you referring to, Mr. Burgos?"

"My ex-wife is gone, God rest her soul. But there was plenty of violence in that home before I showed up."

"If this is before the birth of the child in question it's not relevant."

"Not before, after. Ask Aracely."

"The court is not going to take testimony on alleged domestic violence from a young child."

"Anyway, Dreema wanted me to discipline Aracely. She didn't want her to grow up like a spoiled brat."

Minoa whispered into Georgia's ear, "Did Dreema ever tell him it was okay to hit Aracely?"

"Of course not. It's true her first husband, well, he gave her some bruises, but she would never have allowed anyone to hit Aracely."

"Hitting a child is abuse even if someone told you to do it and even if the mother gave implicit consent," the judge told Amilcar.

"Okay, I get that. But where are you gonna place my daughter if you take her away from her only living parent?"

"We have the question of custody to deal with as well. You do not have legal custody, Mr. Burgos, yet the child was with you when CYFD took temporary custody. How did that happen?"

"She told me to take her." He pointed at Georgia. "She begged me to take her. Now that Dreema's gone there's nobody in that house to take charge of the kid."

"Ms. Adkins, did you ask Mr. Burgos to take Aracely?"

"Yes."

Minoa turned to look at Georgia, who stared at the judge.

"Tell her what happened," Minoa whispered.

"The question was for Ms. Adkins," warned the judge.

She ruffled through some documents and then looked up.

"Mr. Burgos, you've already been through a regime of supervised visits and parenting classes due to an earlier CYFD investigation. So I can only assume you didn't learn much the first time."

"Look, your honor, I'm not perfect. But I'm doing better. And you don't want to place the girl with her grandmother, I can tell you that."

"Can you provide a reason why I should not do exactly that?"

He pointed at Georgia. "I'll tell you why. That's a violent family. Ask Georgia why she was living with Dreema. Ask her."

Georgia was sinking down so low in her seat Minoa feared she'd slip under the table. The pink scarf tied around her neck slipped up over her chin.

"Is this relevant to the case at hand?"

"Yeah, because it shows how Aracely is exposed to more violence at my ex-wife's house than at mine."

"Mr. Burgos, if CYFD determines both households are unfit, the child will be placed in foster care and CYFD will initiate a case for termination of parental rights."

Georgia pushed herself to her feet.

"It's alright. I'll just withdraw my petition. Aracely lost her mother. Maybe it's best that she be with her father."

Minoa glared at her.

"See what I'm saying," Amilcar beamed.

The judge looked back and forth between the two of them.

"Ms. Adkins, are you aware of any violence in your deceased daughter's home?"

"No, your honor, of course not. Everyone adores Aracely."

The judge looked from one face to another.

"This is my ruling. Having heard testimony from Minoa Diamond, a family friend who documented abuse of the minor child in question, Berta Cordova, an investigator with CYFD, Georgia Adkins, the child's maternal grandmother, and Amilcar Burgos, the child's biological father, I find that domestic violence has occurred and a temporary Civil Order of Protection against Mr. Burgos is warranted. A subsequent hearing will determine if a permanent order is to be issued. Regarding custody of the minor, temporary kinship guardianship will go to the child's grandmother, Georgia Adkins."

Without turning to look, Minoa was aware of the rage growing in Amilcar as if heat radiated from his body. The judge finished her ruling, focusing on him.

"Do you understand, Mr. Burgos? No contact of any kind, neither directly nor through a third party."

"But she's my daughter!"

He slammed a fist down on the table.

"Silence."

He fumed, then suddenly launched himself toward Minoa at the other table. Grabbing her they fell to the floor, Amilcar raining punches around her head until Minoa thrust a knee into his groin. He fell back moaning. She rolled over and pinned his arms, but he wriggled free and started a thrashing match, the two of them rolling across the courtroom floor in a chaotic whirl of blows. The deputy trundled over and started slapping at arms as he tried to capture Amilcar's wrists. After more flailing, Minoa and the deputy together subdued Amilcar. The deputy rolled him over, clipped cuffs on his wrists behind his back and pulled him to his feet.

"Ms. Diamond, I suggest you go directly to the DA's office to file charges for assault," said the judge. "Mr. Burgos will be held awaiting my decision as to how to proceed."

Minoa straightened her clothing, then she and Georgia left the courtroom. Outside, walking past territorial-style state government buildings on their way to the parking garage, Georgia made a few noises as if she had something to say but couldn't get the words out. Minoa decided not to bother with pressing charges against Amilcar — it would worsen a situation already teetering on the edge of disaster. She'd succeeded in returning Aracely to Grandma for the moment. But the violent unpredictable Amilcar now had more reasons to hate her. And how would Georgia care for Aracely without an income and soon without a home? But that wasn't all.

When she'd driven out to Tierra Feliz to pick her up for the hearing, Georgia had appeared at the door with the pink scarf around her throat. When she slid into the passenger seat, Minoa demanded that she pull off the scarf. Georgia surrendered revealing horseshoe shaped bruises. She burst into tears.

"You've got to report it," Minoa said.

"We're all stressed beyond what we can stand. I don't want to make things worse by putting Brereton in jail."

Minoa had started up the truck and gunned it down Camino de Destino.

"Listen, if he's ready to attack you for refusing to go back with him, don't tell me you'll go back thinking that will end the violence."

"No." Georgia's voice was a tiny squeak. "I won't go back now. He's gone too far. I just hope he doesn't blame you. I shouldn't have mentioned your name. I'm sorry."

Minoa stopped the truck just outside the adobe walls at the neighborhood entry.

"Uh, what did you tell him about me?"

"I was excited, I guess, and I told him you'd encouraged me to file a DV case against Amilcar and that you had taken me to see that lawyer, the one that represents accident victims, and that you would help me keep the house. He won't blame you for the separation, will he?"

"How should I know?"

Minoa had smashed her foot down on the accelerator.

Now she and Georgia drove along Alameda toward the foster care home. Aracely was jubilant to see them, throwing her plump little arms around Grandma's neck and prattling all the way back to Tierra Feliz. Maybe this will work out, Minoa told herself, doubting her own words.

After dropping them off, she walked around to the back of the house. A car track circled behind the yard and continued into the desert. She walked along it humming a tune, swinging her arms high. After it petered out she continued to the hill where the homeless fellow in a derby hat had surprised her. No sign of him now. From the top she surveyed the view, keeping her back to the city and its sprawling periphery of developments.

Off to her right stretched the indigo Jemez Mountains, below and closer the charcoal cliffs of the Rio Grande Valley edging a jumble of table-top mesas. To her left splayed the trailing end of the Rocky Mountains leading down towards the Sandias. Between facing mountain ranges a hushed emptiness poised on the baked earth strewn with bunch grass and cholla cactus.

She skipped down the hill to a ledge overlooking the arroyo where tire tracks from the snake trapper's SUV still channeled the sand. Plopped down onto a flat rock after checking underneath. Tried to think. Mind didn't want to. Tired maybe. She ought to feel satisfied she'd blocked Amilcar but didn't. Why not? She'd helped Georgia find a lawyer and obtain a protection order. Now she could end this trip back in time and return to solving her current predicament. She stood up and kicked a rock into the air to fall to the riverbed. Time to move on. She headed up the slope detouring around a cluster of yucca crowned with elliptical ivory blossoms.

Cresting the hill she started down the other side, steps drawn into a gully that widened to an arroyo aiming back toward the neighborhood. She was near enough to the houses to hear kids laughing in a backyard down the row when something glinted behind chamisa bushes lining the arroyo edge. Parting stems she saw a metal animal cage. The door on the top hung open. She reached down a hand but stopped in midair. A scent emanated from the cage, like a combination of wet dog and rotting vegetables. She dropped the hand to her side and stood rigid, wondering, as her resolution to forget about Dreema's strange death crumbled. Finally she pulled a tissue from her pocket and picked up the cage using the tissue to cover the handle.

Back at Dreema's house she was walking down the driveway when Brereton Senior pulled up in front. She waved and opened the truck door, setting the cage on the bed behind. Brereton stepped out of his car and paused, staring at her. She pretended not to notice, climbed into the truck and drove off, eyes straight ahead, determined to avoid a conversation with him. Destination? Santa Fe Police headquarters.

Chapter Twelve

"I have information about a suspicious death."

The clerk tipped one ear in Minoa's direction from behind a barrier of bulletproof glass.

"Have a seat. I'll see who's available."

She placed the cage on a built-in countertop with a couple pens dangling on ball chains and sat beside it. A few minutes later a fresh-faced young man in street clothes walked out.

"I'm Detective Ricky Martinez. Please come with me."

She followed him through a security door and down several hallways into a small office. Greenish walls checkered with wanted posters. Gun metal gray office furniture. She tried not to stare at Martinez, intrigued by his lush eyelashes and chubby cheeks shaded with bluish-black stubble.

"Which murder do you have evidence about?"

"It's not listed as a murder yet."

She noticed a film sliding over his baby brown eyes. As a junior member of the investigation team, he probably had to filter out the crazies who came in to report alien spaceship landings or cartel hitmen following them as they ran errands. She hurried to summarize the circumstances of Dreema's death, talking faster as his eyebrows drew closer together gouging furrows into the plump space between.

"Let me get this straight." He leaned back in his chair. "You're alleging that a case of death by snakebite is actually a murder because you found a discarded animal cage nearby?"

"Snake cage. In combination with other factors. The venom was a type that is unusual in this region. A witness says that someone, or possibly more than one person, went around the back of the victim's house on the night of her death. And there was at least one person who hated her and benefited from her death."

"Listen, Miss, I appreciate your concern over your friend's death." He smiled too broadly, nodded in a fake gesture of empathy.

"But here's what must have happened: some kid had a snake for a pet and it got loose in the house one too many times, so his mom made him take it out to the desert. Or maybe he put the cage out there with some bait hoping he'd catch himself a bull snake and when he never caught anything, he forgot about it."

"Little kids don't usually keep Mojave rattlers as pets."

"Exactly. That's why it's unlikely this cage ever contained one."

He rose and moved toward the door. She stood.

"Detective Martinez, are you saying a woman dies in her own bedroom by the bite of a rattlesnake whose normal range is southern Arizona and California, a discarded snake cage is found in the desert behind her house, and that's not of interest to the police?"

He paused with his hand a few inches from the doorknob to think it through. When he pulled open the door it looked like he'd decided.

"This case is not being investigated as a homicide. Frankly, I can't imagine how even the most evil animal trainer could convince a rattlesnake to slither into someone's bedroom and strike on command."

"That's not what I'm suggesting."

"I can't just send a cage to the overworked state forensic lab and ask them to test for species DNA and fingerprints when there is no murder to investigate. If we had the capability to carry out a manhunt for the rattlesnake, I would gladly have the culprit put to death."

He flashed a sarcastic smile. She spun around, stormed out the door. Outside in the parking area she dropped the cage on the truck bed and jerked open the door. As she picked her way through the rush hour free-for-all on Airport Road, she admitted he was right. An empty cage, even an empty snake cage, proved nothing. Obviously no snake would carry out the will of a murderer. So forget the cage. Even forget the snake. But the notion of a killer wouldn't go away. Could a killer have used a venom-filled hypodermic? The coverup for that kind of murder was perfect: a rattler had already entered the house and Dreema complained about it to a lot of people. Then she supposedly left her door open at night with tragic consequences. A perfect crime.

She shook her head, telling her mind to shut up. There was zero proof for that hypothesis. Why was she complicating an obvious case of accidental death? Because hopeless investigations were her specialty, like her years-long study of the Huaorani which had produced zero job offers? Whatever. Best course of action now, she decided, was a long run, then dance and drink to oblivion.

Chapter Thirteen

Funk carioca mixed with tropical house surged down her veins like an infusion of Lethe water. Arms waved like the undead in revolt, bodies huffed, footwear pounded the beaten up dance floor at Many Moons. Manufactured bliss was cooking on high until some drunken college students tipped over flattening half the dancers. Screams and laughter. After a promising linebacker rolled off Minoa, she scrambled to her knees and stood up, shaky, dusting off her leggings, hand lingering on the hip bone that had scraped across floor planks. She limped to the back of the club, sat on a bar stool and ordered a club soda lime no ice, then told the bartender to just make it a draft.

The madness on the dance floor was back in flow with a scooped area where the collapse had occurred. At the front of the crowd, crammed up against the stage, she spotted Rich doing that flat-footed shuffle that was his signature style no matter what the music, grinning at a twenty-something blonde. Suddenly she remembered his text from before she learned of Dreema's death. She'd forgotten all about it.

As she scanned back through messages on her phone she noticed the fellow on the next bar stool playing a native flute, a hand carved affair with a couple dangling feathers. The band was so loud she couldn't hear him but he seemed to be immersed in his playing. With his black ponytail and earth-toned skin he looked the part, despite the bright red UNM Lobos tee shirt.

She must have been staring, for he set the flute on his lap and gave her a look like three dots followed by a question mark.

"I just wondered why you chose this place to practice."

"I'm not practicing."

"Okay, no problem."

She looked away, sensing the hair on her forearms stand up and then roll over like hay under a mowing machine. Probably irritation. She took a swig of beer and focused on the bandstand. The musicians were propping guitars on stands, adjusting amplifiers. As they headed off stage she heard a flute melody, swooping and falling over and over like swallows at twilight. It was pretty but she avoided looking his way. Then he stopped.

"Are you a tourist or do you live here?"

She frowned, asking herself if she was obligated to respond. Finally she flashed him a glance.

"Both."

He grinned.

"Me too."

Now she bobbed her eyebrows for a low-commitment question.

"It depends on how you define here," he said. "Or whose 'here' we're talking about."

"Meaning you're New Mexican but not part of the Santa Fe imperialist class?"

"Not exactly. I'm Hopi. I work with Santa Fe's wealthy set."

"You sell real estate?"

"Art gallery."

"You own a gallery?"

"Someday. Right now I work at one."

She nodded, took a sip.

"I do installations, deliveries. It's a way to learn about fine art marketing. I'm a painter."

Familiar territory. Half the people she met at parties were artists.

"What kind of art do you make?"

"Surrealist hyperrealism with a message."

"Cool."

"What do you do here in 'the city different'?"

"Uh, I promote alcohol consumption for Lucky Coyote Inc." When he continued to stare she added, "I'm bartending at the casino. Got a degree in anthropology but couldn't find a job."

He levered his torso away from her, face contorting.

"Anthropology? You study Indian stuff? Analyze other people's way of life as if they were ants in an ant farm?"

She raised a hand to press her forehead, fearing a headache. This wasn't the first time she'd encountered this attitude. She considered using one of her stock responses but decided to wing it.

"I suppose that's why you have a good shot at making money off your art."

She capped that with a look and turned away. If he sold one lousy painting he'd make more than she ever would off the years devoted to coursework, grant and post-doc apps, articles, conference presentations, along with years eating grubs and yucca and monkey meat in an Amazonian village with a bunch of barely reformed homicidal maniacs. Hunched her shoulders and poured a long drizzle of beer down her throat.

"Do anthropologists ever wonder whether the people whose hospitality they're enjoying would be better able to describe their own customs?"

She swung her head back.

"For your information, anthropologists have agonized over that question."

"What's to agonize? Why not just agree to respect each other's privacy and stay home?"

"Look, you can study Anglo culture if you want. Nobody's stopping you."

"Wouldn't it be more efficient to study one's own cultural practices? Why don't gringo anthropologists write about nuclear war or sex slavery?"

"Look, I agree with you. And I think native peoples should publish their own observations for balance. Aren't the Hopi into balance?"

"You're sinking to that cultural stereotype?"

"Sorry."

She turned away, resolved to end the conversation. After a moment she heard his voice.

"Relax, Margaret Mead, I don't hate all anthropologists."

She clenched her jaw pretending not to hear.

"So what do you do for fun?"

Looked like he wasn't going to give up. She looked over.

"I spend a lot of time trying to figure out what to do with an anthropology degree other than bartending." Was he smiling? "I like to run."

"Me too. My high school cross country team won State a million times."

"Congratulations. My team at Santa Fe High never won a thing."

"At least you still run."

"I don't have much else to do. I mean, recently I had to deal with a death. A friend of mine died."

She asked herself why she told him that. Concluded she was stressed and ... lonely.

"That's too bad. A car wreck?"

"Rattler."

She glanced at him to check his reaction. He was waiting for her to continue.

"Since her unusual death I think about rattlers a lot. I even started dreaming about them."

"Dreams are powerful. You'd better pay attention."

"It's nothing. The first time I hadn't slept much. The second time, well, anybody would be affected. Dying by snakebite is ... revolting. And tragic."

"You think dreams are meaningless?"

"Of course not. I analyze dreams with friends sometimes. We take dreams seriously. We read Jung."

"Just not this one?"

"Look, these images popped into my mind for an instant. I don't know why I mentioned it. Could we talk about something else?"

"Anything other than snakes, right?"

"My friend died of snakebite. I'm stressed. Unrelated situations."

"Anglos seem to think that the material world and consciousness are separated by an impassable wall. Unless you have the weapons to impose your vision on others. Then your wish becomes their fate."

She squinted at him sideways while sipping her beer.

"People who think their thoughts alter the world are considered insane."

"That's everybody I know. Anyone who believes their thoughts are ineffective has a license to think whatever they want."

She gazed around the club. Lots of people chatting, drinking, forgetting the past and the future. Why was this guy pressing her?

"Look, I'm just trying to be logical."

"Anglo logic is a cool toy but it doesn't explain meaningful connections, does it?"

"I don't know how we got off on this topic."

"You said Indians should study Anglos, right?"

"I guess I did. Okay, Jung talked about synchronicity, you know, meaningful connections that can't be explained by scientific causality."

"And?"

"My point is that my old friend died of a rattlesnake bite. By pure chance I'm back in town and her brother I haven't seen in years finds me and invites me to the wake and then her ex- shows up with a knife and later attacks me in court and meanwhile I see a senior citizen poaching rattlers and end up finding a reptile cage behind her house and now I can't stop thinking about rattlesnakes."

"And dreaming about them."

She scowled at him.

"None of this is mere coincidence, is it?"

"I don't know what it is. I should just stop thinking about it."

"But you can't."

"Is this a Hopi version of therapy?"

"Reverse fieldwork. You're my informant."

"Honored."

She checked to see if the band had returned from break.

"Am I making you uncomfortable?"

She turned back to him.

"Do you really want to know what I think or are you just trying to prove that anthropology and anthropologists suck?"

At that moment Rich walked up, forehead crinkled beneath a retro poof of brown hair. His eyes flicked between her and the flute player.

"Hey, Minoa, I didn't know you were here."

His voice sounded warped.

"I saw you up front but you were busy."

"You never answered my text."

"A lot has happened, Rich."

"Aren't you going to introduce me to your friend?"

"We just met."

Rich walked over and leaned his backside against the bar between their legs.

"Rich," she cautioned.

He stretched out his hand, tipped sideways and righted.

"I'm Rich. We might as well get acquainted since looks like we're both friends of Ms. Diamond."

"Rich, you're drunk and you're being ridiculous."

"The name is Lewis." The Hopi guy stood up stretching an arm to indicate his stool. "The grand *Pahaana* would probably like to sit down. It's been a pleasure, Minoa."

He walked away, disappearing into the crowd. She turned a furious expression on Rich.

"Maybe you're so wasted you don't realize you're acting like a jerk."

"I've been missing you so I was drinking to console myself."

"Did it work?"

"Now that you're here."

He smiled a sloppy grin. She looked out at people moving onto the dance floor.

"I've been super busy."

"Me too."

"That rich dude up above Abiquiu?"

"Yeah, you should see the railing I carved for him on a curving staircase. Looks like cougars leaping. He's pretty impressed."

"Maybe he'll become your patron."

"Patron? Don't know about that. But he invites me in for drinks after work and lets me drive his Aston Martin into town sometimes."

"Invites you in? Is he gay?"

"What do I care? He wants me to cast a big piece for his estate."

"More pouncing predators?"

"It's work and we both know how hard that is to come by."

"I guess he's your ideal market demographic."

"Not ideal just ... Santa Fe."

The band members on stage fiddled with amplifiers, guitars.

"Where'd he get his money?"

"He said he was on Wall Street. Hey, I've got the funds for a nice dinner. How about the coyote tomorrow night?"

"Are you kidding? What, did he set up a trust fund for you? Look Rich, I'm in the middle of something."

"More job apps?"

The band launched into a clunky rock version of *El Gallo Celoso*.

"My old friend was killed by a rattlesnake," she yelled over the music.

"What?" he screamed back.

"I said a rattlesnake. Oh, forget it."

Chapter Fourteen

S lices of a rainbow, refracted through a crystal-decorated dream-catcher dangling before one window, danced on her eyelids. Minoa squinted open, rolled sideways to avoid the glare, stopping just before she bumped into a white whale on her bed — Rich's broad-backed form under a sheet. Squeezed her eyes shut, determined to go back to sleep. Didn't work.

She stood up, pulled on shorts and a tee, surveyed the cluttered guesthouse, clothes dropped on the tile floor, a row of books domino-tipped across the desk, dishes in the kitchenette sink. Gazed at torrents of solar waves pouring through window glass. She scribbled on a piece of paper: 'Had to check on a job. M.' Laid it on her pillow. Then grabbed her keys and was out the door before Rich stirred.

The truck was unlocked; she'd come home tipsy enough not to notice. She climbed in, noticing a faint odor of rattlesnake that reminded her of the cage in the back. Where to, she asked herself? She sensed that familiar itch that always started back of her navel and spread to her extremities, that urgent need to go somewhere, anywhere. Problem was she'd run out of places to run to. She buzzed like a loose electric wire until an idea came to her. She'd head to the University of New Mexico library in Albuquerque for some job research. Maybe she'd poke around for information on rattlesnake deaths as well.

Driving south out of town she put in a call to Georgia to see how little Aracely was doing. As the phone rang out from the cell sitting on her lap, she spotted the area far out on the Caja del Rio plateau where Tierra Feliz hunkered, midway between I-25, the Rio Grande and hell. No answer. She'd assume that Georgia hadn't overdosed and Amilcar hadn't burst through the front door with a loaded rifle.

She coasted down La Bajada, the big descent from Santa Fe to the lower elevation region around Albuquerque, staying in the left lane far from the drop-off along the right side of the highway that could launch a car all the way to Cochiti pueblo land. Then up and down the rollercoaster ride to Albuquerque, crossing terrain gouged by one dry watershed after another. Near the midpoint of the hour-long trip she noticed the funky gas gauge, needle bent sideways from a quarter tank to nothing, which she'd learned through painful experience meant about two miles from a long walk. There was nothing on the road until Bernalillo, north of Albuquerque, except an abandoned outlet mall. Her brain fired up, cranked out an estimate of miles and fuel.

"Crap," she muttered, picturing a choice between a hot bushwhack to Santo Domingo Pueblo somewhere to the west or a terrifying hitchhike on the side of the interstate.

But wait. What about the Cochiti Pueblo casino? She hadn't passed it yet and it included a truck stop. So she held her breath and crawled over the next few hills until, topping one, she spotted it. Eased onto the exit ramp, rolled down and had just passed the stop sign when something caught her eye on the floor on the passenger's side. In an unthinkable instant a wedge-shaped head appeared from under the seat, forked tongue flicking, followed by a long muscular diamond-back body that methodically began to coil itself on the passenger side floor mat.

In a nanosecond the blood in her veins froze and her muscles locked down as her mind sped up thousands of times faster than normal.

It will sense my body heat. How long until it strikes? I can't take my foot off the gas pedal or the movement will attract a strike. Could I jerk open the door handle and hurl myself out before it strikes? Don't be absurd. A rattlesnake strikes faster than the eye can follow. I'd be bitten before I hit the pavement.

So her panicked thoughts raged as the car rolled under an overpass heading toward the casino. While minutely adjusting the steering wheel, her eyes roamed the scene framed by the windshield. Casino, abandoned walkway in front, a row of heat-shriveled bushes, asphalt expanse dotted by scattered light posts. No one to call on for help. No security guard or passerby. Not that anyone outside the car could act in time to save her.

The snake emerged from under the seat, all five feet of it, completing its spiral. *Perfect position for striking,* she screamed at herself. It seemed to stare at her although she knew it was probably sensing infrared radiation with the pits below its eyes. Perhaps the vibrations of the moving car pacified it. What if this snake was a Mojave hybrid with neurotoxic venom that would paralyze your muscles so you couldn't even cry out for help? She'd slump over the steering wheel and they wouldn't investigate, taking her for another drunk who'd lost her last dime at the casino and indulged in one last binge — they saw it every day of the week.

There must be some way out. Throw her bag at its head as she pitched herself out the door? Crash that side of the truck into a light post, stunning the snake to give her time to escape? Scream so someone from the truck stop would come running and save her? Blast the horn to confuse the snake? Ridiculous. Through this horror movie cut flashes of her life seen from the perspective of an early death at age thirty-six. Would anyone think it bizarre that childhood best friends died of the same rare cause within two weeks of each other?

Clamping her jaw, squeezing the steering wheel, she smashed the gas pedal to the floorboard and headed toward a light post. A memory strangely flickered for an instant, a recollection of one day in Ecuador when a twenty foot long boa constrictor swirled down toward her dreaming head and one of the Huaorani women had to pull her to safety, amusing the group of mothers and children. That story had been told and retold in the evenings to hysterical laughter.

At the moment of impact she screamed. The right front end hit a post, whipping the back end around in a semicircle. As the truck spun she jerked open the door handle and flew out noting a flash of movement to her right.

She rolled across the parking lot to stop in a dizzied heap. Groped her side for puncture marks, blood, swelling, something to tell her if she would live or die as awareness of the sizzling asphalt percolated into awareness. A few more heartbeats and she perceived a shadow across her eyes. Squinted up at a figure towering above.

"Help."

The croak barely squeezed out of her thickened throat, already closing up, she thought, from the effects of the venom.

"Do you need a hand?"

She reached up an arm to see if the muscles obeyed. The figure knocked the car door shut and pulled her to her feet. Though shaky, she stood.

"Wanna tell me why you were hauling a rattlesnake around in your truck?"

"But ... was I struck?"

She ran a hand up and down her right arm, patted the right side of her hip and torso.

"Only if it went for you before me."

"What?"

He shepherded her dazed self over to the sidewalk in front of the casino and pushed her onto the curb. She crouched there, unable to form her mouth into the shape required to pronounce a word, internally scanning her body for symptoms. Then she peered up at him.

"You? Why are you here?"

He barked a laugh and kicked the pavement. Then drilled her with his eyes.

"Probably to save you from a sorry fate."

She examined his face, black level brows that tipped down in the middle as if he never stopped thinking, plain brown cheeks cut hard at the jawline, eyes ironic.

"You're the one ... from Many Moons."

She struggled to sort image pieces into recognizable stuff: a parking lot, a building, a gas station, a desert. And the Hopi flute player from last night. Was this a dream? Was she comatose and delusional? Or already dead?

"I was standing by the highway trying to hitch a ride. When you drove by I ran over to see if you might give me a ride south. But you took off on that kamikaze attack on the poor light pole. When I looked through the passenger window your friend struck at me. If he hadn't hit the glass I'd be lying on the pavement with a head the size of a watermelon."

A revised picture of what had happened rearranged her thoughts. It was a miracle. The crash had bought her a moment to escape while Lewis approached from the other side of the car and drew the snake's strike. She stared out at the desert landscape surrounding the casino and truck stop, buoyed on an upsurge of gratitude until a falling anvil of guilt smashed down. What if the window had been lower? What if Lewis had been struck in the face? But luck had been with them both. He was walking around the truck, peering in.

"Why the hell did you take it out of that cage? Do you think rattlesnakes are pets?"

"The cage?" Then she remembered the cage sitting in the truck bed. "It was never in the cage. Somebody put that snake in the cab of my truck."

He hooked thumbs in jeans pockets and squinted at her.

"You better explain."

She stood up and started pacing back and forth in front of the casino. A few diehard morning gamblers had to scuttle to one side to avoid being run over. Finally paused and faced him.

"This proves it!" she yelled.

He stared at her, his expression contorted.

"I'm not crazy. Dreema was murdered."

Chapter Fifteen

"A re you saying that rattler already killed somebody and then you turned it loose in the cab of your truck?"

"What? No, I'll have to fill you in. But first we've got to cage that snake so I can drive to Santa Fe police headquarters and present it as exhibit number one to justify a murder investigation."

"You're going to file charges against a snake for murder?"

She stopped pacing and stared at him.

"Sorry. I'm confusing you. I told you an old friend of mine died by rattlesnake bite in her bedroom. The police labeled it an accidental death."

"And you think it was murder?"

His words carried a hint of sarcasm. She frowned at him.

"Somebody put that snake in my truck to kill me, the same way he put a snake in my friend's room."

"Or like you said last night, you're attracting rattlesnakes."

"I didn't say that. I said I had a couple dreams. But this is not a dream. This proves my friend was murdered."

"What's the proof?"

"The proof is the improbability. Rattlesnakes don't slither into bedrooms or trucks. Yet that happened to two high school friends within days of each other."

"And when the police suggest a snake crawled into your car on its own? Or maybe you contrived the whole thing to get attention?"

She sank back down onto the curb and propped her chin on her hand.

"The brilliance of using rattlesnakes as a weapon is that nobody imagines they could carry out the will of a human. And they're so common. Still, with photos of the snake in my car the police will understand."

She stood and walked over to the truck, glancing in through the driver's side window. Her cell phone was sitting on the seat. His voice followed.

"Just don't mention the cage in the back."

She turned around and stared.

"That cage makes it look like I was carrying a snake around in my car, like I'm the one who's turning rattlers loose everywhere." She circled the truck a few times. "Is there no way to prove somebody put that snake in there to kill me?"

Lewis crossed his arms and waited.

"Detective Martinez already thinks I'm deranged. If I claim this was a second attempted murder by rattlesnake, he'll probably have me committed."

She moved around to the passenger side and looked in the window without getting too close. The rattler flicked its forked tongue at her.

"I can remove the snake, if that's what you want."

"You can?"

"Are you sure you don't want to take this snake to the police?"

"What good would it do?"

Without another word he walked along the sidewalk in front of the casino and disappeared around the far corner where open desert loomed against a background of Sandia Mountains foothills. A few minutes later he came walking back down the sidewalk carrying a stalk of dried yucca flowers in one hand and a stick with a fork at one end in the other.

He inserted the yucca stalk through the partially open window and shook it, rattling the dried pods with seeds inside like maracas. As the snake focused, Lewis used the forked stick to pin the snake's head to the floor. Dropping the yucca stalk his hand went in and caught the snake just behind the head. He pulled the entire length of it out and held it up in midair with the thick Diamondback body flexing up and down in angry S curves, rattle shaking ferociously. Minoa pulled her cell out of the truck and snapped a picture. He walked out into the desert and returned in a few minutes, empty-handed.

"That was amazing. You probably learned how to do that at the Snake Dance."

"Probably."

He stared out at the scene beyond the casino parking lot where a wide dry wash led down to buttes lining the Rio Grande. A few horses grazed alongside the arroyo.

"I can give you a ride to Albuquerque."

"Sounds good."

He found an electric cord in one of the trash cans at the gas station and tied on the bent bumper. After filling the tank she headed back onto the highway, nerves still buzzing but grateful to have someone sitting beside her. He rode without speaking, looking out the windows as mile after mile of rangeland slipped past. Even when she continued west of Albuquerque on the highway to Gallup he didn't say anything. She wondered if he was angry at her for almost getting him snakebitten or just avoiding conversation with a supposed anthropologist. As they approached the eggshell cliffs outside Grants, she had to speak.

"I'm sorry that snake struck at you but it wasn't my fault."

He turned a bemused expression on her.

"I see that hanging out with you could be dangerous."

"I don't usually travel with Diamondbacks."

"You dream about them."

"That's not my fault either. And I shouldn't have mentioned it. Anyway, thanks for saving my life."

"What's your next move?"

"No idea. The only thing I know for sure is that I'm sick to death of rattlesnakes."

"Careful what you say."

A tiny pulse of anxiety coursed down her limbs to disperse into the lukewarm air trapped inside the truck cab, desert heat neck-and-neck with a clunky AC.

"Can we talk about something else?"

He grinned at her.

"You always want to escape."

She swallowed hard, focused on driving. She would not allow this guy to therapize her even if he had saved her life. By accident. The conversation sputtered out until driving onto the old Highway 66 in Gallup.

"What do you think I should do?" she ventured as he stepped down into the parking lot of Rudy's Coffee Shop, a down home affair with a neon slice of pie on the roof.

He scuffed a boot toe on the asphalt, then answered with that habitual sarcastic smile.

"Walk carefully and carry a forked stick."

She grimaced a fake-grin and turned away, resentment and gratitude lobbing grenades at each other in her mind. He shut the truck door, shouldered his bag and headed down the sidewalk, lifting a hand in a backwards goodbye. He'd said he knew someone in Gallup who could drive him home. She cranked up the truck and pulled out, careful not to look his way.

***

Cars, RV's, semis streaked down the interstate toward Albuquerque, their speed reduced to nothing viewed against the vast encircling horizon. Traveling in the wind-whipped truck, still tainted by the odor of rattlesnake, Minoa's jangled nerves quieted as her thoughts sped up. Who put that giant rattler in her car? It had to be the same person who killed Dreema, someone who didn't want her interfering. But with everyone convinced Dreema's death was an accident, why would the killer risk another rattler attack? She must have crossed some line. What had she done that made Dreema's killer think she had to be eliminated? Was this Amilcar's response to the protection order that jerked custody of Aracely? Or some rattler-obsessed psychopath with an irresistible compulsion to kill? Either way another attack was likely. Where would she next encounter a rattlesnake? The thought sent a seismic tremor down her backbone.

Staring out the dust-laced windshield at mile after mile of stark desert, she offered the powers of the desert a deal: If she agreed to tolerate the rattlers slithering in and out of burrows all over this sun-scarred country, would they please please please keep them away from her? No response.

When she reached Albuquerque, with slice-of-watermelon mountains looming over acres of shabby stucco developments and refurbished strip malls, Georgia's civil case popped into her mind. She was filing suit against the subdivision developer for negligence that led to Dreema's death. Morrison had spoken of a big award if they won.

What would happen if it turned out somebody put that snake in Dreema's room? Homicide invalidated a civil claim. She grabbed her cell and dialed Chet Morrison. He was one of the few men on her contacts list, she noticed. Now Lewis' name clung to the list although she'd only taken it to be polite. After a screening, the receptionist put her through to the man.

"Minoa, good to hear from you."

She could see him perfectly: five hundred dollar cowboy boots crossed on the mahogany desk, tie loosened, cappuccino in hand, staring out the floor-to-ceiling windows of his suite at the same craggy rose-hued cliffs she was skating by on I-25 north.

"I just wondered if there is any news on the case."

"We've had an investigator in the neighborhood interviewing people and our construction consultant inspected Ms. Adkin's house. He found some code violations. Too soon to get your hopes up but the evidence begins to accumulate."

"Fantastic."

"The real estate developer, T. Reddy Shauvenupp, is a character. He confronted the investigator and sent some tattooed goon to chase him away." Morrison paused for a guffaw. "Not to worry. That kind of defensive reaction usually stems from ignorance of the law which will work to our advantage. And if he obstructs or gets more aggressive, we'll use it against him."

"I sure hope no more rattlers appear in that house."

"*Au contraire,* that would help our case. I'll have my paralegal call Ms. Adkins so she knows to notify us the minute she hears a rattle."

How fast would Georgia's reactions be in the moment of a snake encounter if she were in the grip of another valium overdose? She probably overdosed on a daily basis. And if Aracely ran into another rattlesnake in the house? Unthinkable.

"Maybe they should move out for now?"

"Much better to stay on site and collect evidence. Another snake attack could cinch the case."

"I suppose it would strengthen the case if another member of the family dies by snakebite."

Morrison laughed.

"The odds of that happening are steeper than me winning the New Mexico state lottery, not that I didn't pick up a ticket this morning when I stopped for gas."

"How long before the case is resolved?"

"These are just the preliminary steps in a process which will take several years."

"Several years? Isn't there any way to speed this up? Could you maybe offer Shauvenupp a deal? Ms. Adkins has a dire need for money."

"Hold your horses. This is not the moment to negotiate. First we turn up the pressure. When Shauvenupp gets a clearer idea of the legal costs and negative publicity involved in contesting our complaint, then we make an offer to settle. Even if he refuses and we go to trial, we'll have an edge. Juries hate to see mothers of young children die. They want somebody to pay big for that poor orphaned kid. We're looking at a bigger award if we win than some poor schmuck who gets crushed by an earthmover at a construction site — possibly hundreds of millions."

"And if we lose?"

"You're not out a dime. No fee unless you win. Listen, my secretary will be in touch. Just trust your hired gun to clean out the rustlers."

She pictured him offering a grinning thumbs up to the mountains as he pushed the call button to his secretary and instructed her to transfer future calls from Minoa to the paralegal. She hadn't forgotten to tell him about her own rattler encounter, just decided it was inopportune. The wrongful death suit could win a lot of money for him and Georgia. Neither of them would make a cent off a murder case. She'd walked herself into the role of saving Dreema's bereaved family. Would she turn around now and ruin Georgia's chances for a judgment to compensate her and Aracely for their loss? No, everyone would be better off with no talk of murder.

Besides, she reasoned, the two rattler encounters could be unlucky accidents. She'd heard of improbable things happening twice, like someone struck by lightning on separate occasions, or two members of a family dying in unrelated airplane crashes. Perhaps a Mojave hybrid rattlesnake slithered through a gap in the flooring into Dreema's bedroom and curled up under the bed. When Dreema's arm dropped off the side of the bed as she slept, the startled snake struck. Feeling threatened, it slithered back into its hole.

Then she or Rich left the truck door open when they returned to her guesthouse last night. On a chilly desert night a rattler would seek the engine's warmth. *Voila*! A reasonable explanation that allowed the legal suit to proceed. Minoa's brush with a rattlesnake was just more of the bad luck she'd tried and failed to escape by moving to New York, to Ecuador, back to New York and then back to Santa Fe. Another failed geographic. Anyway, there was no synchronistic meaning in all this, despite what Lewis suggested. Just a pile-up of bad luck. She drove north out of Albuquerque, checking the gas gauge, determined to forget about rattlesnakes.

Chapter Sixteen

T. Reddy Shauvenupp was standing outside his Wild West office when she turned into Tierra Feliz. How perfect that he and Cowboy Chet ambled toward a showdown. All that lacked were a couple of six-shooters and ten-gallon hats. He was talking to the tattooed young man beside that turquoise vintage truck. Shauvenupp gave her a venomous look as she drove by. In the rearview mirror she saw him snap a cell photo of the back of her truck. Was that a threat? That assistant was the one who had been firing into the air as the old snake woman collected rattlesnakes off Tierra Feliz land. So instead of shooting snakes to carry out his employer's 'reptile elimination program,' he must be selling them on the sly. She filed that deduction for later.

After parking in front of Dreema's house she launched a search on her cell for information on Shauvenupp. He had worked for the New Mexico Chapter of the National Association of Commercial Real Estate Developers, lobbying state lawmakers for passage of the Tax Increment Development Act. A bit of noodling revealed that the law allowed developers to finance the construction of infrastructure, such as streets and sewage, with taxpayer money. So Schauvenupp was a former lobbyist for the real estate industry. How had he accumulated the capital to pay down on Tierra Feliz? Was that an informal 'thank you' from some multi-million dollar developer for helping to shift millions in costs to New Mexico citizens? Carter would love to hear about this.

Rubbing her eyes she noticed the brownish stucco houses circling like a herd of giant horny toads dozing in the buoyant August air. How long had she been sitting here in the truck in front of Dreema's house? She grabbed a pair of sunglasses for the trip inside, protection against the onslaught of Georgia's woes. As she trudged up the inclined drive-way she saw Aracely standing rock still, her back to Minoa, right hand raised as if waving a fist in anger.

"Aracely?" she called out as she approached.

The girl didn't budge. Minoa circled in front of her and paused. Aracely held a popsicle stick in her raised fist. The popsicle had melted, coating her fingers in electric blue goop that puddled on the cement drive. Tears bathed her face. She stared down to where a piece of blackish garden hose lay on the driveway.

"It's just a little piece of hose," Minoa said.

When Aracely remained frozen, Minoa picked up the hose and threw it across the front yard.

Aracely bolted to the front door shrieking, "Snake! Snake! Snake! Snake!"

When Georgia opened the door, Aracely collided into her. After regaining her footing Georgia scooped her up, stroked her hair and disappeared down the hallway. The cacophany of screams diminished until a shut door stifled it. Minoa wandered into the living room to find Berry standing there.

"Aracely mistook a piece of hose for a snake. Poor kid."

His eyes bulged but he turned around without a word to stare out the glass door on the back of the house. She moved to a chair.

"I imagine we're all seeing snakes everywhere."

"Damnit!" He spun around to stare at her with eyes of fire, making her lurch as she was sitting down. "That worthless scumbag Amilcar must have scared her with snakes."

She reached out a hand to the coffee table to steady herself, classified his words as grief-provoked temporary insanity and modulated her voice to pacify.

"Her mother's death has traumatized her. She might acquire a phobia of snakes as a result. Maybe some counseling?"

"It's all his fault. I should have killed him when I had the chance."

His fists clenched, unclenched, clenched.

"What makes you think Amilcar frightened her with snakes?"

"I never liked him." He tucked his chin into his neck as if he would like to eat the collar of his navy polo. "First he was dealing and taking Dreema around all the traffickers and addicts he hung out with. We only found out later, after they arrested him. Otherwise I would have killed the wetback rat on the spot and avoided all this."

His hands rigidified as if by electro-shock, then went limp and dangled at his sides.

"After they settled his case — the incompetent D.A. turned him loose with two years of probation — he flip-flopped, got religion and joined some fanatical cult up north. Could have been the *Penitentes*, the ones who nail some poor fool to the cross every Easter. But there are rumors some splinter group up north engages in snake handling just like in the backwoods of Appalachia, where my dad grew up. That bastard probably made little Aracely participate in some sick cult. If I'd have been here in town, I would have stuffed him into a rattler hole, head first."

He slammed his fist into the sliding glass door he had turned back to face, making the safety glass shudder. Minoa stared at his back, pondering.

"Do you suspect Amilcar exposed Dreema to a rattlesnake?"

It was as if an alpine wind whooshed down off Santa Fe Baldy into poor forgotten Tierra Feliz. His frame sagged. When he turned around again frost crystals laced his eyes.

"What kind of stupid loser am I that I treated this like an accident? Of course he did it. Why didn't I realize that right away? It was obvious from the minute he pulled a knife on his own brother-in-law. I'm such a coward. All these years I left Dreema alone to cope with that psycho trafficker while I just did my life in OK City. If only I'd ended this long ago before he had the chance to kill my precious sister."

He raised his hands to his temples and swung his head back and forth, emitting a high-pitched moan. When he paused he stared right through her.

"Sweet jeezus, I'm going to kill that weasel-faced devil."

At that moment Georgia shuffled in.

"I'm sorry. I have to calm Aracely down before Brereton picks her up for his visit."

"No problem."

Berry stormed past them, slamming the front door behind him.

"Where's he going?"

"Give me a minute."

Minoa ran after. She reached his rental car as he threw it into gear and grabbed the door handle. He rolled down the window.

"Let go of the car, Minoa."

"Berry, we have no proof yet that Dreema's death wasn't an accident. And another violent encounter with Amilcar could get you killed."

"That bastard is the reason this happened to Dreema, whether he held fangs to her or not. He did nothing but drag her down. And I didn't stop him. Two worthless sons of bitches abused my only sister over years and I did nothing." He pounded fists on the steering wheel. "I didn't do a goddamned thing to protect my sister."

He busted wide open, puking a torrent of sobs, slamming his forehead into the steering wheel. Minoa stuck her arm through the window and pulled out the key. Berry looked up to see her ducking out and tried to grab her arm.

"Give me that key!"

"Could we please talk for a few minutes before you decide what to do? Think how your mother will feel if something happens to you."

"I don't care if he kills me. I want him to kill me. Then the cops will arrest him and at least he'll go to jail. That's better than having him free to steal back Aracely."

"The judge denied him visits."

"That won't last. At some point he'll keep his ugly nose clean long enough to get custody. Then he will have killed my sister and stolen my niece."

He hunched over and coughed out more sobs. Minoa's line of sight rose to the housetop rooflines and beyond to an afternoon sky studded with lines of cloud puffs like the remnants of smoke signals.

"I suffered a snake attack today."

Berry hiccuped and looked at her, his cheeks gleaming.

"What?"

"Don't tell your mom. This is between us."

"Tell me what happened."

"A rattler in my truck. My first thought was that the same person who murdered Dreema by putting a rattler in her bedroom tried to kill me by putting one in my truck. But it's possible Dreema's death and my snake encounter were accidents, a freak coincidence."

Berry gripped the steering wheel.

"That monster is going to kill all of us, one by one."

"Look, why don't you let me investigate? If I can't find out anything in the next couple days, you can take whatever action you like. But give me a little time to try."

He stared out the windshield like a house god facing down the evil spirits of the desert.

"Go ahead. Do whatever you want. I'm not promising anything."

She waited for a minute, then headed back up the drive to the house.

"I'm leaving now," she called in the front door.

Georgia came padding to the threshold, squinted at Berry sitting in his rental car and turned back to Minoa.

"Do you know where he's going?"

Minoa handed her the car key.

"Keep Berry occupied for the next few days. Yard work, house repairs, closing accounts, whatever."

"Maybe he should go back to Oklahoma City?"

"Whatever it takes to keep him from driving to Amilcar's place."

Georgia's eyes stretched longways. Minoa headed back down the drive, steps picking up speed. Berry was still sitting in his car, stiff as wood. As she settled into the driver's seat of the truck she blew out deep breaths causing a haze of dust particles to levitate up from the dash. What the hell had she gotten herself into now? She took another breath sucking in a mouthful of dust. Coughed until her throat hurt. Then she fired up the engine and sped away.

Chapter Seventeen

S he drove out Camino de Destino scouring her brain for ideas and turned onto the county road. As she drove past trailers on parched squares of land and stucco houses fronting barbed wire pens holding a couple bored ponies, interspersed with salt cedars wherever water seeped, nothing occurred to her. Only one thing was clear as an artesian spring: she wasn't driving out to Amilcar's place again. Where the county lane met the frontage road she paused, looked right and left. About a quarter mile down to her right she glimpsed a flash of turquoise. Felipe's classic truck turned out of a side road and headed south. He was leaving Tierra Feliz during work hours, going out of town, not into town to pick up supplies or run errands. What was he doing? The only routes ahead of him would be the interstate south to Albuquerque or southeast on the Turquoise Trail, a two lane back country highway that wound through a couple of reclaimed ghost towns around the back of the Sandia Mountains on its way to Albuquerque or the Manzano Mountains farther south. She followed.

He veered onto the Turquoise Trail, driving through rangeland speckled with the modest homes of people escaping the pumped up real estate market in Santa Fe. On the flat stretch by the state penitentiary she let a car slip between her truck and his. Then, where the road bucked like a green colt, she pulled back behind him, slowing as she approached the top of each hill until his truck vanished over the next one. He continued past a ladder of side roads to coast into a broad valley bordering the Ortiz Mountains. Sailed past the turnoff to Cerrillos, a cluster of century old adobes that had served as a set for old westerns.

When the road rose, zigzagging around hillsides glittering with the minerals which once drew prospectors, she floored the accelerator. But though she sped, nearly skidding a back wheel off the switchbacks, she couldn't catch sight of the turquoise pickup. Rolling into Madrid, a jumble of retrofitted shacks by an old mine shaft, she concluded she'd lost him.

She turned around and wound back through the hillocks. As she emerged onto the valley floor, a road she hadn't noticed before caught her eye, Gold Mine Road. She turned and headed down its lonely stretch, accompanied on the left by barbed wire fencing and occasional ranch gates, on the right by mottled gray hills.

Suddenly, up ahead where the road met the horizon, a turquoise dot surfaced. He was coming back. She braked, pulled a U and headed back to a dirt track leading up into the hills. As the turquoise dot reappeared topping another hill, she turned onto the track and made it up a rubbly incline to park behind a pile of boulders. Dashed over, scrambled up a boulder and crouched there, spying across the rocks as he drove by. In the truck bed she spied a wood frame box. Had it been there before?

The turquoise truck disappeared from view and once again a dazzling silence filled the cavern between bleached land and electrified sky. Thunderheads were gathering over the distant Sangre de Cristos, midnight blue with ruffling black edges. She picked her way over the boulders, climbed in the truck, then pumped the brakes down to Gold Mine Road and turned right.

Within a half-mile Gold Mine Road ran into Vista del Oro and that road soon dead-ended. Where could he have gone? Retracing her path she noted the turnoff options: a gate with 'Triangle Y Ranch' carved into the arch, a cattle guard with a peeling sign beside it for 'Ortiz Mountain Horse Shelter,' a track with a 'No Trespassing' sign leading to a vintage airstream house trailer hooked to a geodesic dome, and finally a faint road with no marking that meandered up into the hills. Looked like the only option so she parked the truck and strode up the slope. At the first curve she began bushwhacking through the hills just out of sight of the road.

She traversed around the sides of hilltops, kicking steps into thick gray dirt that blew puffs of dust into the air with each footfall. Soon she eased to the top of a hill and scanned the terrain. In a draw she spotted a cluster of buildings nestled into the side of a cliff, a house with outbuildings. Didn't look like a ranching operation, she'd seen plenty of those. No stock corrals, no piled up hay bales with tarp cover or pavilion roof, no stock tank, no forklift. Wasn't a horse breeder either: no arena, no horse walker, no barn with stalls. She'd heard of a growing dairy goat industry in the area but saw no sign of goats. The smaller buildings looked slapped together out of plywood and corrugated tin. Could it be the retreat of some hermit survivalist? But Felipe had been going somewhere with that cage in the back of his truck. She saw no dogs, so she decided to swing closer.

After jogging to the far side of the hill, she picked her way down a cascade of rocky terraces clogged by chamisa flocked with masses of tiny gold flowers. At the base, where the ravine opened into a valley floor thick with native grasses, she walked around the hill until the buildings came into view. Still no sign of life until, moving closer, a tickle in her nostrils stopped her cold. She scanned the ground but saw no 'narrow fellow,' as Emily Dickinson put it. The odor filtered from a hut set off a bit from the other structures. She padded over to a dust-clouded window on the back of the shack, peered inside and froze.

An old woman stood with her back to the window, a kerchief on her head, gray braids hanging down her back. She wore a man's Khaki work shirt over a calico broom skirt and Wellingtons. Minoa ducked behind the wall, took a few fast breaths and then sneaked one eye around the window frame to spy. The old woman was pulling something out of a box, cupping it in her hands and placing it inside the door of one of the stacked wire mesh cages lining the walls. A skinny hairless tail poked out of the woman's hands, whipped back and forth. A mouse. The cages, in stacks of six, rested on legs raising the structure above the ground about a foot and a half. Her brain pinged: snakes. These were snake cages and the old woman was feeding them live mice. There must have been thirty snakes in the hut if all the cages had occupants.

She sank back against the wall feeling as if she'd drunk something rotten, wondering if feeding live rodents to snakes was standard practice for reptile care or sadistic animal cruelty. Couldn't see the face but the woman's gray hair said this must be the snake trapper she'd seen in the desert near Dreema's place. What was she doing living out here in the hills with all these snakes? No sign on the drive, this was no legitimate business. A horrified fascination caused her to lean back around the edge of the window frame.

The woman had turned sideways revealing wrinkle-sliced skin, drooping eyelids and the muscular jaw line of someone who does physical work. She placed several more trembling mice in cages, turned her back and stepped out of view.

Minoa stood hesitating, transfixed by the creepiness of the situation as questions ricocheted around her mind exactly as she imagined those desperate mice were bouncing around the cages. Should she report the woman to animal protection? And what was she doing with all these snakes? Then it came to her: she must be selling snake venom. Not a bad venture for a pensioner. Snake venom sold for around fifty thousand dollars an ounce, as she recalled. And if she paid no taxes on it ...

Without warning a circle of cold metal bumped into her spine. She petrified, then words started spilling out of her mouth.

"Excuse me, I'm so sorry. I was taking a walk and happened to see your place and thought I better take a look to make sure no one had suffered a heart attack or some terrible accident. But if there's nothing wrong then, no problem, I'll just be on my way."

The metal only pressed harder into her vertebrae.

"What the hell you doin' here? If I take you for a robber I can shoot you by law."

"I'm not a robber." Minoa's voice cracked. "Really, I'm just curious, I've always been curious. And I like to walk, and I thought I'd just walk by and ... I'll never come back, I promise." She was blubbering, so she shut up, thoughts rocketing every which way.

"You like snakes?" It was an odd question so Minoa pondered what the right answer would be. 'I hate them' might insult the trapper's enterprise while 'I like them' could make her suspect Minoa wanted to steal her snakes. She equivocated.

"I don't know. I never thought about it."

"Wanna find out?"

A jolt of electric current surged up Minoa's spine.

"No, I don't. You can't hold a gun on me this way. I don't care if I wandered onto your land by mistake. Assault with a deadly weapon is a serious crime and you're risking a prison sentence. If you let me go right now, I'll forget about it."

Her answer was to shove Minoa around the shed with the gun barrel. At the door Minoa balked, trying to decide if she had a fraction of a second to dive and roll before the old woman's reflexes hit her trigger finger. Concluded she didn't. Then did a lightning scan of all the judo throws she could remember, cursing the black belts at the dojo for never teaching her how to defend against a gun at close range. While her panicked thoughts collided, the woman reached out one hand in a worn work glove to the door latch, maintaining the pressure of the gun barrel on Minoa's back around the level of the heart.

"Long as you're here you might as well take the tour."

The door swung open and the gun barrel thrust her into the shed so hard she stumbled and caught herself by grasping the wire mesh of the snake cages, shaking the pine and wire structure. A bedlam of frenzied rattling broke out, shriveling her skin with horror. The door slammed shut followed by the sickening click of a stake shoved into the latch. She spun around and beat on the door with both fists.

"Let me out of here, you psychopath!"

The only answer was a raspy trill of demented laughter. She glanced around assessing the situation. The shed was nothing but plywood sheets nailed onto posts set in the ground, a door of reinforced plywood and a roof of corrugated tin sheets. She judged she could take the whole thing down in fifteen minutes. But could she do it without knocking over the cages?

"What do you want of me? I said I'd go away and never bother you again."

"Getting a teensy bit scared?"

The old lady laughed. This was probably the most fun she'd had in years. Living out here alone in the creosote-peppered hills with a bunch of rattlesnakes for pets would probably drive anybody out of the land of the normal.

"If you don't open that door I'm going to knock down this whole shed."

The only response was a sing-song chant. She scanned the interior. A metal bucket sat on the ground near the door next to a long metal pole with mechanical tongs on one end. She picked up the pole and smacked the window glass but it held. A flicker of movement spied out of the corner of an eye caused her to turn her head. On the far end of the banks of cages a bottom cage door hung open and a Diamondback was gliding through. The head was too far out to slam the door shut with her foot.

"Ayyyy!" A scream cleaved her down the middle. "Let me out of here! There's a loose rattler!"

More giggles from outside. The terror turned her senses chromatic and her muscles bionic. She grabbed the bucket by the handle and crashed it into the glass, once, twice, three times. The glass shattered and the bucket went flying outside, leaving a rim of shards lining the window frame. The snake was gliding across the dirt floor towards her, head lifted, tongue flicking. She placed her palms on the jagged glass points, hoisted herself up and dove through, catching a flash of movement on one side, raking shoulders and hips across the sawtooth edges.

She hit hard, rolling across pebbled dirt. In a flash she was on her feet, running straight up the steep hillside, following a line that would keep the shed blocking the woman's view for as long as possible. As she neared the crest of the hill, shots rang out. Pitched herself over a rock and tumbled across the rocky ground to stop with her arm impaled on a barrel cactus. Her breath was coming so fast and furious she hardly noticed. She crawled back to a jumble of rocks at the lip of the incline and peered over.

The old woman was standing in the packed dirt clearing outside the shed, rifle pointing at the crest of the hill. She fired again. The bullet pinged off a nearby boulder causing Minoa to jerk her head down into the cradle between her shoulders. Then she heard a scream like a mountain lion that coagulated into words.

"I'll find ya' if ya' tell anybody!"

Peeking around the edge of the rock, she saw the old woman taking aim. She ducked down, lizard-walked across the hilltop and took off sprinting down the back side of the hill.

Chapter Eighteen

A scarlet drop oozed from under a strip of ripped T-shirt tied around her arm, meandered down to her elbow and plopped onto a white linoleum floor. The nurse glanced at it.

"Maybe you should've gone to ER."

"Couldn't afford it."

The nurse nodded, handing her a paper dress.

"Think you can get this on by yourself?"

"Of course."

She gave her a doubting look and went out, calling over her shoulder, "The doctor will be in soon."

With a thumb in the money pocket, Minoa enlarged the waist of the jeans as they came off. Some long bloody scratches on the sides of her hips. Punctures on the palms of her hand leaked blood as she pulled. Her upper arms sent SOS signals from scored skin. The denim looked as if a puppy had pulled the jeans out of the laundry basket and had a good teething session before anybody noticed. As she tossed the pants on a chair, it registered in her consciousness that there was a scrap of paper in the money pocket. She extracted it, unfolded and read the words printed there.

If you do not know your own origin, it will poison you.

It took a moment to recall. Inanna's gathering. The paper Marian the Librarian gave her that she'd crammed into her pocket and forgotten. She'd asked the oracle why Dreema suffered snakebite. What did this fake maxim have to do with her question? A fatal snakebite was not fate's punishment for ignorance. Maybe Inanna's hoodwinked acolytes would buy this kind of flowery archaic-sounding pronouncement. She threw the piece of paper into the trash basket. Then worked the shirt over her head, wrapped herself in the paper gown and lay back on the examining table.

It was chilly with bare legs and air conditioning. She shivered, glanced at her wounds a few times. Another trickle of blood meandered down one arm. She caught the drop before it fell, wiping the red onto the paper sheet. Then lay back and stared at the ceiling, white with gray flecks. Her eyelids fluttered, closed for a moment. She pried the lids open before they drifted down again to rest on the lower lashes.

A mottled white surface faces her. It's a white door, chipped paint revealing gray metal underneath, three dead bolt locks in a row. The door swings open. Aunt Wanda stands there, hennaed hair curling up on the ends, fierce gaze nailing her dad while flicking commiseration at Minoa.

"She wouldn't have wanted you to come here."

Her dad, rumpled, tenuous, puts a foot on the threshold.

"Minoa has a right ...."

Minoa feels pressure on the small of her back. Steps inside.

"You get out or I'll call the cops."

Aunt Wanda takes a fly swatter from a nail on the door jamb, slaps his head and shoulders. He smacks the fly swatter aside, careful not to touch her. Minoa takes a few steps in, looks around.

"Dad, it's okay. Please just wait outside."

The door swings shut.

"Look around, honey. Take whatever you want. Sure it's a mess, but she didn't know this was coming."

India print cloths swirl on a bed, stacked dishes teeter on a kitchenette counter. Canvases lie stacked on a utility table, easels spattered with paint lean against walls. The windows look out on a brick facade checkered with rows of identical windows. Unframed paintings cover the walls, surreal portraits with random elements floating around the figures: a beer bottle, a car, a Dachshund, a bouquet of daisies, a Virgin Mary, a teddy bear.

She tiptoes around, hands clamped under armpits, stepping over books, shoes, paint tubes. Sees nothing to remind her of the mother she once knew and nothing to remind her mother of her. Did she forget about Minoa when she ran off to New York to be an artist? That meant Minoa was easy to forget, easy to leave. But Minoa had never forgotten her, not for one hour of one day. She'd survived adolescence by planning to run away to go live with her creative mom in the big city. She'd made one try hitchhiking that didn't turn out well, but that didn't stop her. This time she'd saved enough money to buy a cross-country bus ticket. Then the news came. Now her dream is dead. She feels dead. She tells herself it doesn't matter, that she can still escape. She'll just have to do it alone.

She peers into a bathroom with vintage fixtures. On a frosted glass shelf below the mirror lies a hairbrush, a tousled mass of auburn hairs curling up out of the bristles. She scoops it up, holds it next to her hair, looking in the mirror. The hair color is her own. She presses the bristles into her cheek, squeezing her eyes shut. A couple tears leak out. Followed by a wave of heat rolling up her face, exploding in russet fireworks behind her eyelids, pumping blood into her skull until the pressure threatens to crack her cranium.

Clenching her jaw she mutters, "Stupid, stupid, stupid."

When she walks out of the bathroom, her face is smooth as porcelain. She stands in front of Aunt Wanda.

"Tell me again what happened."

"Honey, it's better not to talk about it. What's done is done."

"Tell me."

"She shouldn't have been carrying that heavy portfolio. She came out of the Bedford Avenue station and walked right into the street. I don't know if the portfolio was blocking her view or she was so anxious to get to that gallery. Anyway, that damn taxi driver should have seen her. He's real sorry but what good does that do?"

"Was she selling her paintings? Was she gonna be a famous artist?"

"Oh sure."

She stops in front of a painting of a woman looking back over her shoulder at a girl on the far side of a canyon who is reaching out both arms, leaning over the edge. Objects swirl from foreground to background: a kachina, spurs, a spider and, between the mother and daughter, a coiled lariat. She steps closer. Not a lariat, a coiled rattlesnake.

Arms encircle from behind.

"Your mother missed you so much."

She shakes herself and pulls free.

"Right."

"Why don't you take that painting? She would have wanted you to have it."

"I don't want it."

The aunt reaches for her shoulders. She flops side to side flinging her arms.

"Get off me!"

"Calm down, honey."

"Let me go! Let me go!"

Struggling, twisting ... she wrenched her arm free. Opened her eyes to see a woman with graying hair in a white medical coat scrutinizing the cuts on her upper arm.

"I'm sorry, did I hurt you?"

The doctor smiled.

"It's okay."

She willed her arms to lay still as her mind writhed. Was that a true memory or another hypnagogic hallucination? Had her mother painted the two of them with a rattlesnake between? Or was she so obsessed with rattlesnakes she was seeing them everywhere, even inside her own memories?

"Did you suffer a knife attack?"

"Uh, I got locked in a shed and had to escape through a broken window."

"You couldn't go out the door?"

Minoa gave the doctor a wizened look.

"Someone was standing on the other side with a shotgun."

"I see."

She let them work on her, relieved to be pricked by needles and then gloriously numb. The doctor cleaned the wounds, added stitches here and there, bandaged everything. When she was done, she put her hand over Minoa's and said, "If you get into trouble again, call 911. That's what it's there for."

She walked out of the room and the nurse handed Minoa one printed sheet on wound care and another on domestic violence.

"The stitches will dissolve. Call us if there's any redness or swelling."

"Thanks."

"Be careful next time."

'Sure thing, next time I get locked in a shed with a couple dozen venomous snakes,' she whispered as she walked out of the clinic.

Outside she paused to look around the backside of a shopping strip, unpainted walls rising from a field of asphalt. The anesthetic wasn't wearing off yet but she already felt angry about the coming discomfort, angry about the gall of people threatening her with rattlesnakes, angry that an old friend who'd suffered a lot had to die so young. Angry about more stuff going back in time and angry about having to think about it all. The parking lot bled into house clusters cowering beneath a mountainous horizon so choppy it looked like some giant had gone after it with a monstrous hatchet. Above, the azure sky blasted caustic light that nearly made her eyes bleed. Dammit! That demented old woman had tried to murder her. Should she head to a police station and file a report? Was there any charge — endangerment with a deadly reptile? — that would get her arrested? Was it illegal to keep a bunch of venomous animals on your property? Or to force someone into contact with them?

She climbed into the truck — no blood stains on the interior that she could see — and checked her maps app for the state Game and Fish Department. Headed for the Relief Route, turned off at Caja del Rio Road and took Wildlife Way. Inside the office she approached a woman standing behind a counter with an elaborate pile of frosted hair above a crisp gray uniform.

"I'd like to notify you about someone who keeps thirty or more rattlesnakes in cages in a shed by her house. And I've seen her out trapping snakes on private land near Santa Fe. She must be breaking laws."

"Does she have a commercial collecting permit?"

"How should I know? Even if she does, would that allow her to keep so many rattlesnakes in a shed in her yard?"

"Does she live within city limits?"

"No."

"Then she can keep animals as long as they pose no threat to public safety."

"So a concentration of lethal creatures isn't a threat to public safety?"

"There is no legal prohibition against owning rattlesnakes, as far as I know. Are you her neighbor? You might be able to file a nuisance report with police."

"So there's nothing to stop her from caging as many rattlers as she wants?"

"She may be an amateur herpetologist."

"Do you really think she's keeping thirty rattlesnakes as a hobby?"

"Breeders of non-domesticated animals must obtain a breeder's license. Do you suspect she's a breeder?"

"I think she's selling venom."

The woman raised her eyebrows.

"Unless you can prove she caught snakes on federal public land and sold them for profit, which is illegal although rarely investigated, your only option may be to report her to the humane society. You'd have to suspect she's not providing adequate care."

"Is feeding live mice to snakes adequate care?"

The woman's eyes stretched wider.

"Like I said, try the humane society."

"What about trying to kill me with her rattlers?"

Now she backed up a step.

"Uh, that would be a matter for the police."

"Okay, thanks."

Minoa turned to leave but after a few steps spun back around.

"By the way, do you have any information on the spread of neuro-toxic rattlers in New Mexico?"

That question made the Fish and Game agent flip her extra long bangs out of her eyes.

"I've heard something about that."

"Or statistics on cases of snakebite in New Mexico by neurotoxic rattlers?"

"I don't think so."

"If a cluster of neurotoxic rattler bites turns up in Santa Fe, will Fish and Game take action?"

"If a noticeable increase in rattlesnake attacks occurs, we'll issue an advisory warning."

At the truck Minoa paused, squinted into a summer day going sour. Why had the snake woman warned Minoa not to tell anyone about her place? Was it to avoid detection by the IRS? It sure wasn't to avoid law enforcement. Nobody cared what she did with her rattlers out in the hills. Unless her snake-pets killed Minoa and a few others. Then maybe Fish and Game would issue an advisory warning. Yahoo.

All she'd found out was that Felipe was selling rattlers to a venom trader in the Ortiz Mountains. These transactions with the snake lady showed that Shauvenupp had access to rattlers. The rest required convoluted suppositions to explain how he came up with the idea to use a rattler to eliminate a homeowner. Maybe his success made him think he could get away with doing the same thing to Minoa whom he blamed for the looming legal suit. Amilcar's motives for both rattler attacks were simpler: he was angry and violent. No matter. She lacked any proof she could show police to get Amilcar arrested. She needed to clear her mind.

Chapter Nineteen

A few blocks from the plaza she turned into the library parking lot. Inside she sat at a computer terminal, opened an article database and typed in keywords. 'Killing with snakes' turned up little apart from a couple news reports on murders in India where family members purchased a cobra to eliminate an unwanted family member. But there were lots of hits on ancient warfare. Tipping arrows in snake venom had occurred in every war from Carthage to Persia.

In the library catalog a search on 'killing with snakes' turned up one book. After winding up and down stacks unable to find the call number, starting to notice an empty sensation in her stomach, she located the frayed tome on dusty shelves in a spillover storage room at the back of the building. She grabbed it and headed to a reading room. One other person sat at a table, a woman perusing a tabletop volume of abstract art reproductions. Just past her spiky gray pixie-cut Minoa glimpsed pages of brightly colored stripes and splashes.

The cover of the book below its title, *Rattlesnake Lore of the Southwest*, carried an embossed sketch of a buckaroo twirling a rattlesnake like a lariat. Inside the back cover an old-fashioned tattered paper checkout log gave the date of its last checkout as February 29, 1984. February 29? How improbable was that? The book contained a collection of fantastical stories of encounters with rattlers in frontier days, like cowboy stories of encountering a king rattlesnake longer than two ponies and broader than the back of a dog or sighting a ball of snakes stuck together rolling down a hill.

Glancing up she saw the art lover paging through a book of Georgia O'Keefe paintings full of colorful cliffs, magnified flowers, longhorn skulls. Beyond her a row of windows high on the wall framed squares of a sapphire sky. An image of a Mexican combo plate with enchiladas, tamales, refried beans and rice in a lake of green chile flashed across her mind but she stiffened her will.

Skimming past more picturesque anecdotes – a Comanche dish prepared by mixing chunks of rattlesnake meat with wild vegetables and boiling it inside a buffalo stomach, a mother snake swallowing baby snakes to protect them from danger, one rattlesnake tall tale after another – she came to a chapter on hunting with venom. Here a frontiersman reported Indians would tie a deer's liver to a stick and move it in front of a rattlesnake. After several strikes they would dry the venom-filled liver, grind it into a powder, mix it with sap and paint arrowheads. These arrows produced a wound that killed in seconds.

Setting the book down she leaned back and stretched. Could the snake lady be aware of this old-fashioned practice? Did she sell concentrated venom? Extra-strength neurotoxic venom would likely produce immediate paralysis and yet be indistinguishable from normal snakebite in an autopsy.

The art lover had left, the window-squares of glowing sky had darkened. She listened for activity in the library but heard nothing. Most people were home by now with their families or dog or favorite streaming series. She pictured her empty guesthouse, the kitchenette invaded by snaking lines of tiny black ants, and decided to surf on. Heading back to a computer terminal she searched for websites on snake symbolism.

Most of the results took her back to the ancient Near East. In Mesopotamian religions snakes were seen as symbols of rebirth and rejuvenation since they shed their skin, and as mediators between life and death because they moved between the underworld and the surface of the earth. Temple statues often depicted goddesses holding snakes. In the temples of Asclepius, a Greek god of medicine, snakes were free to slither around the floor to promote healing. She thought back to the Women Rising gathering at Inanna's place in Pojoaque. Her invented ceremony evoked the cults of the ancient world. Maybe she told Dreema to imitate those goddess figures by holding Basmu in her hands? Or she turned Basmu loose in the house to facilitate healing? Just how crazy was Inanna?

Minoa blew out a sigh. Everybody she knew viewed rattlesnakes as dangerous pests remembered only when they crossed paths with humans and quickly dispatched. But ancient peoples had wrapped their bodies in snakes and kept poisonous asps like modern people kept poodles. Like the Hopi, who collected rattlesnakes for their Snake Dance, housed them in a kiva and then danced holding them, even in their mouths. Lewis would have insight into people who were comfortable with rattlesnakes. Maybe she should ask him for advice? No, he saw her as just another intrusive anthropologist. She almost savored his negativity. At least he viewed her as an anthropologist rather than a part-time casino bartender.

She looked around. Not a library patron in sight. Had they closed the library and locked her inside? Suddenly she jerked her feet into midair and peered under the table, realizing she'd imagined a rattler. She stood and shoved her chair too hard. All this talk of rattlesnakes was getting to her. Hurrying to the exit she sighed with relief when the door swung open.

Outside, a topaz sheen coated the darkening sky. The thought of her one-room guesthouse still inspired claustrophobia so she started walking toward the plaza taking deep breaths to clear thoughts of snake-murder from her brain. At the square, vintage street lights illuminated people in cheerful vacation clothing milling about on their way to a New Mexican food dinner. She slid into a bench and watched, eyes roaming over the adobe buildings surrounding the plaza.

The Governor's Palace, its long portico sustained by wooden pillars, empty now of the jewelry vendors who spread their merchandise on Indian blankets each day. Picturesque, but it had seen executions, fraudulent land grabs and Confederate takeovers. Over one corner towered La Fonda Hotel, only lacking burro trains in front to recreate the endpoint of the old Santa Fe Trail. Who remembered the lynching in the back patio or the territorial judge shot in the lobby? Beautiful artifacts saved from the destructive passage of time created a pleasant experience of history that erased the painful bloody episodes. That's why all these people came to Santa Fe on vacation, to experience this sanitized mockup of the past. But when she returned to her childhood home, all she could remember were the distressing experiences. On top of it she was hallucinating rattlers everywhere she went.

She felt herself leaning toward escape and indulgence but a thin clear filament of who-knows-what pulled the other way. Okay, okay, she had a choice: she could dog paddle around her pool of self-pity and spend the rest of the evening anesthetizing her wounds. Or she could try to keep Berry from getting himself shot. Berry thought Amilcar belonged to some splinter faction of the Penitentes that handled snakes. It sounded about as probable as getting locked in a hut full of rattlesnakes or being murdered by someone brandishing a hypodermic full of concentrated rattler venom. But it looked like the improbable was taking over her world. She'd get some sleep and head out tomorrow for a bit of improvised fieldwork.

Chapter Twenty

The next day was clear and sunny like three hundred sixty other days of the year in Santa Fe. Wounds had scabbed over which Minoa took as a good omen. Driving north out of the historic district, the Santa Fe Opera to the west and Tesuque estates to the east soon gave way to billboards for casinos, sandblasted dwellings and the occasional rusting trailer. In Espanola she took a wrong turn, passed a liquor store with bars on the windows, a drug treatment center, old houses converted to home daycare, shoe repair, beauty salon. Found her way back to the northbound highway and settled into the spectacular climb out of the Chama River Valley, colored cliffs beneath a turquoise sky so entrancing she almost drove past the tiny sign for Abiquiu. She gunned the truck up a rutted road to a dirt square surrounded by adobe buildings and a mission style church. The punctures on her hands ached when she took them off the steering wheel.

The only newly plastered building housed an art gallery. Just beyond she spotted the local library, a flat-roofed adobe with fading murals on the front walls. Inside a smiling woman with hair striped silver and pewter offered to help find a book. Minoa eased into her fieldworker persona.

"I'm doing research on religious practices in northern New Mexico. Would you know of any local groups with unusual rituals, maybe something to do with snakes?"

"I can show you a reference work on the history of religious traditions in our region. Maybe that would help?"

"I'm sure your personal knowledge would be more valuable. I've heard of the Penitente morada in town, but you may know of other groups?"

"The brotherhood is secret. I couldn't provide information on that."

"No problem. What about unofficial groups, maybe with ties to militias or fundamentalists or polygamists or ... snake-handlers?"

"Most everyone around here is Catholic, or at least their parents or grandparents are."

"Maybe a splinter group that broke off from the Penitentes with extremist beliefs?"

"There would be no need for a group to carry out secret rituals like in the old days. The Church has permitted the brotherhood public celebration of services since 1947."

"What about rattlesnakes? Hear of any group handling rattlers?"

Her friendly face stretched in horror.

"Rattlesnakes? I could help you search for something on that topic through interlibrary loan. Otherwise I have no idea."

"Okay. Could you tell me where to find the morada?"

With a skeptical frown she drew a cross on a photocopy of a town map and handed it to her.

"Are you sure you don't want directions to Georgia O'Keefe's house? That's the reason most visitors come to Abiquiu."

"No, this is fine."

"Then take care. The *hermanos* aren't friendly to visitors."

Minoa headed down Palvadera Road and soon spotted Georgia O'Keefe's house. Farther down the road a couple of kids playing tag in the road stopped and stared at her. Soon it turned uphill and, after a short climb, she faced three rough hewn crosses skewed out of a cluster of bunch grass and prickly pear cactus. Just beyond sat a tin-roofed adobe with straw sticking out of patches where the mud plaster had fallen off. The windows were tiny chinks, the ceiling low. Pickup trucks sat in a flat area behind.

She pulled out her cell and geared up to improvise. Started snapping photos. After the first half dozen she pretended. In a few minutes she heard footsteps and then two middle-aged brothers stood in front of her.

"You can't photograph the morada without permission," said one fellow with a white-tipped goatee cut in the triangular style of a conquistador.

"I'm not hurting anything."

"This is a religious center, Miss. You have to have permission." The second fellow, round face circled by a fan of silvering hair, looked friendlier. She focused on him.

"Can't you give me permission?"

"You have to request it in advance in writing and wait for written approval."

"That's awfully complicated for a few shots on my cell. Just for personal use. I won't publish them, I promise." She smiled at the nicer fellow. "And I'm very interested in your services. Would it be possible to attend one?"

Don Coronado took control.

"That's not possible. You could check with the women's morada."

"But the history here is so rich."

"You'll have to go."

A couple young bucks turned the corner of the morada and hurried towards them. With a shock she recognized the developer's assistant, Felipe. The other young man was skinnier, tattoo-less.

"I know her," Felipe barked. "She's been causing trouble where I work, too."

"Amilcar told me I could take photos."

The *hermanos* exchanged glances.

"Amilcar doesn't –," the young man lacking tattoos paused mid-sentence at his elder's gesture.

"And he said you have fascinating services where you handle rattlesnakes."

"Rattlesnakes?" Felipe stabbed a finger at her. "You're crazy." He looked at the others. "She's lying. Amilcar hates her."

She returned his menacing look.

"You've been harvesting rattlesnakes from Tierra Feliz land and selling them on the sly. Did you bring snakes up here for Amilcar?"

Felipe's expression exploded.

"What are you talking about?" He turned to the other men. "*Es una gringa loca.*"

The two older men frowned at him.

"Do you have a dispute with this woman?"

"She knew that woman who got snakebit where I work. Now she's trying to sue my boss. She's the one who's harassing me."

"Wait till I tell him you're selling snakes off his land to a venom trader and pocketing the money."

"Ya-you can't do that."

Felipe squirmed under the men's questioning looks.

"*Quítale de su cámera.*"

Felipe's skinny buddy didn't bother to lower his voice. The gringa wouldn't understand the suggestion to grab her phone.

She tightened her grip. Felipe's hand shot out and took hold of her cell. They tussled, hauling back and forth, elbows flapping, until Minoa crashed onto her backside. As she pushed off palms to her feet, she became sure somebody's foot had hooked around her ankle and pulled the foot out from under her. She regrouped. Felipe was scrolling through the phone's camera roll. His friend smirked at her.

"*Cálmense.*" Don Coronado gave the two younger men a stern look.

"You can't delete my photos." Minoa turned to Don Coronado. "That's my property. He just stole it. Aren't you going to stop him?"

Felipe's blustery face morphed from outrage to perplexity as he paged through the photos accumulated since Dreema's death. Minoa followed along in her mind, recalling the images he must be seeing: Amilcar's slap of Aracely, his own turquoise truck, the developer's office, Lewis holding up a Diamondback wriggling in midair, the snake lady's rattler hideout.

After a moment he looked at her. "Are you an investigator for that lawyer that's trying to sue my boss? Or an informant for the cops?"

All the men turned to stare at her. She struggled to read their expressions, ransacking her memory for information on the Penitentes. At the end of the nineteenth century they'd gained infamy for nailing young men to the cross on Good Friday to reenact Christ's passion, a practice which led to several deaths. During the first half of the twentieth century there'd been reports of violent attacks in response to unwanted photography of their ceremonies. Surely they weren't still violent to intruders?

"You don't understand. I suspect Amilcar had something to do with his ex-wife's death, so I came up to find out more. I thought he belonged to your group."

"That's a lie!" shouted Felipe.

Don Coronado palmed downward several times, gesturing to calm him.

"Give my phone back. You already deleted the photos of the morada. It's my property."

She put out her hand.

"*Devuélveselo*," said Don Coronado.

"*Si, hombre*," said the gentler older fellow.

Felipe made a show of looking through the camera memory for another half minute, then slammed the cell down in her hand so hard she almost dropped it. She turned on her heel and sauntered down the road. Didn't look back until she'd rounded the corner and could see the O'Keefe estate ahead. A violent gust of wind shook the branches of acacias along the dirt street and flattened bunch grass in the open desert beyond. No one had followed.

She headed back to the plaza wondering what she'd learned from this encounter. If Berry wasn't imagining Amilcar's involvement in some fringe snake-handling group, at least she knew it wasn't the Penitentes. But now Felipe had more reason to distrust her. Would he tell his boss the gringa was spying? No, he wouldn't risk revealing his deal with the rattlesnake lady. He might tell Amilcar she'd showed up in Abiquiu asking questions about him. What would Amilcar's response be? Would he show up at the guest house in the middle of the night with a syringe full of extra-strength venom?

Chapter
Twenty-One

A t the truck, scanning the crumbling adobe buildings encircling the plaza as she opened the door, her eyes met those of an aged gentleman. He was standing in the door of a tiny souvenir shop. How could he possibly run a store out here? He drilled her with a smile so commanding she hesitated to look away. She was probably his only shot at a customer for today so she gave in and walked over.

"*Bienvenida, señorita.*"

He made a dramatic bow with an arm flourish as she stepped under the overhang, an adobe portico slipping sideways in geologic time. Tufts of his steely hair pointed heavenward while lower lip, jowls, arm flesh all dangled down toward the flaking concrete step.

"Welcome to my shop."

He opened the door for her. The interior was a surprise. Cool and sprayed with colored light from a stained glass window on the back wall, a historic collage with figures bent over hoeing, raising a cross, leading a donkey train. Shelves in the whitewashed shop displayed traditional New Mexican crafts, carved images of saints, hammered tin art, stamped tile images of the Virgin. One shelf held a scattering of candy remnants from her dad's childhood: faded packs of red hots and sweethearts and twist-wrapped chunks of bubblegum.

"You have come to our village to learn about local history?"

"I'm searching for information about —"

"You've found your way to the perfect spot to learn about this fascinating topic. The history of Abiquiu is a microcosm of the history of New Mexico, a clash of three cultures over five centuries. Longer if you consider the Tewa pueblo which thrived here from the 1300s until the 1600s."

"How intriguing. I'm inquiring about a guy named Amilcar. I thought he belonged to the Penitentes but maybe not."

He leaned so close to her face she could smell the tamales he had for lunch. His remaining teeth poked out at crazy angles.

"*La hermandad* is secret. In the old days you could be killed for trying to find out its secrets."

She backed up.

"Of course I didn't mean to invade anyone's privacy."

Now a smile stretched his grizzly cheeks.

"Don't worry. I, Juan Carlos Esteban de Cortes y Saavedra, will help such a charming visitor to our village. Who would bother to kill an old man so close to the reaping of *Doña Sebastiana*?"

Her brow crinkled with the effort of sizing up Don Juan Carlos. She took a turn around the shop to consider her approach. That brought her to a display of ornamental ceramics. Nearly half the brightly glazed figures were rattlesnakes, coiled, strung out with head raised, a couple biting a boot that stepped on it.

"Gee, look at all these rattlesnakes. I bet some people around here keep rattlers, or trap them or something, right?"

"The *señorita* need not worry that you will encounter a *culebra* on the streets of Abiquiu."

"That's not what I meant. I heard of someone in Abiquiu who sells rattlers to a venom trader. Do you know of anyone here involved with rattlesnakes?"

"In all my years as self-appointed local scribe I haven't heard of such a thing. What I can tell you, my young friend, is that the pressures of neocolonialism leave us few economic options. Our land would have been stolen long ago if it wasn't held in a land grant, a communal ownership structure the gringo capitalists can't understand and haven't been able to eradicate."

"So you don't know of anyone keeping rattlers around here? I'm ... uh, doing research for my dissertation."

"Wonderful, an intellectual. Then you understand how corporations poison our land to extract uranium, natural gas, molybdenum, copper. The United States government appropriates our forests where we hunted and grazed our livestock for centuries. Meanwhile, our impoverished culture withers leaving only these tokens to sell to tourists bored by the world this rapacious despoliation has created. Perhaps some local entrepreneur found a method to extract a marketable commodity from one of our most abundant resources, rattlesnakes, and so create wealth for the local people. Chicano ingenuity!"

"Ingenious, yes. Perhaps as local historian you know of an earlier use of rattlesnakes in rituals?"

"So you wish to investigate how the historical dynamics of colonialism have molded our local traditions?"

"Something like that."

She feigned interest in some notebooks with hand carved leather covers to avoid his blistering gaze. Don Juan Carlos was still staring with an all-knowing expression when she looked up.

"Abiquiu is the Spanish transliteration of the word Avéshu, the Tewa name of the pueblo established here in the fourteenth century.

When natives abandoned the pueblo in the seventeenth century, many traveled west and joined the Hopi. Then when the governor ordered the resettlement of Abiquiu in the 1740s, Fray Francisco Delgado, a Spanish friar, went to Hopiland. He found the descendants of the Tewa migrants living as the Asa clan and brought some back to resettle their ancestral lands."

"You mean that Abiquiu was settled by Hopi?"

"By Hopi-Tewa and *Genízaros*."

"What are *Genízaros*?"

"Indians who were sold to the Spanish as a kind of slave."

"So Hopi-educated Tewa came to Abiquiu in the eighteenth century. Do you think anyone around here still considers themself Hopi?"

"Ay, *señorita*. It has taken genetic testing for local people to acknowledge their indigenous roots."

She scanned the book titles on a scant shelf.

"Do you know someone named Amilcar?"

"I may have heard the name. But don't you want to know about the witch trials?"

"Witch trials?"

He squinted at her, then waved his arms in the air. His iron brows bristled, his eyes smoldered.

"Sorcerers, witches, accused of casting spells to kill a Spanish priest and other evil witchcraft. Jailed, flogged, pagan idols destroyed." He leaned closer, blowing a crop-withering breath across her face. "Maybe burned at the stake, skin shriveling in flames as they screamed and begged their heathen gods to save them."

She swallowed.

"That was several centuries ago, right?"

Don Juan Carlos relaxed back and chuckled.

"I'm kidding. When you mention witch trials to Anglos they think of beautiful young women consumed by flames as sadistic priests leer. No one was burned in Abiquiu, as far as we know. But church authorities did their best to suppress the indigenous spiritual practices of the *Genízaros* and Hopi-Tewas."

"The Hopi have a ritual where they dance holding rattlesnakes. Do you think the priests tried to stop the Hopi-Tewas from doing that here?"

"You ask an intriguing question, young lady. The Tewa grandchildren would have learned the ceremonies and religion of their Hopi hosts. Returning to Abiquiu they must have continued these practices. And the friars would have been scandalized by Indians playing with rattlesnakes, the symbol of evil in the good book. That would be seen as consorting with the devil, the very basis of an accusation of witchcraft."

"So it's plausible that the snake dances continued in secret after the witch trials ended. You haven't heard of any modern day witchcraft around here or people doing blasphemous things with snakes?"

"You postulate that local people in the twenty-first century still carry out snake ceremonies?" He threw back his head to laugh, revealing an Adam's apple like a knotted rope. "I see that you have the imagination of a visionary. The study of history requires imagination. On the basis of so little we must reconstruct stories red with steaming blood and knife-edged with pain in order to understand the lives of our *antepasados*."

"But no signs of snake handling around here?"

He shook his head.

"Nothing I know of but little kids playing with bull snakes."

"Not even some offshoot of the Penitentes?"

"*Señorita*, even if I knew of such an aberration, would I tell a young Anglo visitor to my shop, possibly leading to my death? Worse, would I put the life of an educated young Anglo woman in danger by revealing to her such a dangerous secret?"

Minoa struggled to decode the ironic smile flickering across his dead worm lips.

"Thank you so much for the information. You've been very kind."

She took a few steps toward the door.

"If you want to learn about the Penitente brotherhood, I have this lovely history."

He picked up a thin monochrome text off a bookshelf and thrust it at her. She accepted the book in her hand sensing a layer of grit on the cover. Entitled *The Penitente Brotherhood: Nativist Resurgence in Territorial New Mexico*, the cover displayed a black-and-white photo of men kneeling, stripped to the waist, black hoods over their faces, flagellating their backs with barbed whips.

"If you'd prefer something more extensive with color plates?" He pointed a knobby finger at a tabletop volume entitled *Cultural Syncretism: Religious Pageantry of New Mexico Since the Reconquest*.

"No, I'm sure this is fine."

He smiled devilishly when he told her the price, obviously a huge markup but the poor fellow was probably living on canned beans and tortillas out here. He stuffed a flyer into the bag as he handed it to her.

"You must come to the festival of *Santa Rosa de Lima* on Saturday. And visit my shop again. I have much more to tell you."

The shop door closed with the tinkling of ceramic bells tied to the door. Minoa hurried across the deserted plaza to the truck, slid into the driver's seat and cranked up the motor. Down the steep entry road she went, kicking up a trail of drought-fluffed white dirt, to slide to a stop at the side of the highway. Her breathing relented as the motor sputtered to a growling idle. She stared across the tawny valley to the cliffs on the far side, striped with pink and gold, cliffs that led north to Ghost Ranch, site of legendary ghost sightings. Pausing there between witches and ghosts she glanced down the black strip of highway, stretching in a straight line to either side, seeking reassurance that the twenty-first century was just a short drive away.

'What now?' she asked herself.

Berry's hysterical accusation of Amilcar had gone nowhere. The fact that Hopi helped found Abiquiu in the eighteenth century was a historical curiosity with no relevance for Dreema's death, right? Despite learning nothing of value on her trip to Abiquiu she smiled. Wandering around unknown territory trying to understand events and behavior that seemed incomprehensible reminded her of doing fieldwork in Ecuador, of the sense of energized aliveness, interspersed with confusion and discomfort, she'd felt doing her ethnographic research.

She pulled the book out of the bag and flipped through its historical black-and-white photos. The word rattlesnake in a caption caught her eye. The photo showed a group of men gathered in a rocky canyon pulling ropes to raise a crucifix carrying a nailed figure in white robes. Below: "Charles Lummis 1889: 'Where the rattlesnake is god.'" Rattlesnake gods here in New Mexico? Had the early Penitentes viewed rattlers as divine manifestations, perhaps as fallen angels reemerging from the earth? Or had the Tewa migrants brought Hopi ceremonials with rattlesnakes back to Abiquiu? From witch trials to live crucifixions to rattlesnake gods. A colorful history of local religious practices, but what could it have to do with Dreema's death?

She dropped the book into the bag and pulled out the flyer. *Fiesta de Santa Rosa de Lima* headlined the top, followed by a grainy picture of a saint statue wearing a wreath of roses on her head. Procession to the *Iglesia de Santo Tomás*, food and music on the plaza. Sounded insufferably boring. Another ritual decayed over the centuries. No one would be flogged or burned or crucified at this event. Customs which once commanded fear and awe had deteriorated into excuses to drink beer and snap selfies. A postmodern world of dulled meaning. Maybe handling rattlers provided needed excitement?

Out of the corner of her eye she noticed someone in a car next to her waving. She grasped the steering wheel, poised her foot on the accelerator for a quick getaway and turned to look. It was only Rich, smiling up at her with a daffy grin from the driver's seat of some European sports car convertible.

"Hey there. What are you doing sitting by the side of the Chama highway?"

"Rich, you startled me."

"Sorry."

"Where did you get those wheels? Did Art in America profile your work and now your walking sticks are selling for a grand each?"

"Very funny. No, it's the boss'. I just took it for a spin to go home and shower after work."

"So you're still getting perks from that rich guy? Didn't you finish that predatory staircase?"

"You should see it. As you climb up the stairs it gives you the impression that one big cat after another is leaping at you for the kill."

"I bet the rich dude loves it."

"He's pretty pleased. He wants me to cast a piece to put in front of his barn. Hey, I'm going up there right now for an event he's having out at the barn. He said it would give me some ideas for the piece. It's more than a barn, really. It's a fancy indoor arena with padded seats and a bar in one corner. Why don't you come along?"

Minoa hesitated. Rich advanced, she retreated. Or thought about it. Time for a straight talk, tell him the truth: she and commitment were oil and water, electron and proton. But meanwhile, what were her options? She could head back to town, microwave a frozen enchilada and waste the evening on the web. Or she could head over to the mythical estate she'd heard so much about to see how the point one percent amused themselves in their country manors on a free night. She'd make a date for that serious conversation with Rich. Soon. Real soon.

Chapter Twenty-Two

Wind tousled her hair as she leaned back in the bucket seat of the convertible and watched cumulus barges bump each other in an azure lagoon. Rich cranked the wood-handled gear shifter, whipping around switchbacks above Abiquiu Reservoir. He paused near the top of black rock ridges lining the western side of the reservoir. The surface of the water mirrored the sky, so the cloud barges floated down there as well.

"Is it much farther?"

"Just a few minutes."

At the top of the ridge he sped up on the flat section, weaving around rock outcroppings. Topped a rise and there it was. Encircled by a high adobe-style wall, the estate included a southwestern palace and numerous smaller buildings. At the entrance Rich punched in a code, a massive black metal gate swung open and they were inside. They parked to the side of a two story glassed entry, scintillating with floodlights. Rich walked around the side of the house.

"I'd like to show you the staircase but Randy said to go straight to the barn. He values his privacy."

"I would guess so, living out here alone. No wonder he wants your company."

"Now don't start on that again. The guy's okay."

Behind the house they passed a horse stable and an art studio with a clerestory before reaching the arena. Entering she saw that a partition closed off the back part of the building. Glass panels topped by wire mesh enclosed the arena, leather seats encircled it. At one end people gathered at a bar, sipping drinks.

"What do they do in here?" she whispered.

"How do I know? Randy just told me to come get some ideas for the bronze piece he wants to put in front."

The two of them slid into seats. Minoa fiddled with buttons on the side of the seat and found that it reclined.

"Hopefully the waiters will come around soon with champagne and caviar."

"No, you have to get your own drink," Rich said, oblivious of her sarcastic tone.

More people filtered in the front door, picked up a drink at the bar and took their seats.

"Have you noticed there are no women here?"

"Uh, yeah, I did notice that."

"What's going to happen when your Cosimo de' Medici walks in and sees me sitting here?"

"My who? Oh, I don't know, but I doubt he'll say anything."

"Did you ever wonder what they do in this place?"

"I just assumed it was some kind of animal show or competition, you know, horses or dogs or something."

"You'd have trouble getting more than a couple horses in that ring. And is he worried they'll leap out and attack the spectators?" She pondered the glass-encircled ring. "Does this guy raise roosters?"

"What?"

"Cockfights are legal and popular in Ecuador so I've seen some. Maybe this guy Randy breeds cocks for sport. Although that wouldn't explain the high walls on this arena."

"Gosh, I have no idea."

"To justify this ring he would have to be raising genetically altered monster roosters."

Rich smiled with one side of his mouth. A few more well-dressed men walked in. The place was nearly full and every guy in the room shot surreptitious glances at her every half minute or so.

"Rich, are you sure this guy's not into live pornography, some kind of bestial sex show or something? I mean, why is everyone in this room except me male?"

"Uh, maybe you were right and he's sexually weird. Do you want to go?"

"Not yet. I'm dying to solve the mystery of what they do here."

At that moment a Viking throwback dressed in white slacks and a black silk shirt strode into the building, waving at the men lining the arena like a campaigning politician. His eyes surveyed the crowd and came to rest momentarily on Minoa, causing a brief furrowing of his pale brow. He composed himself instantaneously and addressed the crowd.

"Tonight we're going to witness a spectacle which I hope will make your drive worthwhile. You know, in the modern world we enjoy many conveniences and an unprecedented level of personal security. It's truly the best of times, as I'm sure you all agree. But we tend to lose touch with the power and majesty of nature and the necessary cruelty and savagery which underlie that power. For those of us in business, we need to have our batteries recharged with that energy so that we, too, can reenter the economic arena inspired to battle and win."

Minoa poked Rich in the ribs.

"Is he going to present fights between people, like gladiators?"

"Look, he didn't tell me much about this but I thought it had to do with animals."

"Rich, do you think he could be involved with drug cartels or the Russian mafia? I mean, where did he get all this money?"

"He said he made his money on Wall Street."

Randy took a seat at one end of the arena. Now a Latino guy in a cowboy hat drove a golf cart into the arena. He stopped, unloaded two cages, setting them on the floor of the arena and then, standing on the back of the cart, used a long pole to open both cage doors. An enormous diamondback rattler slithered out of one cage. When nothing came out of the other cage, the caretaker used the pole to push out a gargantuan black snake with whitish bands. The rattler hissed, skittled backwards. Testing the air with its tongue the black snake began to glide toward the rattler.

"What the hell?" muttered Rich.

"Do you know what the black snake is?"

"Looks like a king snake. We played with them when I was a kid."

The rattlesnake had slithered across the arena and coiled up against the glass wall. When the serene king snake approached, it hissed, struck at it and shot past.

"If the king snake isn't venomous why doesn't it flee the rattler?"

"Rattlesnake venom doesn't affect king snakes." He spoke without moving his gaze from the reptilian duel.

"You mean the king snake can kill the rattlesnake?"

"That's why some people keep king snakes around their property."

The king snake pursued the diamondback, head leading, tongue flicking, long body undulating behind, following as the rattler reeled and lurched, striking and retreating, scooting one way and another. After a frenzied zig-zagging pursuit, the king snake finally managed to loop around the rattler's body just behind its angular head. The coil tightened. Now the rest of the rattler's body flipped and flopped, slapping onto the arena floor over and over, rattle twitching. The king snake wound itself around its victim, one coil after another, until only the head and tail of the rattler were visible, squeezing tight and then waiting.

In her life Minoa had never felt anything for a rattlesnake but fear and some archaic sense of repulsion. But now she felt sorry for the poor creature having the life squeezed out of it by an animal immune to its defenses. She sank back into her leather armchair, deflated, disgusted.

"Do you want to leave?"

Rich put a hand on her knee, peering into her eyes. She stared straight ahead, face stiff.

"Wonder where Randy gets his snakes."

The keeper drove into the arena and shoveled the wound-together snakes into a cage, then used a crank on the back of the cart to raise it. He drove to a door in the partition at the back of the arena and disappeared inside.

"Look, I'm sorry about this. Why don't we go?"

"This guy needs to be busted."

"This is a private event and I ... I don't know."

Soon the keeper drove back into the arena. He lowered a cage to the dirt and opened it. Out popped a roadrunner, instantly running at full speed, its stick legs a blur. It charged toward the far end of the arena. Minoa gasped as the bird's pointy beak slammed into the glass wall. The bird teetered, dazed, then took off running along another beeline and slammed into another glass surface, careening backwards. Gamely the bird recovered its footing, heading off now in another direction.

Randy walked to the arena wall and waved at the keeper, who pulled a large hand net out of the cart and went after the bird. That led to several minutes of slapstick comedy with the keeper slamming down the net on turf vacated milliseconds before by the terrified bird, its slender crested head and brown herringbone body elongated by speed, darting this way and that in an instinctually choreographed dance to evade predation. Guffaws from the audience erupted every time the keeper swung down the net onto empty dirt. Randy's tanned features leaked irritation. But when he addressed the guests, his voice was as smooth as the surface of Abiquiu Reservoir.

"Gentlemen, this isn't the show we had planned for you. But hopefully it will provide a few moments of entertainment before we move on to the next combat, which I'm sure you're going to enjoy. Feel free to get another drink while we set that up for you."

Waving at a few people as he passed, Randy walked straight over to Rich.

"Hello, Rich. Aren't you going to introduce me to your friend?"

"Uh, this is Minoa Diamond. She's ... a friend."

"I gathered that."

He offered Minoa his hand, enclosing hers within his two palms. His skin was dry as the desert yet soft as yucca petals.

"Very pleased to meet you, Miss Diamond. Are you enjoying the show?"

"It's ..."

"It's designed for gentlemen. It may be a bit on the wild side for ladies." He turned to Rich without letting go of her hand. "Rich, what were you thinking bringing a lady to something so crudely masculine?"

"I didn't know."

"Why don't you take Miss Diamond to the house and show her your masterpiece?" He turned back to her. "Your friend is a gifted artist. You're going to be impressed by the unique piece he created for my home."

Rich stood. Randy finally released her hand. Walking out with Rich she noticed the keeper driving his cart toward the back of the building. He must have caught the roadrunner while they were talking. When they reached the door of the barn she ducked to one side and peeked around the doorframe. Rich continued a few steps and called out in an anxious whisper.

"Minoa, come on. Let's go."

She shook her head. After a moment the keeper came back. This time he had a friend with him. As the cart neared the arena gate she gasped. The other animal keeper in the cart was Amilcar. She watched as they placed two cages inside the arena. The first keeper levered open one of the cage doors while Amilcar stuck a pole through the bars to prod the animal. Out darted a bobcat to lope around the arena, sizing up the environment. After a hushed moment Amilcar prodded a brownish furry creature out of the other cage, maybe a mink. The bobcat paused and pricked its ears. She watched it take a few steps toward the other animal. She turned around, leaned her back into the doorframe, blew out a long breath.

As she walked toward where Rich waited, she glanced around the corner of the building and saw a silver pickup truck parked behind. She took off at a trot with Rich's 'wh- wh- where are you going?' trailing after.

Behind the building quiet reigned. She snapped a photo of Amilcar's license plate with the barn as backdrop. Then pulled open a sliding panel door and stepped into a bestiary of calls and snorts and growls and spurts of frantic movement. The place looked like intake for a zoo. Cages of varying sizes lined the walls. In the dim lighting she saw pairs of yellow eyes following her movement. A row of cages along the left-hand wall housed small furry creatures. In a large cage she spied two coyotes pacing back and forth, sidling against each other as their paths crossed without altering their route by a hair.

Suddenly she heard a murmur of excitement from the crowd; maybe first blood had been drawn. She focused her cell phone and started snapping shots.

In a large pen in the corner an animal bolted a few strides to the far side of the pen and froze there, dark eyes wide, nostrils quivering. Minoa approached. It was a juvenile mule deer, her large velvety ears turning first one way and then another as she sought information on the unknown threat she faced in this inscrutable environment.

"This is awful," Minoa whispered.

She opened the gate of the pen. The deer bounded out and disappeared through the barn door into the night. Snapping photos she moved past the cages until a low snarl stopped her. She traced it to a tarp-covered bulk near the entry. Approaching she grabbed a rake leaning against the wall. With the rake handle, she threw off the tarp off revealing an enclosed cage.

A mountain lion stood unmoving behind bars, liquid brown eyes fixed on her, the tip of its tail flicking. Just then a cry broke out from the spectators inside the arena, catching the animal's attention. The cage door had a lock. She jiggled it, then scanned surrounding walls and spotted a ring of keys. A couple of thick ropes hung down from the ceiling over the cougar's cage, perhaps for winching. She grabbed the keys and started trying them in the lock. When the lock slid open, she removed it from the latch on the cage door and climbed on top of the cage. After draping one of the hanging ropes over her shoulder she maneuvered the rake handle through the cage door and levered it open.

For an instant the creature crouched. Then it leaped out of the cage and paused, turning to look at her, sleek body stilled, sizing her up. Minoa grabbed the rope and started climbing up when she heard the whir of the golf cart.

"Get out of here," she hissed, kicking her legs in midair to spook the cougar.

It crouched lower just as the golf cart burst through the portal from the arena. The two gamekeepers jumped out of the cart and started running toward it. When the cougar crouched even lower, baring its pointed incisors, snarling, the two men stopped dead, hands up in front.

"*Tranquilo, tranquilo,*" the first keeper muttered.

Amilcar stared at her.

"What the hell are you doing here?"

An instant after the mountain lion whirled and raced out of sight, she kicked off from the wall and swung out the door opening, letting go of the rope at the far point of its arc. She tumbled through space, landed hard and rolled to a stop. She was up and sprinting down the alley beside the building when Amilcar dashed around the corner of the barn.

Swerving around the front corner of the building she almost ran into Rich standing in the same spot where she'd last seen him, arms hanging, brow furrowed.

"Let's get out of here fast."

His face came alive.

"My truck's near the gate."

They took off running. When they curved around the drive and saw Rich's junkyard pickup parked beside the mansion, she glanced back to see Amilcar racing toward them with a pole in his hands. They made it to the truck, jumped in and chewed dirt over to the entry gate where, for a moment, she feared they might have used some emergency lockdown system to trap them inside. But the gate swung open.

"Can you prop it open?" she said.

As Rich jumped out and grabbed a two-by-four from the back of his truck, Minoa saw Amilcar come around the corner of the house, racing toward them with the pole balanced on his shoulder like some prehistoric spear, ready to launch. Rich inserted the board above one of the gate hinges and sprinted back to his truck door. He ducked in as the pole sailed past stabbing through the space where his head had been an instant before, clattering to the ground up ahead.

Speeding away Minoa looked back to see a tawny blur fly up and over Amilcar as he crouched with hands on his head. Soon they were flying down the access road under cut glass spattered blackness.

"That was wild, wasn't it?"

Rich flicked eyebrows at her.

"That's an understatement. I'm going to have Randy busted."

"I know his hobbies are a bit over the top." His smile curved up seeking company. "But he's got a lot of money to throw at art."

She caught the subtext loud and clear. For Rich it was kick up a fuss with the authorities about Randy's private entertainments and it would be back to selling hand-carved walking sticks at crafts fairs. If he kept his mouth shut and cast that massive bronze piece Randy wanted, it might catch the eye of some other rich collector and lead to another commission and then maybe another and then an article on his work in Art in America and then no more takeout burritos for dinner and maybe his very own sports car to drive around.

She took a breath of deep blue air, whistled it out with a whoosh. She wouldn't criticize Rich for his fawning tail-wagging and she wouldn't jeopardize his career chances by reporting Randy. No promises about anonymous tips to either Game and Fish or the police, although New Mexico might not prohibit wild animal combats just like it didn't prohibit keeping a shed full of rattlers in your yard. Was anything illegal for the filthy rich? How about for their workers? Did the wild animal shows give Amilcar the idea that you could kill with impunity by using animals to do the killing for you? Maybe it gave him a source for acquiring rattlesnakes as well.

She hadn't confirmed Berry's belief that Amilcar participated in some diabolic rattlesnake cult. But what she'd seen made her more convinced that Amilcar had killed his ex-wife with a rattlesnake. If only she could prove it.

Chapter Twenty-Three

S he woke heaving, spasming in disgust. Jerked the sheet off and
pushed up to sitting, head hanging inside a prison of hair. Shook
her head to forget but the memory stuck to the edges of her fuzzy
consciousness. She levered eyelids open and spied out the window of
this high end afterthought addition where Rich ate, slept and created. Outside, a new morning tiptoed sweetly over the housetops of
rich people's second or third vacation homes clustered along Acequia
Madre, the mother ditch that ran through Santa Fe's historic section.
Lids snapped back down before daylight dragged her out of the dream
world.

Might as well remember the damn nightmare. She rubbed her temples until ... there it was, that vile revolting image. But how had her
dream self ended up there? She traced back to the preceding image,
then the one before that, and before that to find herself in a house,
a stucco family home like much of Santa Fe's south side but walls
cracking like an eggshell tapped with a knife, jagged lines racing down
sheetrock panels that break apart spewing dust and bits of lumber,
insulation, wiring. She sprints out a back door to escape.

Now she's barreling through the desert pursued by a shadowy figure, running up an arroyo, laboring through deep sand as the cliff walls
rise and rise to finally join in a rock wall blocking off the canyon, a
slender stream of water twirling off the edge to splash in a pool below.
She scales the cliff emerging on top to see a couple figures squatting
over a flat rock. An old woman in a deerskin dress, a man in a short kilt,
black hair bound by a cloth band around his forehead. Approaching
she spots a rattlesnake laid out on the rock. The old woman lifts a flint
blade, then slits the snake's belly long ways, plunging her hand into
the snake's innards. This was the sickening image that had jolted her
out of sleep, made her gag with revulsion. The old woman pulled out
a bloody wriggling mass, wiped it with her other hand to reveal a tiny
struggling miniature of ... of Minoa.

She stood up. Rich hadn't budged. The guy could sleep through a
lightning strike. The walls pressed in, the clutter suffocated. Here she
was again, mind like a summer dust devil, trapped in a petrified forest
of old misunderstandings and white lies. She had to get out of here, go
somewhere, anywhere. She pulled on her clothes, grabbed her keys and
headed out. Inside a window in the main part of the house she spied
Helen, the fifty-something widow who rented Rich his apartment,
wearing a bathrobe, hair askew. Rich had avoided saying how much
he paid for this place. A story there. When she reached the truck she
texted Carter:

Meet me at OJ Juanita's for coffee?

Didn't need to wait for an answer. Carter never slept in.

Chapter Twenty-Four

A tourist — Bermuda shorts, visor — ran up Water Street, glancing side to side, wide-eyed, panicked. Around the corner of Don Gaspar stepped a guy in a black leather jacket and western hat. A revolver hung from one hand. Spotting the woman, he ran up the block toward her. She banged on the locked door of an art gallery, screaming, then ran around the side of the building heading toward the Santa Fe River. Part way across the lot she tripped and skidded to the ground. In a few strides the man stood over her, pointing the gun at her head.

Minoa and Carter sipped coffee without taking their eyes off the scene. They sat at an outdoor table by a coffee takeout the size of a tool shed a couple blocks from the plaza. Near where the man aimed at the fallen tourist a group of people stood behind a camera. Over where Don Gaspar hit Alameda a bus and trucks blocked off the street. In front of the bus, groups of extras gathered around a folding table set with coffee urns and snacks. Scattered spectators stood around the perimeter of the block observing the film shoot.

"It's a horror flick," Carter said, rotating her head of brown curls in Minoa's direction.

"Carter, that guy in the black hat and cowboy boots looks like a *sicario*. It's a thriller about cartels."

"Why would a Mexican assassin kill an innocent tourist? Makes no sense."

"Maybe she's a Walter White figure, you know, middle-class wife and mother starts cooking meth to pay for her daughter's cancer treatment or something."

Now a woman in a white veil and dress slipped around the corner of the art gallery and pointed something like a stick at the killer. The man collapsed, started writhing and groaning as if possessed. The woman in white helped the cowering tourist to her feet. As the tourist ran off, the woman in white aimed at the man in black again and this time he arched, froze, collapsed and remained still.

"I win." Carter jabbed her index toward the scene. "She fried him with magic. That's a supernatural twist. Couldn't be a trafficker movie. It has to be paranormal horror."

"I guess you're right. A La Llorona *bruja* cursing a bad guy. *The Vengeance of La Llorona* or somesuch."

Now a car squealed around the corner, careened into the lot to stop beside the lifeless gunman. Doors flew open and two guys ran over, picked up the killer, hauled him into the back seat of the car and sped off.

A guy in a black tee shirt walked around the camera and said, "Okay, let's run this one more time."

The La Llorona figure walked out of the alley behind the gallery holding a hand to her head.

"This veil keeps slipping."

Two people ran up to her. A woman pulled off the veil and squatted down beside her bag. The guy started touching up the actress' make-up. Her black hair was pulled into a bun at the nape of her neck. When she turned away from the sun to accommodate the makeup artist, Minoa got a good look at her face. Familiar. The woman opened her eyes leaving no room for doubt. Huge blue orbs like turquoise nobs. Even with a black wig there was no mistaking Inanna.

"Carter, that's the New Age diva who runs that goddess group where my friend went the night she died."

Carter squinted at Inanna.

"She's an actress?"

"Maybe she gets roles in local productions to help fund her goddess therapy startup. Or the New Age crap pays her rent while she tries to get acting jobs."

"I know you think the ex-husband killed your old friend. But this lady looks capable of doing serious damage. And she's an actress, so she's a good liar."

"What do you think of that dream I had? Me in the belly of a rattlesnake?"

Carter squinted at her over her coffee cup.

"I think you're in too deep. It's sweet of you to help your old buddy's family. But it's giving you nightmares. And worse than that, you're attracting Diamondbacks."

"Carter, I didn't attract that snake into my car. Somebody put it there."

"Maybe. Or maybe snakes don't like feeling cold at night, so sensing a warm motor nearby they crawl in."

Minoa glared at her.

"So you think I'm imagining everything, just like that detective? Just like everyone, actually."

"I didn't say that. It's just that while the rest of us imperialist invaders seem to forget rattlesnakes even exist, you run into them everywhere."

"So I'm a snake magnet."

"I didn't say that either."

"Then what are you saying?"

"Maybe rattlesnakes are your white whale?"

Minoa's face screwed up.

"I'm Captain Ahab cruising the desert sands in search of the rattler that crippled me? Explain your analogy."

"Minoa, take off your boxing gloves. I'm not criticizing you. I just think rattlesnakes have psychological meaning for you and that's the real reason you're pursuing this snake murderer."

"If it's all in my head, what killed my friend?"

"I'm not denying material reality. Psychological symbols can make use of real facts to convey something. In your case rattlesnakes probably stand for scary stuff from your childhood or something,"

"There was that camping trip with Dreema where ... a snake crawled into the campsite and I didn't protect her."

"OMG. Why do you always think you have to protect people?"

"So what do you think the dream means?"

"I don't know but it's hopeful."

"What's hopeful about being born from a rattlesnake cesarean?"

"Look, you're the mythology expert. But isn't it an image of rebirth? You're reborn out of a snake's belly. Ergo, the snake investigation will lead to a new Minoa. A happier Minoa."

"Maybe a Minoa with a reasonable job or, god forbid, life."

"What does your career matter in the face of climate crisis, world poverty and impending World War III? Bigger things are at stake, Min, than redeeming your damaged ego."

Minoa gulped a sip of coffee

"You're cruel."

"It springs from love. Anyway, I gotta take off. We're doing a Trombe wall construction workshop this weekend and some of the supplies haven't come in yet."

"You're doing enough selfless world-saving for both of us. Happy solar energy trapping."

"Take care of yourself."

Carter stood, plunked her coffee cup in the trash barrel beside OJ Juanita's order window with an exemplary jump shot and strode away.

Minoa sat watching the film shoot as the morning sun turned up the pressure. Rattlesnakes as her Moby Dick? No. She refused the idea. This whole snake mess wasn't just her working out the neuroses that being back in her hometown kicked up. No, her friend had died. That was real. And she was pretty sure she hadn't left the truck door open that night when the rattler got in. No, not pretty sure. Real sure. She wouldn't accept Carter's suggestion that she was searching for an external evil to distract from the pain of her old emotional wounds. Okay, she hadn't turned up any solid evidence Amilcar caused Dreema's death. But she'd traced him to a job working with wild animals and experienced his violent outbursts more than once.

Still, Carter might be right that she was looking in the wrong direction for Dreema's murderer. Dreema had been near a rattlesnake at Inanna's place on the night of her death. And Inanna was no New Age ditz. How could she find out more about what went on at Inanna's gathering that last night of Dreema's life? She picked up her phone and started searching for the Women Rising website. A semi-transparent image of a Mesopotamian ziggurat with a snake coiling out the top overlay the homepage. Photos showed groups of women at the site in Pojoaque. Clicking on more pages she found out that, in addition to the oracle get-togethers, Inanna offered private vision creation sessions, weekend trance workshops and native wisdom coaching. Her bio said she was an initiated shaman with a teacher from the Tewake Pueblo lineage. Sacred stone divination therapy and mythic life story consulting were available as part of wellness packages offered by the Cosmic Energy Day Spa in downtown Santa Fe.

She noted the address, tossed her cup and walked several blocks to where the truck sat. Drove down Agua Fria, veering east on a narrow street lined with luxury condos crammed between aging adobes, then a couple more turns to park on Ambrosio Lane. Down the block she spotted a yard with a many-armed statue spouting water from fingertips into a pool. A sign on the graveled yard said Cosmic Energy Day Spa and Rejuvenation Therapies. Approaching she saw that the front door of the newly plastered house was open. She walked in.

No one sat in the waiting room. A sign on a reception desk said 'Please take a seat. Your therapist will be with you shortly.' She peered into a display case at an array of crystals, fetish stones and beaded jewelry. Several doors led off from the entry room: a closed door with a white noise generator beside it, an open door through which she glimpsed a massage table and an entry to a hallway. She listened hard at the closed door and then tiptoed down the hallway. Inside the first room she spied what looked like a dental chair in southwestern print surrounded by a profusion of tubes. The next room contained a large native drum and a hanging gong. Throw pillows on the floor circled a brazier of artificial coals. In the corner a diffuser puffed little steam clouds like doll-size Indian smoke signals. She glanced up and down the hallway, then ducked in.

On a small desk against the back wall sat a stack of invoices bearing a letterhead for Women Rising. She fanned the pages, glimpsed amounts from $400 to $1250 but didn't see Dreema's name. In a file drawer she thumbed through tabs from 'A' to 'Z' without discovering one for Dreema Adkins. Some of the names were not typical:

Koyangwuti, Atabey, Ereshkigal amidst others like Pullman, Jane and Banneker, Evelyn. Maybe Dreema had used a goddess name in her dealings with Inanna. If so, she'd have to read every file with a goddess name to find it. But wait. At the back of the file drawer among the spare file folders she spied Adkins, Dreema.

The first few pages in the file contained personal information. Under children she'd listed two: Aracely and a boy eight years older named Oliver. She described herself as separated. For education she listed Santa Fe High and a certificate from the community college. A questionnaire asked about Dreema's goals for transcendental therapy. One question said, 'What do you wish to be free of?' Dreema had written 'I don't ever want to feel sinful again.' After 'what I dream of achieving' Dreema had written, "I want to become strong and brave like my friend Minoa." Minoa closed her eyes and squeezed the bridge of her nose. She felt her diaphragm cramp but pumped a few breaths in and out, pried her eyes open and kept reading. Next came a spreadsheet listing monthly amounts ranging from $175 to $400. A few sheets of handwritten notes followed.

Conclusions:

First husband = Zeus figure, godly powers expressed through military background

Theft of boy child = patriarchal expropriation of fruits of women's reproduction

Second husband = Hades trying to steal Demeter's daughter Persephone

Mother (Georgia) = water nymph raped by Cronos

Impulse to sacrifice self to break curse on her family - must realize it's violence of patriarchy that has harmed her

Suggest transformation ritual with Basmu or Musmahhu. Possible descent into underworld ceremony with passage through seven gates,

symbolic three days on meat hook to clear guilt followed by restoration
to light with sisters present to induct her as priestess of the goddess.

To heal Dreema, Inanna was prescribing an enactment of the ancient Mesopotamian myth of the descent of the goddess Inanna into
the underworld. Minoa knew the myth from courses on mythology at
Columbia. There were no serpents in the story, as far as she remembered. But maybe Inanna improvised. And how was she planning to
hang Dreema on a meat hook, even symbolically? Inanna seemed more
and more like a megalomaniacal cult leader.

After returning the file to the drawer she checked the other drawers
but found only office supplies and a bag of polished stones on beaded
strings. On the desk top she noticed a stack of brochures propped
in an organizer and pulled one out. The cover photo showed Inanna
dressed in a fake snakeskin mini skirt and bustier, a snake looped
across her chest and around her neck. No rattle on this snake. Below:
Sacred Snake Ceremonies with Shamaness Inanna/ Experience Divine
Ritual and Connect to Feminine Power. The text inside promised participants would experience dissolution of unconscious blocks along
with enhanced intuition and more sensual romantic relationships. By
invitation only. Who would pay for that? Dreema didn't have the
money. She stuck the brochure back in the slot, noticing a different
brochure in the next slot. Pulled it out. It was a schedule of the yearly
cycle of dances at northern New Mexico Indian pueblos. One of the
upcoming events, a corn dance at Tewake pueblo, was circled with a
few words scribbled beside it: "Meet Richard at noon."

Steps tick-tocked through the waiting area. She shot up and glanced
around the room looking for cover. Saw nothing so she dashed down
the hall into the next room. In the middle sat an enormous metal
box with doors on the front and a round hole on the top. She pulled
open the doors, squeezed inside and pulled the doors shut just as steps

came down the hall. Inside she huddled on a bench in the dark, head crammed against the top. Sounds from outside were muffled so after a moment she pushed her head up through the hole until her eyes and ears emerged. She heard a door by the waiting room open followed by two women conversing. Then a door closed.

After a moment, steps clicked down the hallway again. She ducked just as someone entered the room. The intruder pushed buttons on the box causing a few beeps and then steps retreated. She poked her head up again. More voices drifted out of the waiting area. She noticed she was sweating, though she felt no heat. Soon sweat trickled down her face into her eyes, dripping off her chin. Her tee and shorts dampened.

She pushed hard on the doors of the box. Nothing budged. Lifting a foot she kicked the door with all her strength. The doors jiggled but stuck. She had to blink over and over to squeeze the perspiration out of her eyes. She poked one arm out the hole on the top but couldn't reach the buttons. Her head popped up again and she pressed against the box with hysterical fury. When that didn't work she froze for a moment, then sucked in a lungful of air and disappeared inside.

A long hoarse screech peeled out of the box filling the renovated house. Then a howl split the air, a sound that merged a screaming infant with an outraged tomcat, followed by snarls. Fast steps, then somebody started punching buttons on the box. The doors flew open and Minoa leaped out, shoving a red-haired woman to stumble backwards and splat on the floor. She raced to the front door, flew across the yard and jumped into the truck, catching sight in the rearview mirror of the woman bursting out the front door of Cosmic Energy Day Spa.

She popped the clutch and accelerated a few blocks to a skidding stop a few inches from Agua Fria. Took some deep breaths, checked her face in the rearview mirror: a minute's drive through zero humidity air had dried the skin. The material under her armpits and around the waist of her shorts was still wet. What the hell had that contraption done to her? She chuckled recalling those endless days spent with Huaorani children learning to imitate the red howler monkey, the scarlet macaw, the jaguar. Not entirely wasted.

Hearing a siren she shot across Agua Fria into the parking area behind a house converted to a French restaurant. Then wound around to a shortcut into the backside of a shopping center. Hunkered there while the siren grew louder. Police must have arrived at the day spa. Had the woman seen her license plate? Could she identify her from a dash across the front yard of the spa? She drove up and down a few alleys to end in the parking lot by the Shrine of Our Lady of Guadalupe. Got out, still breathing fast, and walked over to sit on a bench at the feet of a giant statue of the saint.

She thought over what she'd seen in Inanna's shamanic treatment room. Looked like snakes were an effective marketing tool for her. She owned more than Basmu because she hadn't wrapped a rattlesnake around her neck for that photo on the sacred snake ceremonies brochure. She prescribed healing ceremonies for her clients based on bastardized versions of ancient myths. She'd even suggested Dreema should 'hang on a meathook' for three days. But no suggestion she should subject herself to snakebite in order to be healed of her psychological distress. And that note about the meeting with Richard at Tewake Pueblo? Could he be her snake supplier?

Sitting there pummeled by bullet-strength sunshine she let her mind drift, her unfocused gaze resting on the statue of the compassionate lady ... until a thought popped up out of the dusty mental storage rooms she'd crammed full during those years at the university. As she recalled, Our Lady of Guadalupe had miraculously appeared in the fifteen hundreds to Juan Diego, an Aztec who'd converted to Christianity, on the site of an Aztec temple, a temple to the goddess Coatlicue. Coatlicue dressed in a skirt of serpents, an Aztec snake goddess. Crap. Even a Catholic saint had her roots in snake worship. She stood up and headed back to the truck. Like Carter said, she was turning into a snake magnet.

Her spa invasion hadn't revealed much about Dreema's death. Maybe Inanna's followers would betray information about what happened to Dreema at the Women Rising event on the night she died. She scanned back through the photos on her cell to some shots of license plates. Leaning the phone on the steering wheel she began an internet search for the vehicle owners. She came up with a couple names, Josephine Steadman and Debby Romero. Checking for social media she found a Facebook page on Josephine and realized she was Marian the Librarian, Inannaz's helper in the oracle hut. Josephine liked cats, roses and romcoms and worked at a brokerage near the plaza. On Tik-Tok she found a bunch of videos made by Debby Romero. With a little searching she linked her name to a touristy ceramics shop downtown.

Chapter Twenty-Five

G iant modernist doors swung open under a bronze plaque with raised lettering: City Different Investments. Inside, leather and stainless decor screamed big city while a courtyard of brick walkways and flowering vines, visible through floor to ceiling windows, murmured upscale provincial. At the back of the waiting room sat Josephine Steadman, AKA Marian the Librarian, her lined complexion stretched by a high traction bun.

As Minoa approached, passing glass-topped coffee tables carrying the Wall Street Journal, Economist and Forbes, a series of reactions passed across Josephine's face: surprise, doubt, fake courtesy. She must have concluded Minoa was a wealthy potential client of the brokerage with a passing interest in goddess worship. She forced a smile.

"Hello. Can I help you?"

"Hi. You recognize me, don't you? What a surprise. It's great to see you."

"Lovely, I'm sure. Do you have an appointment or would you care to speak with an investment advisor?"

"I was hoping you'd have a moment. I'm interested in Inanna's program and would love to ask you a few questions about it since you obviously know so much."

"Well, I'm at work now so it's not the best time."

"Just for a moment."

"But would you like to speak with one of our investment advisers?"

"Perhaps. But first, I'm fascinated by Inanna's serpent. Does she use Basmu in any other ceremonies? The presence of an authentic viper elicits such primordial feelings."

Josephine glanced around. One graying fellow in denim shirt and top siders reclined on a couch flipping through a magazine. She lowered her voice.

"It's an ancient tradition. Snakes were sacred to the ancient goddess religions of the Near East, you know, before patriarchal tribes crushed matriarchal societies."

"Did you know Dreema Adkins, the young woman who recently died of snakebite? She was a member of your group."

"Yes, we're all so sorry."

"Perhaps she found inspiration with Inanna before her death. Do you know if she had any special sessions with the snake? It might have given her a vision to help her passage to the other world, don't you think?"

"I believe Ms. Adkins was one of the women interested in the community Inanna is developing. I wouldn't know if she received other teachings."

"Community?"

"We're fundraising to construct a womanist community at the site in Pojoaque. It will be off-grid, collectively run, for women only, with a mission to provide a model for peaceful matriarchal cohabitation as a means to avoid eco-suicide and nuclear destruction. Inanna is holding a meeting for potential investors next Thursday. Perhaps you'd be interested in attending?"

"I might like to go. But first, the article I read said that the unfortunate young woman spent her last evening in this world at the

Women Rising gathering. Do you remember how she was doing that last night?"

"She was fine."

"Did you see her leave?"

"I'm not sure why you're asking me?"

"If I'm to consider investing in the community, I would need assurance that safety protocols are observed around the snake."

"Of course they are. She had her turn in the oracle hut like all the rest."

"Please think back. She didn't try to approach Basmu or even fall in?"

Josephine squinted at her.

"Of course not."

"I've always had a vivid imagination. I try to picture how she could have been snakebitten that night. Don't you?"

"Not at all. I understood she was in her own bedroom when the tragedy occurred."

"Who told you that? It wasn't in the newspaper."

"I don't know. People talk. I must have overheard something."

"I'm sure the women from the Tuesday group discussed her death."

"It was a shock."

"Who takes care of the snake?"

"Several of us keep a rotating schedule. It's a privilege."

"Was Dreema on that schedule?"

"Not currently, I don't think."

"Did you ever wonder if maybe she went back by herself late at night to, I don't know, ask the sacred serpent a private question?"

"That would be ... unheard of."

"As a womanist collective I'm sure you all work together for common ends?"

"We don't subscribe to a philosophy of self-interest, if that's what you mean."

"So all of you must agree to do whatever is best for the group?"

"We strive to embody an alternative to capitalism."

"Would you conceal an inconvenient accident to protect the community?"

Josephine's face stretched.

"I'm sure I've never faced such a choice. Now, may I have your name please?"

"No accidents around the snake?"

"Of course not."

"Like what almost happened to me. You remember, don't you?"

"I'm not permitted to discuss these matters with outsiders. Now if you would care to make an appointment?"

"Has animal control ever been called about the rattler? Do the neighbors know there's a venomous snake next to their property?"

"The neighbors are completely unaware. I mean ..."

"And do you know where Inanna got Basmu?"

Josephine rolled her office chair back a few feet.

"I can help you with an appointment but I can't discuss this matter any further."

"If you think of anything else, please let me know."

She jotted her phone number on a notepad on the desk while Josephine nailed her with eyes flickering between suspicion and fear. When Minoa walked out, the mammoth doors of City Different Investments swung shut behind her with a whoosh of air as if to push her out.

***

"Inanna is going to help me get jobs in movies."

Debby Romero's glossy black pony tail bobbed on the crown of her head as she spoke.

"She's an actress, did you know?"

She propped her elbows on the counter in a crafts shop near the plaza that looked like a whimsical bestiary. Shelves to the ceiling teemed with wooden and ceramic roadrunners, donkeys, gophers, horny toads, rattlers.

"I imagined," said Minoa, distracted by a display of brightly painted carved coyotes behind Debby's head. Each figure showed a coyote in some human pose: playing golf, drinking beer, skiing, at a slot machine, in a hot-air balloon, using a urinal.

"She had a supporting role in *Breaking Bad*, sort of small but, you know, really lit. And if you saw that western about aliens landing in ranch country or something — I didn't really get it — she was the waitress at the diner, the one who says, 'Any alien with a shirt and shoes can get served here.' Funny, right?"

"Very. Do you go to Inanna's goddess events often?"

"When I can afford it. She's great, she gave me the strength to get out of this god awful disaster of a relationship with this dirt bag, I mean, scummiest of the all time most repulsive scum. You can't imagine."

"I was wondering if you remember one of the other women who was a regular at the evening gatherings, Dreema Adkins, tall, blonde, green eyes?"

"Oh yeah, I would have died for those eyes, but hey, with colored contacts we can all be goddesses."

She leaned over the counter batting her eyes, irises the color of muddy rain puddles.

"Sure, I see them: azure, like a cloudless sky. But do you recall the last time you saw her at one of those Women Rising evenings with oracle readings?"

"I know she's RIP. Really sad and so gross. Are you an insurance adjuster or something?"

"Not exactly. Were you there, by any chance, at the next-to-last meeting when she went in for her turn with the oracle?"

"I was there, but no promises what went on. I usually come out of that oracle chamber like shook. Besides, those sacred plants are wild."

"It's important. Please try to remember if you saw her later in the evening after the oracle readings were over."

"Nope, don't think so. Hey, you're not one of those forensic investigators, are you? That job is so sick. I mean if you don't mind blood. I don't. I think blood is gorgeous. I mean there's no dress so wow as a blood red clubber, like bodycon lace or maybe ruched velvet. Yum."

"Did the women talk about Dreema's death?"

"I don't know. I don't hang out with the sisters much. No offense but they're a little old for me. I'm Gen Z and they're like Gen A or B or something."

"Did you ever see Inanna do anything risky with a snake?"

"Wait a minute. You don't think Basmu bit that lady that died, do you? He's sacred. Besides, they feed him all the time. He's so fat he can hardly move. I told Jojo she's gonna give the poor snake diabetes or something."

"Does Inanna ever take Basmu out of his pit in the oracle hut?"

"What, she's not Hercules. Anyway, that lady knows what she's doing. She's an honorary Indian."

"An honorary Indian?"

"She's been initiated and everything."

"Does Inanna do rituals that involve a sacrifice of some kind?"

"You don't sound like a detective. Do you have one of those websites that investigates weird stuff like cattle mutilations?"

"Not at all. I'm a friend of the family. Her bereaved relatives wish to know the details of how she spent her last night in this world, that's all."

"Sure, I guess that makes sense."

"So how about ceremonies with some kind of sacrifice? Maybe a dead animal?"

Debby's gleaming charcoal brows angled down in the middle.

"Yuck. Inanna's not an animal abuser. She loves animals. I'd trust her with my cat, Zoomers. I call him that cause he's so hyper, climbs up and down the curtains twenty times a day. He's my spirit animal and I'd die for him."

"Does Inanna ever do other rituals with the snake?"

"Look, she knows a ton of spiritual stuff. But I can't afford the private healing ceremonies, not yet anyway. Till I land a big role. Then it's Gucci all the way."

Staring into Debby's frank smiling face, Minoa's mind went blank.

"Will you let me know if you think of anything else relevant to Dreema's death?"

"Sure. Hey, I get it. You're one of those true crime writers, right? You know I'd make a great focus for your story and I've got plenty of time for interviews, press conferences, whatever."

"No really, I'm just a concerned friend. Best of luck with your acting career."

Chapter Twenty-Six

Outside the shop she turned down the sidewalk toward the plaza. The tree-shaded square teemed with tourists, bored teens and a few vagabonds in worn jeans tossing a ball for a spotted hound with a kerchief around its neck. She sat on a bench to think. What had she learned? That Inanna was making money off poor Dreema, that she was seeking investors to build some alternative community, that she took acting roles in local film productions. And Basmu was overfed and overweight. Was it strange that Josephine and Debby had little recollection of Dreema on the night she died? Or had the Women Rising participants agreed not to talk about her?

Maybe a walk around the labyrinth at St. Francis Cathedral would clarify her next step. She crossed the plaza diagonally and was just turning the corner by La Fonda Hotel heading toward the cathedral when a door opened in her face.

"Ow!"

She staggered back, hand on her nose.

"I'm so sorry," said the fellow rushing around the door.

Their eyes met.

"Minoa, are you alright?"

"Lewis. You're back?"

She rubbed her nose, staring.

"Here, come sit down for a minute."

He herded her toward the plaza.

"I was just heading to the labyrinth, you know, to unwind my thinking."

"Good enough."

He turned her around and headed up San Francisco Street, arm lingering around her shoulders. At the street in front of St. Francis Cathedral the arm dropped. They slid onto a bench beside the statue of Kateri Tekakwitha, a native American saint, and watched kids race around a spiral labyrinth inlaid into the concrete area in front of the Romanesque church. Tourists milled about snapping photos of the twin-tower facade and rose stained glass window.

"What brings you downtown?"

"Delivering some jewelry for a friend. So what's new with the snake mystery?"

"Too many people with rattlesnakes. Instead of finding one person near my friend who had access to rattlers, there are three or four. And each had some kind of motive. Although there's still no proof anyone murdered Dreema with snakes or venom."

"Maybe you're frustrated you can't cram reality into a neat theoretical box?"

She pressed her lips together to avoid an irritated response.

"I was wondering about the history of the Asa clan."

He straightened, levering down his long brows.

"The what? What's that got to do with snake murders?"

"See, this crazy shopkeeper in Abiquiu tipped me off to a group of Tewa Indians who abandoned the pueblo there and moved to Hopiland in the 1600s. When the governor ordered Abiquiu resettled in the 1700s, some friar traveled to Hopiland and brought back the same Tewa people, or their descendants, now the Asa clan. So there were people in Abiquiu who spoke Hopi and probably practiced the Hopi snake dance at the time of the witch trials in the late 1700s. After that, it's possible the tradition continued secretly through the next couple centuries right up to the present, so there could still be snake dances in Abiquiu and people, like you, who are comfortable handling snakes. Amilcar might be one of them."

He gawked at her and laughed.

"That's the most far-fetched thing I've ever heard."

She glared.

"The migration happened, so it's plausible the Tewa brought back Hopi customs and ceremonies to Abiquiu."

"You're trying to turn a simple case of wife murder into a historical mystery. Are you planning to publish an academic paper on this topic or maybe give a lecture at the Wheelwright?"

"Not funny. I'm trying to find my friend's murderer and avoid another unwelcome encounter with a rattlesnake. I'm not as fond of them as you are."

"Then you probably support rattlesnake roundups where they kill hundreds of snakes and serve them up grilled and barbecued."

"What? I never heard of that. That's disgusting."

"That's how the conqueror race deals with the land they stole: exterminate as many species and extract as many resources as possible. They think we're stupid for trying to coexist."

They both stared straight ahead.

"I don't," she said.

His posture softened.

"So I'm an informant for your rattlesnake research?"

"Listen, the murdered woman's brother thinks the ex-husband is involved in some secret cult around Abiquiu that handles snakes. If it's true, this Hopi connection might explain it. I just thought you could tell me if he's completely off base or not."

"Can't stop acting like an anthropologist?"

"This has nothing to do with being an anthropologist. I'm trying to make sure nobody gets away with murdering my old best friend, or her brother."

"Her brother?"

"He wants to be a hero and confront his sister's killer."

"You'd rather be the hero?"

She stood up.

"I gotta go. I ... I have an appointment."

"Wait. Sorry."

He pulled her hand down toward the bench. She glared at him.

"I understand you hate anthropologists. But I'm not your punching bag for the whole discipline. I don't have any connection to it anymore and I probably never will."

"So you're an anthropologist in recovery?"

He flashed a one-sided grin.

"Recovery? I'm about as recovered as this economy."

She slumped back onto the bench. He ruffled the hair on the top of her head.

"Abundance at the top but a struggle with unmet needs everywhere else?"

"Ha ha. You're a comedian and a social critic."

"Look, I bet you've got more information about this Asa clan migration than I do. I don't read studies of my own people. It sounds like a long shot to me though."

"The problem is, I've found zero solid proof that someone killed my friend Dreema even though I'm convinced that's what happened."

"I've got it. Provoke them, then see who responds with violence."

"You're full of great ideas."

"Maybe I should accompany you to provide backup when someone attacks."

"You seem pretty busy for that."

"Well, you could text me next time you hear a rattlesnake. You've got my number, right?"

He stood up.

"So you're a hero-for-loan?"

"You can consider me a handy sort of exotic *other*. I'll be looking for that help text."

The corners of his mouth were little curlicues.

"If I've got cell service when some snake killer is chasing me."

"You better pray for technology. We've got no coverage at Third Mesa where I'm from so I'm used to using my own senses."

"So I'm just a tech-dependent millennial?"

He was walking away, a hand lifted in that backward farewell he favored. She watched him disappear around the corner of Water Street, fuming. He was insufferable. She decided to walk the labyrinth to clear her mind. But as she stood her cell began to buzz and dance on the bench. She picked it up. Carter was texting.

Scanner pikt up police dsptch. Rattler death Ortiz Mtns Gold Mine Rd.

Now?

Yes. Relevant?

IDK Going up to find out. Thx

Adrenalin whooshed down her veins. Hallelujah for Carter's search and rescue equipment. She shot off at a trot.

Chapter
Twenty-Seven

T he truck fishtailed up the steep road to the snake trader's place, tires spinning on a layer of gravel over baked dirt. Near the top Minoa pulled over and parked, stomping down the emergency brake as far as it would go. Then she walked up to where the road tipped down into the old lady's hermitage valley.

In the dirt area between the outbuildings she spied patrol cars, an animal control vehicle and an ambulance. Figures in brown jumpsuits, yellow firefighter coats and gray-green police uniforms milled around. She walked down the hill and joined the crowd, attracting only a few curious glances. In the central area she spied Detective Ricky Martinez squatting beside a body. A woman in street clothes with a black bag leaned in from the other side. Legs in baggy jeans over a pair of scratched Wellingtons stretched across the packed dirt between the two of them. Moving farther along she caught sight of the snake lady's face. Her head lolled to the side, eyelids lax, tongue tip protruding. Strands of gray hair splayed across the dirt.

She took two steps toward the body before a paunchy cop blocked her way.

"You can't go over there."

"Ricky Martinez asked me to come."

The officer glanced at Martinez.

"Wait here. You can talk to him when he's done."

She sidled around to the far side of the open area and paused where she could hear their voices.

"Any idea how long she's been dead?" asked Martinez.

"Not long. Maybe a couple hours," said the examiner.

"Cause of death?"

"I might have said rattlesnake envenomation due to those fang marks." The examiner moved aside one of the snake lady's split open pants legs. "But the area of the bites displays mild edema and little discoloration. Not what you would expect from a fatal strike."

"But being elderly, rattler venom might kill her fast, right?"

"This envenomation didn't progress to the point of causing death. See these red pinpricks? They indicate a slight amount of internal bleeding. But by the time someone dies of crotalid venom they suffer extensive coagulopathy and necrosis. A leg would swell up to bursting and internal hemorrhaging would compromise most organs.

"This lady called 911 saying somebody tried to kill her. She wouldn't call rattlesnakes murderers, would she?"

"I don't think the snakebites killed her. Look at the flaccid facial muscles. It could have been a stroke that occurred by chance on the same day she received the snakebites."

"You're saying several rattler bites had nothing to do with her death?"

"I don't have any definitive conclusions. We'll have to wait for the autopsy. You asked me to speculate."

"Okay, but would a stroke make her think she was being murdered? Or maybe an attacker scared her so much she had a stroke?"

"Strokes can cause hallucinations."

"They tell me some rattlers in that shed over there are out of their cages. It's pretty hard to believe she suffered multiple bites with minor symptoms."

"These could have been dry bites, no venom injected."

"Dry bites?"

"If the snakes were recently milked, they wouldn't have time to accumulate venom to inject."

"So she was keeping all those snakes for venom."

"There's another possible explanation for the lack of visible symptoms but it's rare. If the snake fang hit a vein, venom might enter directly into the bloodstream. In that case death would be rapid, before the development of visible indicia."

"Still doesn't explain why she called to report a murder."

The examiner surveyed the snake trader's ranchette.

"As a snake breeder she'd likely been bitten many times. She could have developed an immunity to venom."

"I'm gonna guess repeated exposure to rattler venom drives you crazy."

"I don't know about that. But dementia could have contributed to a misperception of her situation."

Minoa glanced around the secluded valley where the snake lady had raised her rattlers, encircled by sandstone cliffs on one side and rocky hills on the other. She'd called to report a murder, then died with no marks on her body except a few fang punctures and some tiny red spots. The medical examiner thought they were dry bites or she was immune to venom and died of some other cause. Maybe, but there was another explanation they weren't considering. She hurried over causing the big-bellied cop to head her way. As she approached Martinez and the examiner she started talking fast.

"You're assuming these are hemotoxic rattler bites but they're probably neurotoxic. She suffered paralysis and respiratory failure and died quickly."

Detective Martinez sprang up.

"What are you doing here?"

"I knew this woman. She was connected to the recent rattler death in Tierra Feliz which was neurotoxic. So that type of venom could be involved in this case."

"Connected? What are you talking about?"

"This woman was trapping rattlers at Tierra Feliz. The autopsy report on the victim in Tierra Feliz named neurotoxic rattler venom as the cause of death. So this woman likely has some neurotoxic rattlesnakes."

While she was talking, he waved his hand to signal for an officer, but the gesture froze in midair.

"How did you come up with this information?" He squeezed his button brown eyes to a line. "And how did you find out about this woman's death?"

"I'm helping an old friend."

The officer reached them, his cheeks puckering purple.

"I told you to stay away."

He poked a finger toward her.

"Okay, okay."

As Minoa walked away she heard the medical examiner.

"We don't see much neurotoxic venom in this region but there may be something in what she's saying."

One of the animal control people standing near the snake hutch yelled to Martinez.

"We need to get inside that shed ASAP. Those loose rattlers are probably killing each other right now.".

"They'll just have to kill each other. Nobody goes in the shed till we examine it."

It took a moment for the significance of that remark to sink into Minoa's brain. Might Martinez collect forensic evidence here, something he'd refused for Dreema's death? She tried to recall the interior of the snake hutch, the construction of the cages, the closures on cage doors, tools propped in a corner. One image crowded out all others: a diamondback sliding out of a bottom cage. A metal piece had hung on a leather thong below the door, jiggled out of a loop catch when she crashed into the cages. Not a secure lock for animals with lethal venom. Maybe the old woman tripped and stumbled like Minoa, causing some cage doors to swing open. Maybe her death was an accident.

But the snake lady was a professional. She knew her way around a rattlesnake. And she knew at least some of her specimens were neurotoxic. Surely she would have been careful, incredibly careful. If she noticed a cage door open, why didn't she escape to the outside? And if she was bitten, why didn't she call for help and inform the dispatcher she needed neurotoxic anti-venom immediately knowing she would soon become incapacitated? Why didn't she have a stock of anti-venom on hand? And why would she say she was being murdered?

The animal control guy stomped around as if he were trying to warm his feet on a frigid day.

"Could your crew get the snakes out without going inside?" Martinez called out. "Maybe open the door and catch them as they escape?"

The animal control guy guffawed. Walking casually Minoa circled around to the back side of the shed. Once there, out of view of everyone, she paused. The window was still broken. The snake lady probably figured a broken window didn't matter too much, not while the weather was still good, not for creatures that slithered on the ground. She peered inside. Several cage doors hung open. It took a moment to spot the escaped snakes. One was curled up in a corner, two others lay side by side along the wall. They weren't engaged in mortal combat just yet.

The situation didn't make sense. This woman was an experienced snake handler. She must have had safety procedures for opening the door. Even if she pulled it open and stepped inside, she would have seen immediately that cage doors were open. And although she had behaved like a madwoman to Minoa, there was no doubt she knew her business. She would have stepped back outside and closed the door. No experienced handler would try to catch rattlers in a confined space without protective clothing and other safety measures. It would be more logical to put on her thigh high leather boots and long gloves and get one of her poles with tongs on the end. That body lying on the ground, peeking through half-closed eyes at the pitiless sky, wore only a cotton shirt, jeans and the old Wellingtons. Minoa looked around the interior of the hut. No sign of the pole with snake tongs she had used to hit the window glass. That meant it would have been outside where the snake lady had access.

An idea crowned over the rocky skyline circling the hidden valley. What if someone had done to the old lady what she did to Minoa? What if someone parked near the road and walked in, opened cage doors and waited behind the shed. As soon as she stepped over the threshold, he dashed around and slammed the door shut, locking it with the stake through the latch. He would have waited long enough to be sure she was bitten several times before pulling the stake out of the latch and hightailing it back to his car.

But that would leave the possibility she would run out fast enough to see who had set her up to die, to call for help and reach a hospital in time to save her life. But if he left the stake in the door latch, it would be clear this was no accidental death. So he must have stood by the door of the shed listening to her screams when she was bitten, implacable before her crying and beating on the door and pleading for her life. When he saw the effects of the venom overwhelm her, he pulled the stake out of the latch and took off. Maybe he miscalculated and she struggled to the center of the clearing and made a call before dying, screaming at the 911 dispatcher that someone tried to kill her. Or maybe she tried to outsmart him. While trapped in the shed, she froze to avoid attracting more strikes and he mistook it for paralysis overcoming her. He took the stake out of the latch and fled back to his car while she stumbled into the clearing between the buildings, called for help and collapsed.

Why hadn't the old woman done what Minoa did? Why didn't she hoist herself out the window already busted by her own captive? Maybe the snake lady didn't have the strength in her arms to pull herself up and out or venom was rendering her muscles useless.

But wait. Minoa checked the shards of glass lining the window frame. Each razor edged fragment was perfectly clean. The window Minoa had smashed was dust-crusted. The snake lady must have replaced the window. Then she broke it herself when she was trapped inside and desperate. If she hadn't been locked in the shed, she wouldn't have broken the new window. And she couldn't have accidentally locked herself in. So the only possible explanation was that someone locked her in. That was proof her death was murder.

Minoa walked around the cluster of emergency response workers, spotting Martinez walking toward the shed. How would she explain this to him? He'd suggest that the window, even if it were new, was broken under unrelated circumstances. He'd say the examiner believed the snakebites were dry bites. He'd say the old lady had dementia or her brain had curdled from chronic venom poisoning. That would be the most logical explanation, he'd say, waving an officer to escort her back to her vehicle and muttering under his breath about the nutcase who kept reporting imaginary snake murders.

Now the old snake lady had reported a murder as well, but he wouldn't care. He'd figure any gray-haired woman who lived alone in the hills with a pack of rattlers for company had to be *loca*. There wasn't any way to tell him. He would have to blunder down his own investigative pathway leading to another finding of accidental death, while Minoa continued down her improvised route to its conclusion, which might be finding a serial snake killer or might be returning to scanning the ads in the Chronicle of Higher Education every day until her tires or her savings ran out. Or could be, she added as she trudged up the pitted dirt drive toward her truck, becoming the next victim of the rattlesnake killer.

Chapter
Twenty-Eight

She reclined on the bed with a shot of B & B in a coffee cup, not the first of the evening to be perfectly honest. She'd watched the late summer sky deepen from baby blue to ultramarine as the sun hit the horizon and spattered orange light like a broken yolk dripping down the window panes of her guesthouse. Now the twilight sky glistened navy with scattered sparkles. She scanned the room. Two windows, one door, the one room structure was a tin can with one way in and out. She stood and walked to the front window, peered outside. Brent's southwestern palace gaped, windows like empty eyes. No cars in front. Had he flown off to Paris or Dubai or wherever multimillionaires went when their home paradise grew boring? He never told his tenant what he was planning. Why should he?

She sensed the closeness of the guesthouse walls, eight paces apart but pressing inward like some industrial size trash compactor. Glanced at her car keys sitting on a stool by the door as the urge to flee oscillated down her nerves. But she willed herself to stay. She needed a plan. Carter said she was in too deep, Rich was now a little scared of her and Ireni couldn't understand why she didn't keep sending out job letters and forget about Dreema's murder. They must understand: this latest venom murder confirmed that a rattlesnake murderer existed and continued to kill.

Or did it? She was the only one who believed that. A belief not shared by anybody else could be an unpopular truth or it could be madness. She lifted her hands and stared at them. Ten fingers, one ringed by that silver spiral she'd bought at the open air market in Quito the day she met Berto. Damn these memories that popped up out of nowhere! She forced her mind back to the present. At least her hands looked normal indicating she suffered no perceptual disturbances. She listened hard, heard crickets chirping. Nothing else. Normal for a summer's evening when Brent was away. See, she wasn't going insane. It was just stress that made the space between her brows and the valleys between her shoulders and clavicle ache as if someone had punished her with a broomstick. She turned and headed to her desk. Time to plan her next move.

Halfway there she heard a noise outside and stopped dead, listening. Couldn't even see the lights of the next house down the road, so there shouldn't be anyone around here. Unless ... she headed back to the door and jerked it open. A wedge of chilled air hit her in the face. She peered into the darkness engulfing a couple light cones projected onto the facade of Brent's house. Listened into a sound cave between surrounding knolls. Nothing. Turned back around pulling the door shut behind her. Had just reached the desk and poised on a stool when a chorus of yipping pealed out from the hilltop at the back of Brent's estate. It must have been coyotes running up the drive, she told herself, one of their favorite alleyways to reach the hills behind the estate.

She focused on her laptop. The screen was blank like her mind. She lifted a hand to type something, paused with the hand in midair. C'mon, she told herself. Get job searching, maybe even peruse one of those dating apps that had taken over social interactions while she was learning to skin a peccary and boil cassava root in the Amazon. Her mind plateaued again. She almost moaned. Why didn't she have a coherent Plan B? Why did she spend all those years chasing an improbable career in anthropology with no thought to what she'd do if it didn't work out? The sheer ecstasy of escape had buoyed her along, her mind crammed with intellectual toys that kept her from facing up to hard realities. That youthful fantasy had died. Now she must give up her old dreams and force her mind away from this distracting story of a rattlesnake murderer. Seek solutions for her poverty, her solitude. Be proactive. High school teaching was her best option. Might be a last-minute opening at one of the area schools for the fall semester. Started searching for websites.

A flicker of movement across the front window caught her eye. She stood up, tense as a rod. Took a few long strides to the window and stared out, eyes moving back and forth, mind stuttering. A coyote wasn't tall enough to block Brent's house lights as it passed in front. What taller animal could be roaming the estate? Did a black bear wander down from the mountains? Passing on four legs it wouldn't block the lights either. Was some burglar prowling around? Should she call the police?

She slumped down into the equipale chair by the window. Tried to remember the symptoms of anxiety disorder. Or incipient psychosis. *Mierda,* she was losing it. Stood and walked herself back to the desk.

At that moment something rapped on the door. Her body zinged like a struck tuning fork. She focused every ounce of attention toward the front of the tiny house, reviewing her memory of the last few seconds. Nobody had driven up the entry road and nobody legitimate would walk into Brent's estate at night. It must be true, the story she kept telling herself to forget. Someone had killed two people with rattlesnakes and he was coming for a third. Why had she persisted in investigating something so dangerous? What could she do now to escape, sealed in a tiny one-door structure with no human being within hearing distance? She grabbed her phone to dial 911 when another rap split the air. Looked around for a defensive weapon. Against a snake or a person? Spied one of Rich's hand carved walking sticks beside the closet and grabbed it. Moved to the door, raised the stick, clicked the knob open and pulled.

"Hello?"

A woman's voice. Minoa stuck her head around the door. Inanna was standing just outside the threshold, filling the door frame.

"May I come in?"

She conducted an internal debate: Was she overreacting? Or was it threatening that Inanna showed up here now? While she argued with herself Inanna stepped inside.

"Uh, how did you know where I live?"

"And how did you know about Cosmic Energy Day Spa?"

"Cosmic what?"

Inanna sat down in the other equípale chair.

"We need to talk."

"About what?"

"It's chilly outside. I promise I won't bite."

Minoa shut the door, leaned the walking stick against the hinges. Sat in the other chair. Made a gesture of 'what gives?'

"You've been harassing members of the Women Rising collective."

"Harassing or talking to?"

"You burglarized Cosmic Energy spa."

"Do you have proof of that?"

"It was clear you read documents from the Dreema Adkins file. I could have you arrested."

"I could have you arrested for keeping a venomous reptile without a permit."

"New Mexico doesn't require permits for rattlesnakes."

"What about exposing people to the rattlesnake, watching them be bitten and then driving them home to die? Might that violate any laws?"

Inanna focused those bulging eyes on her, violet in the dim light.

"You realize you're the only person in the world who entertains that bizarre idea?"

"You planned a snake ceremony for Dreema. Your case notes attest to that."

"It astounds me that a woman of your education would not distinguish the symbolic from the literal."

"Those oracle readings you playact involve a live rattlesnake, real people and some real psychoactive substances. What's symbolic about that?"

"When I met you I scanned your aura. It was clear you were being crushed by the materialist worldview. That's why I invited you to the Tuesday group, to offer an alternative perspective on what is 'real.' But your defensive reaction as you sense the materialist paradigm crumbling is aggressive. You're dangerous."

"I'm dangerous?"

"Perhaps you've so absorbed the patriarchal viewpoint of the university that you can't see our society is in crisis, the entire modern world is in crisis. We must return to ancient spiritual practices to save ourselves and women must lead the way."

"I studied trance, spirit possession, and shamanism in the university and then spent years observing a tribe that still utilizes some of these practices. As a result, I can see when someone in twenty-first century capitalist America is faking a Hollywood version and merchandising it for profit."

"Profit is not the problem. We must act within the current economic order to prepare a better future. We're currently creating a community of sympathetic benefactors to sponsor the construction of a womanist retreat center. Your activities could dissuade potential investors."

"Is that really why you're here?"

Inanna squinted at her, threw an appraising glance around the untidy room.

"I could help you with the complexes driving your behavior. I believe it's something to do with your mother. You probably lacked a positive maternal presence which led you to identify with male dominators. So women dedicated to resuscitating female power threaten your false identification with the oppressor. We remind you of what you missed."

Minoa stood and strode across the room, then spun around.

"Where did you get Basmu?"

"That's none of your business."

"A local snake trader was murdered earlier today. But perhaps you already knew that?"

Inanna stood up, hands in fists, boring her blue laser gaze into Minoa. The two women faced off, hostile vibrations rocketing between them. Inanna relented, took a couple steps to the door and pulled it open.

"Stay away from my clients. Stay away from potential investors. Do you understand? I have friends who could make life ... even more difficult for you."

She marched out and disappeared into the night. Minoa stepped outside the guesthouse and looked around. Heard steps retreating down the drive. Leaned up against a post supporting the overhang on the front.

Empty threat, she reassured herself. What could Inanna do to a part-time bartender washed up in her hometown with a basket of minor psychic maladies: insomnia, fear of commitment, loss of life purpose, possible alcohol abuse, nightmares? Unless one of her rich friends knew Brent and could get her thrown out of the guesthouse. So what? Wouldn't be the first time she'd slept in her truck. Bring it on, Inanna of the underworld. Bring it on.

She shut the door, strode back to her desk, determined to prove Inanna wrong. How dare she insinuate she was some damaged neurotic who'd lost her way in life and turned to stalking imaginary criminals. She noticed that flyer on her desk that Don Juan Carlos had given her at his shop in Abiquiu. The Santa Rosa Festival tomorrow. It couldn't be pure chance that he'd told her about it. Maybe that was his cryptic way of responding to her questions about deviant cults in Abiquiu. Maybe he knew something but hesitated to talk about it. She'd find out. Investigating out-of-the way villages was one thing she knew how to do.

Chapter
Twenty-Nine

They were almost back to Abiquiu from the ruin of the old Santa Rosa de Lima church, walking alongside the highway in a ragged sweaty procession led by a few people in period costume: a friar in rough brown vestment, tied at the waist with a rope; a conquistador in dome-shaped helmet, velvet quilted shirt and blousy knickers, lugging an old sword; girls in peasant tops and ruffled skirts. Several grandfathers shouldered a platform carrying the statue of Santa Rosa. Despite a full length embroidered gown and veil, Santa Rosa looked fresh with her pink porcelain cheeks under a wreath of roses. Everyone else was perspiring like punctured water balloons.

At the turnoff to town the conquistador led the way up the dirt road holding his sword high in the air with the rest trailing behind. Minoa had parked the truck in a level area below the plaza so she left the procession and headed over to grab some water and a snack.

She bolted down a couple of granola bars and was hiking back up the road toward the village when a silver truck came into view below. She continued walking along the side of the road next to a steep incline. As the noise of the approaching truck increased, she experienced a creepy feeling roll up her spine, like a stampede of bugs, and spun around to see the truck driving straight toward her. She dove off the edge rolling over and over down the rocky slope to come to rest on the dirt lot where her truck sat. When she jumped up the silver truck was disappearing around Santo Tomas church.

With sunlight reflecting off the windshield she hadn't caught sight of any faces inside the truck before pitching herself down the hill. Amilcar drove a silver pickup, but then nearly everybody around here drove a pickup truck. Should she have held her ground? Brushing dirt off her tee and shorts she noted scrapes and scratches on her bare arms and legs. She muffled her annoyance and started trudging up the hill again.

When she walked into the plaza girls in red and yellow skirts were spinning around as Mexican folkloric music blared out from a boom-box sitting on the cab of a black pickup. No sign of a silver pickup. A scattering of people stood around watching. Over by the church the older men waited, resting the palanquin carrying Santa Rosa on a low wall. A few hand-hammered booths around the edge of the dirt square sold tamales, corn dogs, soda. She walked around, peeking inside the library and the church. Amilcar was nowhere to be seen. The little girls started another dance, spinning, clacking castanets. Minoa leaned against the low wall surrounding the church.

The dancers finished amidst paltry applause and family photo ops. Minoa felt her spirits sinking. Did someone just try to run her over or not? And what could she find out at this local festival so tiny even tourists at the peak of the season didn't find it? She had started checking her texts when she heard shouting.

Men in leather leggings carrying spears and bows were running into the plaza, howling and whooping like Indians on the warpath. The girls screamed and ran to their mothers who herded them toward ve-hicles. The men stared, their expressions hardening into outrage. The invading Indians dispersed and ran toward people standing around the edge of the plaza, throwing handfuls of leaflets. Then they ran back to the center of the plaza, formed a circle and danced around, chanting in some language that was neither Spanish nor English, waving tomahawks and bows and spears in the air, jumping this way and that. People screamed, waving fists or hurrying away. Minoa crinkled her brow trying to figure out what was going on. Could this be part of the festival? Were they reenacting some eighteenth century Comanche raid from the time of the town's founding?

She picked up a leaflet from the ground and read:

Genízaro Slaves of Imperialism! Rise Up!

Why do we honor the Spanish with our festivals? Spain came to this land to enslave and kill our people. We drove them out once, but they came back, more numerous than ever, to establish a government of oppression. The Yankees continued the exploitation. Abiquiu was founded by slaves -- kidnapped Apache, Commanche, Ute. We are all *Genízaros*! Instead of worshiping Spanish gods, instead of letting the Yankees rob our land and water, we must reclaim our native cultures and our dignity. We have our land grant. Let us demand sovereignty as Indian tribes have done. Why should our native brothers have casinos while we live off food stamps?

Down with Santa Rosa! Up with *Senawahv*!

Looking up she watched the warrior dancers with renewed interest. They were spinning, jogging from one foot to the other, yelling chants punctuated by war whoops. Unexpectedly she was witness to a tiny cultural revolution in forgotten Abiquiu. Maybe she could write this up for *American Ethnology* or *Dialectical Anthropology*. She'd describe the local social groupings and political context, then maybe an analysis of socio-economic conflict expressed through rearticulation of indigenous cultural symbols or something like that. She could even narrate her own participation in the event, including nearly getting run over, a Geertzian thick description of Abiquiu's tiny uprising in the style of his famous account of the Balinese cockfight. But her article would be *estilo nuevo mexicano*! She'd restart her career as an ethnographer right here in her old home state.

One of the dancers caught her eye. He was jabbing at the air with his spear as if skewering a detested enemy. It was Amilcar, wiry shoulder length black hair bound under a white strip wrapped around his forehead, flaccid chest peeking out from a vest of elongated bone beads tied with leather strips, bowed legs pounding the earth.

So this was what he was involved in, not a deviant Penitente cult and not handling snakes in some secret ceremony recreating the distant memory of the Asa clan's time in Hopiland, but imitating enslaved plains Indians. Maybe he and his fellow fake Indians recreated the Lakota Sun Dance while preparing for this doomed occupation of insignificant Abiquiu. Maybe they fasted for three days and abstained from relationships with their wives or girlfriends, smoked the sacred pipe to ask *Senawahv* to favor their attack and then stabbed each other's chests with eagle talons and hung from the roof until they passed out. Maybe Amilcar was counting coup when he ran her off the entry road and she should feel lucky he didn't pause by the roadside to scalp her.

Amilcar's group huddled and then charged full speed at the statue of Santa Rosa de Lima held by the group of grandfathers who now stood frozen, staring at the onrush of wild-eyed Indians. The Indians took hold of the palanquin and overturned it, dumping the precious Santa Rosa doll on the ground. Her bearers yelled in outrage as the attackers stomped and kicked the statue to pieces. A roar of fury rose from the crowd of spectators. The village men charged the Indians and a torrent of fistfights broke out. She prayed Amilcar wouldn't use his spear on two middle-aged fellows trying to throw him down. How ironic that during her years among the Huaorani she never saw a spearing while here in New Mexico a spear-wielding rampage was occurring before her very eyes.

Some of these men were armed or kept guns in their vehicles or nearby houses so this could escalate out of control in short order. She scanned the plaza for a place to take cover. Sprinted for the library, slammed the door shut behind her and looked for a window, reaching for her cell. She wasn't going to miss the chance to document history in the making.

The only other person in the library was the librarian, that same woman with metallic hair that she'd met when she came in search of the Penitente *morada*. She was staring out a tiny window by her desk. They exchanged glances.

"Do you understand what's going on out there?" Minoa asked.

"I heard rumors those lunatics were planning something like this. They're just going to get themselves locked up. And the village doesn't need to lose men of working age."

"Let's hope you don't lose any permanently."

Peering out a window Minoa watched the imitation Indians flee the fights to regroup on the far side of the plaza. She couldn't see what was happening so she stepped back outside. Don Juan Carlos stood under the overhang of his shop front, leaning against the wall with crossed arms, calmly observing the chaos. Had he known what was planned? Was he involved? Is that why he invited her to the festival?

The locals pursued Amilcar's bunch and fights broke out anew. The *Genízaro* throwbacks were waving their weapons and howling like blood-crazed berserkers. One grabbed a young guy by the hair and raised his tomahawk as if to scalp him. With the spear held above one shoulder in throwing position, Amilcar chased a hefty fellow who swerved and headed toward her. His face burst with terror, but a wiry fellow in a backwards baseball cap was running on a line to intercept them. She took off running up a side street, then darted down a dirt alley planning to circle back to the plaza. At the next cross street she noticed a silver pickup parked part way down. She glanced around. Not a soul in sight so she trotted down to the truck, pulled the leaflet out of her pocket and extracted a pen from her wallet. She scribbled on the back of the flyer:

Amilcar,

I am going to report your vehicular assault to the police. They will also be interested in the fight you had with your ex-wife on the night she died. Not to mention threatening her brother with a knife. You will pay for your violent behavior.

Dreema's friend Minoa

She pocketed the pen and reached up to place the note under the driver's side windshield wiper. Suddenly giant pincers seized her and hurled her through the air. She landed hard on the rutted road and lay there, tasting dirt, trying to catch her breath. A second later she clawed partway to her feet, nerves in survival mode. A sharp pain in her neck stopped her.

She froze, shifting her eyes to the side, taking care not to budge. Amilcar stood there in his plains warrior get-up poking the point of a spear into her neck. No witnesses in sight as she verified scanning the street in both directions out of her peripheral vision without removing her eyes from him.

"What were you doing to my truck?" he shouted, jiggling the point of the spear.

She shrank from the spear point.

"Don't move!"

"I can answer your question better if I stand up straight."

He scraped the spear tip up her neck to her jawbone, forcing her to straighten.

"Why are you everywhere I go? Why are you following me? Why are you fucking with my life?"

"Stabbing me won't help anything. If you're innocent of your ex-wife's murder you have nothing to worry about."

"Are you crazy? Dreema died by snakebite."

"Somebody put that snake in her room."

"You're out of your mind. What, did you test the snake for fingerprints? *Eres demente.*"

He moved the spear to her hair, stuck the point under the elastic holding her ponytail and jerked up hard. The gesture chopped through a chunk of hair. Hair and elastic flew into the air, scattering across the ground.

"Get out of my life or the next time it will be your ass."

He lifted a foot and slammed it into the side of her hip, sending her flying. She crashed into the front of a house and slid down. In an instant she was on her feet in a crouch, elbows and knees bent, ready to leap. He lifted the spear handle over his head and swung it down, aiming for her head. She dodged sideways. The spear end crashed into the wall, cracking the wooden handle.

"*Perra,*" he screamed, dropping the spear and diving for her.

She put out her arms, deflected his momentum sideways and tripped him with an outstretched foot. He slid to the dirt but scrambled to his feet and ran at her, driving a fist at her face that ended up punching her shoulder, spinning her sideways. As she stumbled, flinging arms to regain balance, he landed a hook with his other fist into her back. Crouched over she cupped a hand behind one knee and pulled the leg out from under him. He flipped onto his backside, then jumped up with a roar and locked an arm around her neck. As he tightened pressure she dug fingernails into the skin of his forearm and scratched marks that bubbled pinpoints of blood.

Amidst gasping breaths she heard sirens whining in the distance, intensifying as police approached on the highway and turned up the road to the village. She grabbed a couple of his fingers and levered them backwards making him cry out in pain. Then a voice rang out down the street. Amilcar turned to look, loosening his chokehold. Minoa spotted another Indian at the corner waving his arm like a wiper blade.

"Amilcar, *vámonos.*"

Amilcar shoved her to the ground and ran a few strides to the pickup. Jerked the cab door open, jumped in and burned rubber up to where the other *Genízaro* stood. After he jumped into the passenger side they sped away.

She clambered to her feet and stood there buzzing with adrenalin, feeling her neck and shoulder and wheezing breaths. Heard the patrol cars come to a stop in the plaza followed by the screams of the officers ordering everyone down on the ground. Running her hand over her hair, she spied an arc of auburn hairs spread across the dirt.

"*Rayos.*"

The note she'd written was nowhere to be seen so it must have stayed under the wiper when he drove away. Would he read it or would it fly off? Did it matter? He'd attacked her twice, maybe three times if that had been his truck on the entry road. But when there'd been witnesses she decided not to pursue charges, and on the other two occasions it would be her word against his. Anyway, out-of-control behavior along with employment at the rich dude's animal combats didn't prove he'd killed Dreema.

With a muttered curse she grabbed the broken spear and jogged up the alley to the cross street, circled around the plaza on tiny lanes to come out on the bottom side of the village. She hopscotched down the hill to the lot where the truck sat. As she drove away, nerves relaxing, a thought bubble popped into her brain. She'd forgotten she was scheduled to work at the casino bar that night.

Chapter Thirty

S he ran into the back entrance of Lucky Coyote late for her shift. As luck would have it, the floor manager was talking to a custodian when she rushed down the escalator to the bar. She frowned hard at Minoa and walked straight over.

"You're ..." She glanced at her watch, set in a silver band inlaid with turquoise and coral. "You're thirty minutes late."

Minoa glanced at her phone.

"Twenty-six. It's only twenty-six, or seven."

"Either way, it's unacceptable."

"There were unforeseen circumstances. Unavoidable. A riot in Abiquiu and this fake Indian dude nearly speared me."

The supervisor, a statuesque middle-aged woman from Pojoaque Pueblo, arched her black brows.

"A 'fake Indian dude' tried to spear you?"

Minoa talked faster.

"At the Santa Rosa festival. Some people want to revive their Native American heritage so they can have tribal sovereignty and build a casino."

The manager considered for a moment, then the brows slammed down.

"On time or before."

She walked away. Minoa picked up a bar towel and found Scott staring at her.

"A riot in Abiquiu? You need lessons on how to BS your boss. That place is barely big enough to appear on a map."

"For your information it's true. Some people want recognition as a Native American tribe so they can build a casino and get out of poverty. They dressed up like Indians carrying tomahawks and spears and started fights." She pointed at the scab on her neck where the blood from Amilcar's spear tip had dried. "One of them speared me."

Scott's lake-blue eyes stretched wide.

"That's stupendous. I wish I'd been there. Wow, attacked by wild Indians. Did you cop a video of it?"

"I didn't have hands free at the moment. I've got the spear in the truck if you don't believe me."

"No way. Hey, could I take a selfie holding it, you know, for my Insta page?"

"Sure, Scott. Whatever."

A couple of servers plopped down drink orders at the end of the bar so she and Scott went to work. She poured a tray of call drinks for a table of mid-level bureaucrats laughing too hard and talking too loud. The order forced her to concentrate on requests for specific brands, a splash of this or that, rocks or no rocks, wedge of lime, rim of salt, shaken or stirred, straight up or neat, chilled or hot or dry or not, single or double or triple.

She moved onto the next order with a sigh of exhaustion, slipping into the rhythm of setting up, wiping down and starting over. When she finally got a free moment she pulled out her phone and started a text to Lewis.

Hey, update on the Hopi-Tewa question. I found out there are people in Abiquiu who ..."

Paused to notice the lack of preceding messages. Understandable. He hated anthropologists, not that she was one anymore. Why chase this guy? They argued every time they talked. Slipped the phone back into her pocket, cocked her elbows on the bar and watched the gamblers buzzing around the casino floor, making honey for the casino owners.

"I'm on break now." Scott grinned revealing his snowy incisors. "Think I could run out to your truck and get a shot with that spear?"

"Sure. It's on the edge of the lot near the entrance."

She handed him her keys and returned to staring out at the casino.

Suddenly a woman screamed, head bobbing up and down behind a row of slot machines. A blue-haired grandmother jumped up and down like a cheerleader. She must have hit the jackpot. Everyone in the casino cheered and clapped. The woman laughed, cried, hugging strangers, waving her arms like some possessed Pentecostal. She should have been touring the old country or taking care of grandkids or helping with the upcoming election. Instead, she was killing the last of her time on earth awaiting a rupture of the extraordinary into everyday life, punching buttons over and over and over until — no denying it — she finally got lucky.

Minoa filled a few more orders and then searched for the Tewake Pueblo webpage. She opened messages, skipped over the draft to Lewis and texted Carter and Ireni: *Corn dance at Tewake Pueblo tomorrow. Wanna go?*

Then she indulged in some googling on the history of native nations in New Mexico. She'd need to research past efforts to get tribal recognition as background for an article on the revolt at Abiquiu's Santa Rosa festival. She came across a recent proclamation by the governor rescinding proclamations from the mid-1800s that authorized militias to pursue and attack indigenous people. Whoa. She tempered her attitude toward Lewis. He definitely had good cause to be mad. A security guard ran into the bar.

"One of the bartenders had an accident out in the parking lot," he yelled. "He's getting loaded into an ambulance."

"You mean Scott?" she yelled back. "What happened?"

"Seems like he got snakebit or something."

She shot out of the bar, climbed over people riding up the escalator, ran out the front door of the resort complex. Spotted red lights flashing and sprinted toward them. As she arrived one of the EMT's shut the back door of an ambulance and walked around to the passenger side door. Minoa ran up to the driver, slamming into the door. The woman turned to her, eye whites glinting with reflected flashes of red light.

"Wh-what are you doing? Get away from there!"

"Wait, please."

Minoa held onto the door handle, walking beside the ambulance as its wheels rolled.

"Was he snakebitten?"

Her machine gun breaths made the 's' hiss. The driver let the vehicle slow.

"Are you family?"

"No, I'm his friend. Please tell me: did he suffer a rattlesnake bite?"

"He muttered something about a snake. The docs will have to assess."

As she drove Minoa ran beside the ambulance, holding on to the door.

"Tell them the venom is neurotoxic. Remember that. Neurotoxic. Don't forget."

The ambulance driver blinked at her, nodded and drove off.

Minoa clicked on her cell's flashlight, walked over to the truck and circled it, checking underneath. She stopped by the driver's door. It was partially open, keys in the lock. The spear lay on the asphalt. She picked it up, then shined the flashlight around the interior, prodded underneath the seat with the spear. No response. Walked up and down rows of cars in the lot, panning the light across the ground, then tracked the curb banked against open desert. Finally went back to the truck and shined the flashlight around it again.

Shutting the door, she leaned against it and stared up into a crusted black hole with a pointy quarter moon stabbing its way in. Should she have known her truck might be — no idea what to call this anymore — rattler-booby-trapped? Could she finally face up to the danger of having a rattler killer on the loose or would she keep second-guessing herself, chalking it all up to her career-failure PTSD or the lingering nightmares or simply the crazy stuff that happens in New Mexico?

Before she could flash the light around the pavement again the doubts glimmered like ectoplasm. Maybe this latest rattler attack was the equivalent of that grandma who hit the jackpot, an intrusion of the statistically improbable into everyday routines? One evening a guy walks into a parking lot in the middle of open desert and a Diamondback strikes? Nobody was counting but New Mexico must have seen thousands of unexpected rattlesnake strikes over the course of its history. Three or four strikes in Santa Fe in a few weeks among people who knew each other was just a once-in-a-century coincidence cluster. Not murder and attempted murder.

Her mind oscillated back and forth between the alternatives so hard it felt like her brain had come loose and was banging around inside the cranium. She clapped hands to her temples, squinted into the crystal-flecked blackness and squeezed out a tiny moan.

After a few minutes she commanded herself to chill and headed back to the bar, careful to walk where lights varnished the asphalt with a luminescent sheen.

She told the servers Scott had suffered a snakebite out in the parking lot. Everyone expressed horror and agreed to walk out together to their cars at the end of the evening. She nodded though her mind lingered outside, careening laps around the parking lot, asking herself who could have known her truck was parked there, then telling herself to stop conjuring crimes out of bad luck.

With Scott gone the orders piled up, but behind the pouring and shaking and measuring her thoughts geared up again and refused to stop. Could Amilcar have waited outside the village after the police arrived to break up the Genízaro raid and followed her to Lucky Coyote? Did Inanna know she worked at the casino? Maybe Felipe had been at the festival in Abiquiu and followed her? Maybe, maybe, maybe. What was she going to do? Drive home in her truck with the unique yellow wheel rims and spend the rest of the night in her one-door cell? No way.

Chapter Thirty-One

It was after two when she drove down the dirt alley branching from Acequia Madre to Rich's place. High adobe walls lined the track. Apricot branches extended over the wall tops, speckled by a few remaining fruit. She pulled into the back entrance of the yard where Rich rented the addition on Helen's high end territorial revival vacation home. This way her headlights wouldn't flash into Helen's windows. Rich would be glad to see her even if she had to wake him from one of his catatonic snoozes. And the man, or woman, behind the rattler attacks couldn't know where Rich lived, right?

Funny. Rich's refurbished El Camino with the stripe on the hood wasn't there. Maybe he'd left it somewhere for repairs. Despite running a newer engine salvaged from a junkyard, it broke down a lot. She parked, clicked off the motor, climbed out careful to lock the truck door with the key. Walking over to Rich's front window she peered in, palms beside her eyes. Nothing moved. Over at the window overlooking his sleeping nook she squinted inside identifying a pillow, heaped blankets, a chair piled with clothes. He wasn't there. She waited a moment to see if he'd gone to the bathroom. But after her nose tip went numb from pressing into the glass, there was still no movement inside.

She backed up a few steps, peered through the branches of an olive tree at a night crammed with shadowy forms: adobe walls, rooftops, parked vehicles, bushes. A tiny cramp bit her abdominal wall. Surely not jealousy. He had no legitimate reason to be anywhere else in the middle of the night, did he? But she had no claim on him. Hadn't she been on the point of breaking up for weeks, maybe months? Still, she hadn't broken up so she had a right to feel peeved, right? O did he pick up on her commitment allergy and take the next logical step? What the hell was she dithering about? This thing with Rich had been going nowhere for a while, for sure ever since she started spending her free time chasing invisible rattlesnake murderers.

The question was where she could spend the night, somewhere the rattler killer couldn't predict. Carter lived in a remodeled garage off lower Agua Fria. Driving in there at this hour would startle Mr. and Mrs. Romero, her landlords. They might even call their nephew Jorge who worked for the Santa Fe police. Ireni's place was way up the road to Los Alamos. It was only a few hours till dawn. Maybe she could park somewhere and snooze in the truck. But where? Police patrolled the streets to make sure no tourists camped in their cars. She shivered. Summery nights at eight thousand feet altitude sucked the heat out of your flesh in no time. She climbed back into her truck, checked behind the seat for an old down sweater and a space blanket she'd stuffed in there and headed the truck back down the alley.

At the Santuario on Guadalupe Street she found a spot at the back of the parking lot alongside the river where some elm branches draped like a curtain, concealing the truck from people driving past. Wrapped her upper body in down, tucked the space blanket around her legs and curled up on the seat. At first she listened for sounds, but soon fell into a sleep so deep it was like being buried in mud. No sensations, no awareness until... scratch, scratch, ghostly teeth gnawed at the darkness. Her eyelids fluttered open. She sat up and looked around at brown squat buildings lining Guadalupe Street, the adobe church with a double-decker belfry topped by a cross, cottonwoods along the Santa Fe River, and remembered she was in her truck. A band of light glowed on the eastern horizon. She scanned her sleepy mind to see if she'd dreamed of snakes. Not a trace. And she'd made it through another night without getting snakebit. Then she remembered Scott. Could he have survived the night with medical treatment if the venom was neurotoxic? She muttered a prayer to the Virgin of Guadalupe shrine on the other side of the parking lot. Then she started up the engine heading for a breakfast cafe.

***

As servers bustled to the order window, clipping paper checks to a carousel and stacking plates on trays, she hunched over the counter sipping her second cup of coffee. The steaming plates of green chile omelets and blue corn pancakes that the tradesmen on either side were gobbling up drew her eyes for a moment but she didn't feel hungry. On the way over she'd called the hospital and found out Scott was alive but they wouldn't provide details. His family members were probably on a plane from Massachusetts right now. Would Scott hate her? Should she have realized it was dangerous to send him out to her truck? Should she explain to police her suspicions about this latest rattler attack? It all felt impossible. Her brain seized up like a motor that's run out of oil.

Orders went in, plates of food went out. Cups slopping coffee, orange juice glistening in tall glasses, trays of water tumblers with ice cubes clicking. What could she do? She had to do something. After scanning her exhausted mind without results, she decided she'd research the Tewake Pueblo corn dance so she could serve as tour guide for Carter and Ireni. Great use of an anthropology Ph.D. but hey.

Into the search bar on her phone she typed 'Tewake Pueblo.' Scanned the list of search results: the Pueblo's official website, a Wikipedia page, the New Mexico State tourism site, trip advisor reviews, a southwestern history site, stock images, searching, searching as she took another sip of coffee and glanced at a waitress carrying three full cups in each hand, savoring the chatter and clatter of an everyday morning, so safe, so snake-less, until way down the results list she spied a name that brought up a ripple of memory. *The North American Indian*, Edward S. Curtis' massive twenty volume work, published from 1907 to 1930, forgotten until the 1970s, digitalized in 2004, a hundred years after Curtis visited the scores of North American tribes he would attempt to portray before their predicted extinction.

She sighed, glanced at herself in the mirror behind the counter — hair askew, circles under her eyes. Off to one side, through the order window, she spied cooks at a grill. A fellow in a white apron behind the counter yelled in Spanish at the cooks. One responded with a laughing insult. Cheerful banter, steam rising, the kitchen door swinging back and forth. A pleasant morning scene but she wasn't there anymore.

She was teenage Minoa curled up in a chair in a back corner of the library with one of those twenty volumes of Curtis' compendium in her lap, picking tidbits to read or silver and sepia prints to ponder. She'd loved the antique store feel of it, bits of lore, myth, hearsay and observation jammed together like treasures and junk on dusty shelves, a cornucopia of curiosities compiled during Curtis' epic journeys across America to photograph Native Americans in traditional dress and settings before their cultures were destroyed. This was what young Minoa had imagined anthropology would be, free-spirited travel to exotic locales where she would learn about native people, become friends with them, expand her understanding of humanity and culture.

Her stomach spasmed at her ignorance. Later she found out many of the people Curtis photographed had adopted European dress and stopped speaking their native language by the time he showed up. Curtis had to position and dress the subjects of his photos to create the illusion of capturing native peoples untouched by European expansion. He'd died in poverty. Maybe a metaphor for the doomed trajectory of her own career. After failing to snag an academic job or any other useful or lucrative employment here she was sleeping in her truck in her old hometown.

She tried to sip from her coffee cup, choked, spit a few drops onto the counter. The bearded guy in gray coveralls to her left stared. She wiped it up with her paper napkin, fake-buried her attention in her phone again.

"You okay?"

She nodded without looking up. How could she have been so naive? Lewis would call Curtis' work patronizing cultural appropriation or something like that. But then he would ridicule her for even going to the corn dance, right? So what. She was a tourist now, not an anthropologist. She searched the chapter listings of volume seventeen and found a section on Tewake Pueblo. Scanning the index of that chapter she stopped cold at 'S'. 'Snake cult' said the entry. She raced to page 184 and read:

There is no doubt that the Tewake and probably other Pueblos formerly and within recent years kept large rattlesnakes in captivity as creatures to be venerated and propitiated. The Tewake adored, and still adore, an enormous rattlesnake, which they keep alive in some inaccessible and hidden mountain recess. It is even hinted that human sacrifices were associated with this hideous cult, that at intervals a newborn infant was fed to it.

The article quoted Adolf Bandelier, a self-made anthropologist of Southwestern Indians, along with newspaper photographer Charles Lummis. Wait a minute. Wasn't this the same Charles Lummis whose photograph of a *Penitente* crucifixion appeared in that book from Don Juan Carlos, the eccentric shopkeeper in Abiquiu? She recalled that arresting image: in shades of gray, seven figures against a sandy hillside spotted with juniper, a crucified figure in pure white towering over all.

"In the land where the rattlesnake is god."

Wasn't that what Lummis had written? Sacred snakes. Human sacrifice. Rattlesnake gods. Were these the fantasies of white settlers projected onto a colonized other? Or clues to indigenous rattlesnake worship? Suddenly an idea occurred to her. She sat up straighter, waved at the server for more coffee. Why not investigate the topic, pull colorful accounts from travelers, early settlers, priests, magistrates, *genízaros*, literate natives, every allegation of snake-keeping, snake worship and, most of all, human sacrifice to sacred rattlesnakes, and write it up with a trendy theoretical analysis? She'd have to work out the details but the material was priceless.

Hell, she might even find other credible suggestions that early Puebloans sacrificed babies to their rattlesnake gods. And — this would be an unbelievable stroke of luck — what if she happened on some evidence that contemporary Pueblo Indians were still secretly keeping sacred rattlesnakes and sacrificing to them, even if the sacrificial victim was a dead gopher dressed up as a baby or some other substitute for infant sacrifice? That would stir up more than a dust devil at the next Southwestern Anthropological Association conference. And if Minoa's name appeared on the article announcing this to the academic world, her foundered career would take off like a supersonic test missile firing through the New Mexico skies.

She was dying to know if any other anthropologist had picked up on this topic. Luckily she still had her library access code from Columbia. As she waited for the library webpage to load, then logged into Anthropology Plus and typed in a few keywords, her fantasy of career rejuvenation pumped endorphins through her sleep-deprived brain. Surely UNM or the University of Arizona would be interested in someone to provide critical perspectives on the history of southwestern anthropology. No more sweating her way through years in a scorpion-infested longhouse watching aging shamans blow vast quantities of *yagé* up their nostrils. And no more long shifts pouring drinks for demoralized workers pretending New Mexico was Las Vegas. Meanwhile, why continue to chase down Dreema's murderer? Better to pursue this new career idea and rattlers be damned.

She checked the list of pertinent references in the Anthropology Plus database: articles on The Ghost Dance, the Peyote Cult, even the Cult of the Feathered Serpent but nothing on pueblo snake cults. So far so good. Looked like virgin research territory. She couldn't wait to tell Carter and Ireni about it. Or maybe just Ireni. She'd be supportive while Carter would tell her to quit wasting time on escapist intellectual pursuits. She paid the check and headed out to the truck, the brief rush of caffeine-fueled fantasies already fizzling in the ruthless light of a morning without shadow.

Chapter Thirty-Two

The car lurched as Carter veered off the highway onto a washboard dirt road, knocking Minoa and Ireni side to side.

"Careful. Can't you drive like a sane person for once in your life?"

In the passenger's seat Minoa sank into hunched shoulders, frowning. Carter threw her a smirk.

"Lose sleep last night playing with your sculptor boyfriend?"

"She probably had another snake nightmare."

Ireni reached a hand forward from the back seat to pat Minoa's shoulder.

Minoa's face stayed stony.

"He's not my boyfriend anymore."

"I never thought it would last," said Carter.

Ireni kept patting, speaking in a reassuring voice.

"Don't worry. You've got options. What about that guy who saved you from a rattlesnake? That's pretty romantic. I wish some guy would appear out of nowhere to save me from danger. But not a rattlesnake. That's too scary."

"The only danger you're facing is cancer from exposure to plutonium at the Lab. Who's gonna save you from that?"

Carter capped this with a slap on the peeling seat back.

"For your information the employees exposed this year received treatment and they're going to be fine."

"What about when they gear up for the next order of nuclear warheads the Pentagon wants so they can destroy human civilization?"

Minoa slapped her palms to her ears.

"Listen guys, my head is on the edge of an explosion so could we please cut the arguing today?"

"Don't you want to give your opinion on nuclear disarmament?"

"We're going to watch a corn dance. Why don't we just act like regular tourists who don't worry about plutonium exposure or rattlesnake venom?"

Carter caught Ireni's glance in the rearview mirror and flexed her eyebrows as a comment. Then she leaned into the duct-tape-wrapped steering wheel, maneuvering between parked vehicles lining both sides of the road.

"Wow, half of Santa Fe must have come for the dance."

"Maybe we better park here and walk to the pueblo?" Ireni pleaded.

"Don't worry. My burro can navigate challenging terrain."

Carter found a spot farther down where a storm-carved gully had scared off other drivers and pulled in, dipping the front end to a forty-five degree angle.

"Don't worry, I can put blocks on the tires."

She ducked around to the trunk. Minoa and Ireni dismounted and scrambled up the slope to the road. Once Carter had kicked blocks under the wheels, they took off walking. Ireni double-timed to keep up with Minoa's and Carter's long legs. The day was so clear and still that the setting, where Tewake Pueblo tucked into the curve of the Rio Grande at the base of Pajarito plateau, looked like a painting hanging in one of Santa Fe's western art galleries. Lines of people trailed from food stands near the pueblo entrance. Reaching the pueblo's expansive dirt plaza they had to sidle around the perimeter against house walls, looking for a gap in the crowd. Ireni clutched Carter's shirt tail.

"I didn't know corn dances were so popular."

"No art market on the plaza in Santa Fe this weekend, so the tour operators had to program in an Indian dance." Carter paused and pointed. "Quick, over there."

She hurried through a momentary gap as the crowd shifted. Ireni and Minoa squeezed after her. From the front of the multitude they had a clear view of the plaza. A group of men with bands tied around their foreheads were setting up barrel-sized drums at the far end. People filled the rooftops of houses around the square. Pueblo officials kept the crowd out of the central area.

Several Koshare clowns strolled along the edge of the crowd. They paused in front of a nearby family, a couple and two children crowded into two folding chairs. From their feet to their hair, bound in two tufts like horns, the Koshare wore black and white stripes. They pretended to sit on invisible chairs facing the family. The clowns passed around an imaginary pair of binoculars, craning their necks and bugging their eyes to scrutinize the family that came to examine real live Indians in action. Everyone laughed, even the subjects of this parody. Then, pushing and shoving each other in mock dispute, the Koshare strolled on. Ireni buried her gaze in her phone. After a moment, Minoa spoke.

"Hey Carter, Ireni can hold our place. Let's go get coffee and something to eat."

"I could use some tamales myself. Want anything, Reni?"

Ireni shook her head without looking up. As Minoa and Carter wove through the crowd, drumbeats pounded. Through a gap Minoa saw male dancers in cream-colored kilts move to the center of the plaza, jumping from one foot to the other, shaking gourds. A diagonal strap crossed their chests, a sheath of corn dangled.

"I slept in the truck last night."

"How come?"

Carter threw her a glance as they walked.

"Call me paranoid but there have been too many rattler attacks lately."

"Maybe you better move in with me for a while."

"Last night a guy at work was bitten by a rattler when he opened my truck in the parking lot of Lucky Coyote."

"You're kidding. But what does that have to do with your friend's death?"

"Maybe the murderer is after me. Other times I feel like I'm losing my mind, imagining connections when it's really just coincidence. So I flip-flop back and forth, searching for a rattler killer no one else believes in and then telling myself all these rattler appearances are natural. Maybe global warming affecting the high desert ecosystem?"

"A third of all species will go extinct by 2050. But populations that are increasing as a result of climate change? Maybe cockroaches. And viruses. Not sure about rattlesnakes. I doubt the mice population is decreasing so they have a reliable food source. It's intrusion into their habitat that drives them into lethal contact with humans."

"Carter, do you really think habitat loss accounts for three rattler strikes in a couple weeks? Besides, what was a rattler doing in a parking lot late at night? They're reptiles, Carter. They stop moving around when the temperature goes down."

"Asphalt retains heat."

Carter made a 'who knows' gesture as she maneuvered between groups.

"So do you still think I'm chasing white–whales–slash–rattlesnakes? "

Carter made another noncommittal gesture.

"I've wasted my time suspecting Amilcar. He's a bully, he likes to scare people. But if he murdered Dreema, wouldn't he lay low to avoid notice? And if his murder motive was to gain custody of Aracely, would he hit her and then jump me in full view of a judge?"

"Violent men aren't rational."

As they reached the other side of the plaza Minoa saw the male dancers move to a different area, reform and renew the dance.

"As for the real estate developer, his motive is weak. Killing people won't protect him from responsibility for shoddy construction; instead it ups the legal risks he faces."

"Capitalists will attack anything that cuts their profits. And they usually face no repercussions."

"Inanna plays with snakes to provide authenticity for her goddess brand. Maybe she's a sort of New Age Charles Manson?"

"You mean the La Llorona actress? Isn't that her?"

Carter nodded toward the top of the plaza where drummers chanted a droning song. Standing beside a group of native men clustered beside the drummers, Minoa spotted Inanna. She was talking to a man in a southwestern pattern shirt with a turquoise-studded concho belt cinched under a belly as round as a basketball, her blonde locks spilling over his shoulder.

"Get me a coffee and a couple tamales. I'll be back."

She dashed through a break in the crowd. Carter watched her disappear, sighed and headed on.

Chapter
Thirty-Three

M inoa reached the passageway leading into the plaza from surrounding houses where dancers had emerged. Several men
stood on the other side keeping out spectators. Up the alleyway she
caught sight of an approaching group of women dancers in black shifts
with red belts wearing tall blue headdresses with white feathers. She
cut over to the house fronts and waited till the dancers passed the
security officers. As soon as their attention followed the dancers into
the plaza, she dashed across the vacant passage.

Glancing at the drummers she saw the Koshare approach and pause
in front of Inanna and her boyfriend. Was he the Richard mentioned
on that brochure in Inanna's office? Or were the two of them planning
to meet with Richard? The tallest of the clowns wrapped his arms
around the shortest and gave him a puckery stage kiss on the cheek.
The shortest let out a shriek and pranced in a circle, hooting and
patting a hand to his mouth in a caricature of the stereotypical Indian
dance from classic westerns. Inanna smiled magnanimously but her
boyfriend's sickly grin suggested he'd rather be strapped to a pole for
torture. Several of the men standing nearby snickered.

As soon as the Koshare moved on, Inanna dropped a peck on the top of his head. He gave her a meaningful look and the two turned and walked toward the alley leading out of the plaza. Minoa watched for a moment, then followed. Exiting the plaza she looked up at the rooftops of houses, crowded with people sitting on folding chairs to watch the dance.

Among the black-haired Indians a splash of tangerine stood out. She squinted. It was Brereton, Sr. dressed in a tangerine polo shirt sporting reflective aviator sunglasses, holding binoculars. Was this one of the pueblos where he said he was working out a deal to supply equipment for a future casino? He lowered the binoculars and turned in her direction, but with the reflective sunglasses she couldn't be sure if he saw her. She lifted a hand to wave, just in case. It was a good sign that Georgia wasn't there with him. Left some hope she hadn't caved in and gone back to life as a house slave.

The couple wound along dirt lanes between facing blocks of houses, flat facades broken by occasional doors or blue framed windows. Through one open door Minoa spied a dining table with people crammed around it, the sounds of conversation, laughter and clinking pans drifting out into the still alleyway. She peered around each corner the couple turned, waiting until they disappeared before following.

Soon, passing a whitewashed adobe church with a wooden balcony above a carved door, she emerged from the pueblo. A dirt road led through an open area toward cottonwoods alongside the Rio Grande. Inanna and her fellow neared the trees. Minoa hurried after, passing a hand-scrawled 'no trespassing' sign.

On the other side of the sun-bleached field she glanced back. No one in sight except two figures who hurried behind the church. In the cool shadow of the grove she paused. Massive tree trunks surrounded, glistening canopies far above unmoving in the late summer afternoon.

She moved through the trees until coming to a clearing. A small adobe sat in the middle, shut up tight. She made a circuit around the house, hid behind a tree and watched. Soon a horse fly found her and dive bombed over and over. The hot air pressed down, ruffled every so often by a flicker of breeze that set the leaves above chattering. Boredom set in, followed by embarrassment. What the hell was she doing spying on Inanna and her boyfriend? That note on the brochure in her office had nothing to do with snake murder. It was a date. Was this what her search for a rattlesnake murderer had led her to?

The only sound was the tinkle of rippling water. She headed through the cottonwoods toward the Rio Grande, marked by a fringe of river willows. As a burst of wind tousled the branches above, she caught sight of movement on the far side of the trees. She stared. Nothing. Probably a fractured branch waving in the breeze. She passed a weathered picnic table, pushed through the willows and stopped at the river bank. The wide flow burbled, rocks here and there poking above the muddy brown current. On the far side of the river the land rose to Pajarito Plateau, a long flatland with a steep skirt scalloped by canyons. Rock strata from caramel to cranberry striped the cliff sides, iced by white volcanic tuff.

She sat down on a flat rock by the river's edge and stared at the water. Damn she felt tired. Almost tired enough to tumble into the water and just float, let the current carry her south, south all the way to Mexico. The water reflected nothing, concealed its own depths and incessantly fled. Why try to figure things out, why struggle to turn a string of freak incidents into some logical narrative where this causes that? Why couldn't she accept life as it was, haphazard, inexplicable, sometimes cruel?

Suddenly a rock pinged off a nearby boulder and ricocheted into the river. She spun around and caught another stone projectile on her cheek. Exclaiming, she clasped one hand over the injury and scanned tree trunks. She spied a couple of forms moving. One assailant stepped out to launch another rock at her. His silhouette, drawn by back-lighting from the sun-flooded field on the other side of the grove — stiff wedge of shoulder length hair, slight figure, wiry arms — was familiar. Amilcar. A ripple of distant laughter passed over her to lap at the current. He sounded drunk.

She jumped down to the water's edge and squatted behind a caved-out bank, cursing in a whispered stream. This idiot was attacking her again? She doubted he would stone her to death, but she didn't want to take another hit. He'd trapped her next to the river, cutting her off from the road back to the pueblo. Maybe if she ran downstream his drunken cussed self wouldn't be able to keep up allowing her to cut over to the entry road and circle back to the pueblo. She took a breath, then shot up and started running downstream. Out of the corner of an eye she caught sight of another man running through the trees, following her on a parallel trajectory. She estimated whether she could sprint to arrive first at the house where Inanna and Richard were but concluded she wouldn't make it. Within a few strides another rock hit her on the side of her skull, knocking her sideways to stumble into the river.

She fell onto hands and knees on pebbles in shallow water, splashing her front. Staggering to her feet, water dripping down her face, she looked back to see Amilcar jogging toward her, a demonic expression on his face. Without another thought she began sloshing across the river, wading long steps in sneakers that soon felt like bricks tied to her feet. The water level rose to her thighs as another rock skidded past and landed with a plunk in front of her. Risking a glance back she caught sight of Amilcar and Felipe at the river's edge, staring at her.

She picked up speed, striding through waist-deep water like a long distance skater. At mid-point the water surged to her armpits, lifting her feet off the bed. For a moment the current carried her, scraping her across a boulder, mashing her into another. She shoved off a third and maneuvered herself into shallower water approaching the far bank.

As she regained her footing, paddling with her arms, a rock grazed her shoulder. Reaching the bank one smacked her in the back of the head. She tripped forward a few strides, then bolted to the high water line. From behind a man-size boulder, breathing in spurts, she peered around. Amilcar was balancing on a rock part way into the milky flux. Felipe stood on the far bank. Without taking her eyes off them she extracted her phone from her soaking wet shorts pocket, swiped and glanced at the screen. It stayed dark.

After rubbing the back of her head she stared at her hand. The fingertips shone with blood. This was outrageous. If only her phone were working she could snap some photos to substantiate charges. It was time Amilcar did hard time for his evil behavior. But first she had to find a way out of here. She spun around to survey the plateau's skirt ruffling down to the river bank. Then scanned the wide curve of the river rolling south, calculating the distance to where the Los Alamos highway crossed over. The back road from Espanola to Los Alamos stretched across Pajarito Plateau a couple miles up, but getting there required scaling the cliffs. The bridge was farther away but terrain alongside the river would be easier to navigate.

She stepped out of her hiding place and started jogging downstream. Glancing to the side she caught sight of Amilcar wading farther into the river as Felipe ran downstream along the other bank. She pushed harder, dodging cypress branches and rock pile-ups. When she paused to catch her breath, she saw Felipe had kept pace and now stood staring across the river at her. At the bridge, he could cut her off from the front while Amilcar came up from behind.

What were these drunken bad boys planning? Were they vicious enough to cause her serious harm or just making a bunch of bad decisions about how to spend their weekend afternoon? Should she face Amilcar, try to take him out before Felipe could cross over? The thought didn't appeal so she cut right and sprinted up rising scrubland, weaving around yucca spears and prickly pear cactus topped here and there by fuchsia blossoms. As she veered into the mouth of a canyon, facing cliffs shut out all noise except the sound of her hoarse panting. She charged up the ravine to where the slope grew so steep she could use all fours without bending over. At the base of a rock face she paused on a lip of crumbled rock, peering out to the mouth of the canyon far below.

At this distance, Tewake plaza appeared filled with a carpet of insects. She saw no movement on this side of the river but the canyon walls narrowed her view. She heard nothing, no footsteps, no telltale rock kicked loose. Neither banging a thumb on the phone screen nor punching buttons produced any result.

She took off jogging along a lateral path of rock debris. Gaping holes pockmarked the rock wall; along the edge of one she noticed gridlines and glanced inside. Peaked piles of dust and fallen chunks of rock littered the floor beneath a soot-crusted ceiling. She glanced into other caves as she hurried along the ledge and all showed signs of human habitation. Above, the peachy cliff glowed in afternoon sunlight. Turning into a deep-cut ravine, still on the level path, she scoured the fold in the cliff to see if it might provide a channel to scramble to the mesa top. A vertical crack looked promising, but nearing she paused and blinked to clear her vision.

The crack wasn't a crack, it was a pictograph, a long zigzag figure with two lines sticking out of its triangular head, a giant symbolic depiction of Avanyu, the horned serpent. She'd seen the design on native pottery. Beside it climbed two vertical rows of holes gouged into the rock. That must be how the ancient cliff dwellers reached the plateau top but she wasn't about to try it. Cliff dwellers were phenomenal rock climbers who designed their cliffside dwellings to keep invaders out. She didn't like the idea of scaling a cliff clinging to indentations gouged out a few centuries ago, so she continued along the ledge out the other side of the ravine.

Beyond, a car-size fallen boulder blocked the path. She'd have to climb down the rock slide and look for another route up. Or maybe Amilcar and Felipe would have given up by now and she could hike back to the pueblo. She glanced down the slope to the band of juniper obscuring the valley floor from view. Something moved. Felipe stepped from behind a tree and stared straight up at her. Her nerve endings started ringing like a bell choir as she spun around and ran back down the path.

Coming out the other side of the ravine she spotted the cave dwellings ahead. As she jogged she focused on the ruffly incline ahead searching for routes, so she didn't notice movement on her left a split second before Amilcar leaped out of a cave to pose in front of her, lips crimped like barbed wire, dangling hands like claws. He locked hands around her forearms and hauled. She flung them every which way, twisting her wrists, trying to loosen his grip. He launched himself at her, levering an arm around her neck. She sank to a squat as if a trapdoor had opened below, freeing her neck. Launched a shoulder into his gut throwing him backwards and sprinted back down the path.

Reaching Avanyu she glanced back to see Amilcar stagger around the turn and trundle towards her, footsteps irregular. How had he pursued her this far in his drunken condition? He'd never be able to climb, or if he tried it, he'd fall. She stuffed a sneaker toe into one hole, grabbed another with her hand, and started pulling herself up. The handholds were decent, not as weathered as she'd expected. She felt like a four-legged spider and after a few moves sensed a thrill of excitement pulsate through her body. When she dared to look down she almost swooned. The basin, from the river across sage and bunch grass plains to a horizon lined by teal mountains, looked like a diorama sitting in some museum. Below, between the soles of her shoes and the valley floor, nothing but pure thin air shot through with the lowering sunbeams of a ripening afternoon. No sign of Amilcar or Felipe. She was breathing too hard to listen for sounds so she kept moving.

Near the top, handholds petered out leaving her to scramble over the crumbly edge on hands and knees. Once on top she stood and peered over the edge leaning out as far as she dared. The rocky slopes fell to the Rio Grande, its surface like molten bronze. The cars parked along the entry road to the pueblo had thinned. She shook her phone and when there was no response stifled an urge to hurl it over the cliff's edge.

Her eyes traced the plateau to where it curled up into the foothills of the Jemez Mountains. The back road to Los Alamos crossed somewhere up there. A flux of anger roiled inside. This wasn't an expedition she'd intended. How dare those two drunks attack her with stones like a couple of pre-teen delinquents? Maybe she should have confronted them. They might have backed down or run away, although Amilcar probably carried that hunting knife tucked into his sock everywhere he went. It didn't matter now. She wasn't climbing down that cliff. The only way out of here was to hike up to the road and flag down a ride to Los Alamos. The driver would probably lend her a phone to call her friends. What did Carter and Ireni think when she never reappeared by the plaza? They might have alerted pueblo officials about her disappearance, but they'd have no clue where she was. She shrugged, traced a mental route and started walking.

Chapter Thirty-Four

A fter striding through brush until her forehead felt damp and her lips gritty, a form emerged from a grove of spindly ponderosas up ahead. She froze, scrutinizing. As the figure approached she recognized Brereton Sr. Her mind started churning, trying to answer the question: what was he doing out here? He stopped in front of her before she'd come up with a good answer.

"I saw those two degenerates attacking you. I drove out on the back road to give you a ride. My car is up by the highway. I can take you back to the pueblo."

He turned around and started walking back toward the pine trees. She hesitated. Did this make sense? He had binoculars. The sides of Pajarito Plateau were visible from the pueblo. He could have watched her climb, seen Amilcar and Felipe following and decided to help by driving along the back road to Los Alamos, parking on the roadside and walking down to meet her. Didn't seem probable but here he was offering to help. It was better than hiking up to a little-traveled highway and trying to flag down a ride. She caught up and they walked side by side through vanilla-scented pines, emerging into a field of aromatic sage.

"There's something for you to see on the way." He flashed her a smile. "You studied ruins and stuff, right?"

"Actually it was anthropology. Live people, not artifacts."

He walked on without responding. Entering a clearing she spotted humps of weathered adobe walls, grouped in a half moon shape: an abandoned pueblo. A raptor screamed. She looked up, spotted a red-tailed hawk circling, herringbone brown body tapered to a fanned coral tail. It screamed again, a raspy cry that made the hair on the back of her neck stand up.

Brereton moved toward a circular wall in the center of the abandoned village so she followed. It was a kiva, in better condition than the rest of the ruin. Two log rails of a ladder protruded upward from a hole in the roof. The roof, at waist level, looked solid. Rungs of the ladder led down from the entrance hole, disappearing into the darkness of the subterranean chamber.

Atop the far side of the kiva wall she noticed painted sticks. She approached and picked one up. It was less than a foot long, dark blue with a couple downy feathers tied to one end by a cotton cord. Two others lay on the wall, one dark green, one turquoise, both with feathers tied on with a cord. Prayer sticks. She moved back to the kiva entrance.

"Very pretty. It looks like they're maintaining the kiva."

"Take a look inside. They fixed it up real nice."

She tried to peer into the dark interior but couldn't see much. So she stepped onto the ladder, lowered a foot to the next rung, then the next.

Suddenly a rain of black lava crashed onto her head knocking her down, down, all the way to the floor of the kiva. A cacophony of rattling broke out all around. Amidst roaring clouds of incomprehension she rolled onto all fours, struggled to her feet. Through the entrance hole above filtered a gaseous cylinder of light. Enough to see them. Rattlesnakes. Rattlers thicker than tree limbs and longer than a man.

One in a coil, its rattler uplifted and vibrating. Two others stretched across the floor, one with head lifted, tongue flicking in and out.

She grabbed the rails of the ladder and began scrambling. Nearing the top she looked up into the blessed circle of blue sky and saw Brereton staring down. His face contorted with rage, his eyes bulged. In one raised hand he clutched a rattlesnake. The snake's body curled up and down into swirls and curlicues. Their eyes locked, then he looked up and raised the snake high, calling out:

"For the lips of an immoral woman are as sweet as honey, and her mouth is smoother than oil. But in the end she is as bitter as poison."

He leaned over the ladder, thrusting the snake's head at Minoa. Its tail whipped back and forth, rattle vibrating. She backed down the ladder hearing frantic rattling below her feet, mind racing. Brereton was swinging the rattler back and forth so it slapped the sides of her head. She ducked and hung one way and another off the ladder to avoid it. He grabbed the ladder with one hand and shoved it back and forth. Though she locked her arms around the rails, her legs flew free to swing back and forth through the dark kiva interior, echoing the movement of the ladder. The head of the closest rattler jerked side to side following her movement.

When Brereton stopped jerking the ladder back and forth, she stood on a rung and looked up to see him staring down at her, the serpent suspended over her head. She noticed he wasn't holding it behind the head but part way down its body. Both halves of the snake curled in undulations forming fleur-de-lis patterns.

'*Bite him,*' her mind screamed even as she wondered if his careless pose indicated he had gained immunity to the venom from multiple bites or believed himself under God's perfect protection.

"And I will put enmity between you and the woman."

He hurled the snake down at her. The twisting snake body hit her head, slid across her face, undulated along her shoulders and slid down her back to fall to the dirt in a frenetic looping muddle. It untangled itself and raced over to the kiva wall. Looking up Minoa saw Brereton disappear and reappear with a thick stick in his hand. He thrust the point of the stick down at her like a plunger, forcing her to dodge to one side and another. The stick hit flesh a few times, making her gasp. She knocked the stick sideways until he lost his grip, dropping it to the floor of the kiva.

At that instant she scurried up the ladder, but just as she reached the point where she could see over the kiva roof to the surrounding pine forest topped by distant slate blue ridges, he swung a fist down onto her head. Registering a sensation of neck vertebrae smashing together, she tumbled backwards and whooshed to the kiva floor, bouncing her feet along the ladder rungs as she fell. Hit the dirt so hard it felt like a bomb had gone off in her brain.

She levered an eyelid open to see the coiled rattler rearing back its head. Reaching in her pocket for the prayer stick, she tossed it toward the snake which struck at it in midair while she triple-timed back up the ladder. Nearing the top she saw Brereton raising a fist. As the fist came down she plastered her body to the ladder rungs so the blow fell on her back. Then she shot upward like a spear to ram her head into Brereton's abdomen. He stumbled backwards, flapping arms to regain balance, and fell to one side.

She jumped from the ladder and took off running for the cliff's edge, balls of her feet barely grazing the earfth. She dashed through the field of sage and was entering the pine grove when she heard him coming, bellowing like a rampaging elephant. She careened around tree trunks, leaping over fallen logs, then emerged into the grassy area near the plateau edge.

As she sought the spot where the series of footholds down the cliff face began, she felt a hand claw her shoulder, then jerk her down. They fell to the earth, his bulky body on top. She struggled against the weight, the grip on her arms, but he was stronger. He sat on her thighs, knees trapping her arms, and wrapped his fingers around her neck. She squirmed trying to work an arm or leg free, but he smashed down harder. Her frantic eyes scanned his, bulbous in a blustery face, trained on her neck. Suddenly she couldn't breathe. She flopped like a hooked fish, survival chemicals scorching the walls of her arteries, black dots speckling her visual field. Into the wall-to-wall panic intruded a tiny simple thought like a child singing a nursery rhyme over and over: 'It's not going to end like this. It's not going to end like this.'

The thought stilled her mind enough that when he shifted, she jammed a knee into his testicles. Groaning, he tilted to one side enough that she pulled a leg free. She wriggled a hand loose and launched a fist into his nose. When he threw his head back, she pulled the other hand free and peeled his beefy fingers off her neck while pummeling his groin with a flurry of knee blows. He contracted enough that she twisted her other leg free.

She was up and running in a heartbeat. As she neared the edge of the plateau she heard him charging after. At the last moment, when a quick one-eighty would have allowed her to start down the cliff, a blow knocked her sideways. She fell face down, one leg slipping off the edge. Instantly scrambled on two hands and a knee back onto firm ground, rocketed up and took a stride before he wrapped arms around her like a malevolent bear hug. She wriggled and fought but all it did was force his grasp back to a fierce grip on both wrists. Then he started leaning toward the cliff's edge, dragging her along.

They scissored arms up and down as she dug in her heels against his relentless pull. She leaned backward toward trees, civilization, life while he dragged her toward annihilation. Though she resisted with every iota of strength she could muster, diabolical energy powered him. As he gained an inch for every smidgen she recovered, she began to accept the inevitable. She would fly through the air for a couple seconds and then crash onto rocks and die.

When he wound back for a final launch, betraying his plan to swing her in a half-circle and hurl her into midair, she noticed that the tilt of his weight rightward ungrounded his left foot. Then, as he hauled left, he shifted weight from the right foot. He wasn't aware of the imbalance. Why should he be? He hadn't spent years in a judo dojo, several hours a day, learning to detect minute shifts in an opponent's posture so the correct throw could be utilized to exploit that momentary weakness. He had never been trained to respond to such perceptions with a sweep of the foot, a forward thrust of weight, a spinning turn, simple movements that would convert that unguarded instant into a loss of footing, a crashing fall. He hadn't but she had. So despite the firestorm of panic, part of her brain remembered and saw and knew what to do.

When she flew past him she hooked a foot around his right ankle and jerked the foot out from under. Teetering sideways, his right arm released its grip too soon, leaving her left hand free to grab his other forearm in time to keep herself in orbit instead of flying loose into space. His reflex movements, his untutored instinctual effort to regain balance, loosened the grip of his left hand as she fell onto the cliff edge, legs hanging out into space, hands clawing at rocky dirt. But her survival tug on his forearm had jerked him forward, enough that he made an involuntary bow, stumbled and tipped over the edge. Body writhing in midair, arms spinning like pinwheels, he stared straight at her for an instant and then dropped out of sight.

She dragged herself onto flat ground and lay there on her belly, breathing in knife-edged blasts, head turned to stare into the azure-hued updraft rolling over the cliff top, fearing his Beezlebub face would appear at any moment. But no face came over the edge. So after a while she sat up, crawled over to the edge of the plateau and peered down. Below, on that rubble trail beside the ancient cliff dwellings, she spotted a tangerine blob, unmoving. Backed away, checked her phone, still dead, and stood up, hands balled, nerve endings jamming, squinting out into the distance. Few cars remained along the entrance road to Tewake Pueblo, the plaza showed patches of dirt between remaining groups of people. As the sodden sun swelled to bursting, sinking onto pointy peaks in the Jemez Mountains, a wave of crimson light flooded the Rio Grande valley all the way to the Sangre de Cristos on the eastern horizon. Light thick enough to choke on, dark enough to stain. She turned around and started walking upland.

Chapter Thirty-Five

A tomic bombs and rattlesnakes. Not much in common except they had both been used to kill people. Minoa sat staring out at Ashley Pond in downtown Los Alamos, renamed a few years back as the Manhattan Project Historical something-or-other. Naming a small town family park for the creation of a nuclear weapon sent a confusing message. Or maybe that was the point: make horrendous mass murder seem like a family affair. Streetlights bejeweled the pond's obsidian surface, illuminated a surrounding walkway. Empty now. Nobody strolling around the pond in the dark. She had a few minutes to think. Tried but her mind didn't cooperate. Three people dead, one murderer and two victims. Not counting the rattlers as murderers. It wasn't their fault they killed Dreema and the snake lady. They were just doing what nature made them to do. It was a human who encouraged them to murder.

Wait: she'd forgotten to count herself as a murderer. If Brereton was dead, that made two killers. Why hadn't she suspected Brereton? Her mind surveyed all the peculiar things she'd noticed about the rattlesnake attacks. In a neighborhood full of rattlers, in a house where a rattler had already gotten in once before, why would anyone suspect murder? Did Brereton place the first snake in Dreema's house as a murder attempt, only later horrified he'd almost killed his granddaughter? Or had the first snake intrusion been an accident that gave him the idea and the cover? Had he then held a rattler's fangs to his daughter's flesh or injected her with venom or simply turned a snake loose in her room and waited? They'd never know.

Yes, she'd found that snake cage. But Detective Martinez had been right that a snake cage meant nothing. Lots of people kept snakes for pets. Rich said he and his friends had played with snakes as kids. Delete that thought of Rich. Anyway, the desert outside the subdivision was no wilderness. Anybody could have dumped a cage out there.

What about the poor old snake lady? Felipe's deal with her had distracted Minoa from the possibility she sold snakes or venom to someone else. Venom was pricey, out of range for a rep for a gambling equipment company, so Brereton would have purchased a rattler. And although he might not know the difference between neurotoxic and hemotoxic rattlesnakes, the old snake lady did. She would have told Brereton the snake he purchased was neurotoxic. So it couldn't be that he exposed his daughter to a rattler to punish her with the suffering of hemotoxic envenonation, limbs swelling to the point of bursting and amputation, thinking that would force her to return to life as a docile pious woman. No, he planned to kill her.

Or maybe he procured rattlesnakes from one of his contacts at the pueblos. Could her theory about how the snake lady was murdered be wrong? Snakebite was an everyday hazard in her line of work. Maybe there was some other explanation for the broken window on her snake shed. There were lots of possible explanations for what happened and she'd never know which one was true. Brereton might even have stolen a sacred snake from that kiva. No idea if the rattlesnakes around Tewake Pueblo were neurotoxic. Did Brereton know of Inanna, of her connection to a member of Tewake Pueblo. of the rattlesnake she kept at her house in Pojoaque? Since he hated her, he might have figured a rattlesnake murder would throw suspicion on the cult leader his daughter followed who owned a giant rattler.

Why had she wasted so much time investigating Abiquiu, the Penitente morada, Don Juan Carlos' insinuations, the protest at the Santa Rosa festival? A complete wrong turn. She'd misinterpreted everything by letting her anger at Amilcar influence her, imposing her own agenda on what she saw. No self-respecting anthropologist would make that mistake, not that she was one anymore. All the while Brereton was watching her efforts to intercede in what he considered his family domain, watching Minoa convince Georgia to seek a protection order, file a civil suit, establish a life, divorce him. She'd been trying to help, sure, but so many self-righteous plans to help others went wrong for lack of insider knowledge, because some superior-feeling outsider made a clumsy intervention and ended up causing more harm than good. Another anthropological no-no.

Her thoughts U-turned back to her childhood, all the times she'd had a sleepover at Dreema's house, the two of them splayed on the couch together watching a TV show when Brereton came home after work or trying on clothes in Dreema's room and then sneaking out the window after everyone went to bed. And the other memories, why didn't she pay more attention? Like that time Dreema sat in the car putting makeup over a mark by her eye, laughing about a mug her dad threw across the room when she came out dressed in a mini-skirt and halter top. There were others like that, but Dreema always laughed and acted tough so Minoa laughed too.

She should have figured it out. Maybe not as a kid, but when she came back to Santa Fe nearly middle-aged with all her training in observing social practices and all that crap, she couldn't even read her own hometown right? Couldn't understand what was going on in her childhood buddy's family? Just like she never understood her own family. Like all kids, she'd thought it was her fault when her mom ran off, her fault when her dad drank himself into a stupor every night in front of the TV set. An unbearably painful thought so she'd left, tried to become somebody else. That hadn't worked either. Another failed trajectory. She'd gone to college and then spent her twenties and early thirties trying to fight her way into the elite club of college professors only to end up tending bar back where she started, leaving Dreema alone all those years with a series of violent men. Would things be different, might Dreema still be alive, if she'd kept in touch, asked how she was doing, even offered to help? Her lips moved, mouthed a silent vow: she wouldn't abandon a friend again, wouldn't leave someone in bad circumstances while complaining about her own difficulties.

Suddenly two people stood in front of the park bench where she sat.

"You doing okay?"

Carter hunched over to peer at her like an optician examining her corneas. Ireni sat beside her wrapping an arm around her shoulders.

"Is he dead?"

Minoa skewed her line of sight sideways to avoid eye contact.

"EMT's declared it. No pulse, no respiration, multiple injuries."

"It's awful you had to fight him."

Ireni patted her back.

"I threw him over the edge."

Minoa's voice was as monotone as a virtual receptionist. Carter and Ireni exchanged glances. Ireni's hair looked gray in the dim light, Carter's vanished into darkness leaving a pale oval face.

"He tried to kill you, right?"

"*Osoto gari.*"

"What?"

"Major outside reaping throw."

"Meaning?"

"I did a bad job of it, lost control. That's why he fell over the edge."

"You used a judo throw on him? It was self-defense. He attacked you, right?"

"If I'd had a better grip on his arm, I could have kept him from going over."

Carter sat down on Minoa's other side on the bench, peered around her at Ireni.

"She's traumatized."

"Let's pick up something to eat and we'll take her home."

Minoa looked back and forth at their faces.

"The police. I have to make a statement. They're waiting for me, right?"

"Uh, I didn't mention you when I phoned in the dude's accident. No use complicating things." Carter shrugged.

"The guy fell off a cliff. He wasn't supposed to be up there, was he? Reservation land. It's on him."

Ireni threw her palms up.

"I wasn't either."

"Listen, nobody knows you were up there except us three. And two of us only because you say so. You say you dropped somebody off the cliff? I don't believe you. Do you believe her, Reni?"

"No way. You went for a walk behind the pueblo, got lost and had to hike out to the highway. Lack of food and water and a touch of hypothermia make your perceptions unreliable."

"Well said, Reindeer." Carter glanced around the park, still abandoned, huddled closer. "Off the record, Min-min, what happened? Why'd you climb that mesa? Did he follow you?"

"I was running for my life from Amilcar. He and his buddy threw rocks at me."

Minoa felt her cheek, the nape of her neck. Couldn't feel a thing. Had she exaggerated the attack in her mind? Should she have faced them down instead of running away?

"Those bastards. Why didn't you call?"

"My phone got wet in the Rio Grande. Brereton must have seen what was happening with his binoculars. Or maybe he arranged the whole thing. He came around from the highway side to meet me. He must have been to that plateau before. He knew what was up there."

"What was up there?"

Carter and Ireni stared from close, eye whites luminescent reflecting streetlights.

"An abandoned pueblo, several hundred years at least. And a kiva full of ..."

"Full of what?"

"Uh, spirits. Howling spirits."

"Creepy."

Ireni hugged herself.

"Hey, maybe those native spirits shoved him over the cliff. BTW did he kill your high school buddy?"

"Yeah, and maybe an old snake trapper."

"But why?"

"He may have been mad that Dreema sheltered his runaway wife. He didn't like how Dreema was living. He blamed her for the bad stuff that happened to her. He had some extremist fundamentalist views on women and a history of domestic violence."

"Then he deserved to fall off a cliff." Ireni humphed.

"At some point he realized I knew his daughter's death by snakebite was murder. He might have suggested to his son that Amilcar caused Dreema's death hoping Berry would mention it to me and send me off on a wild goose chase. Or maybe Berry's rage at Amilcar after the knife attack led him to assume Amilcar killed his sister. Whatever their reasons I went along with it thinking up crazy theories about rattlesnake-handling cults in Abiquiu. I never did connect Brereton Sr. to Dreema's death."

"Maybe, but if you hadn't tried to figure out who killed his daughter, he would have gotten away with it," said Carter.

"Yeah, and he's been punished so justice is served."

Minoa turned to Ireni.

"Justice? Luckily Scott will survive and the old snake trader knew she had a dangerous occupation that could kill her. But poor Dreema who never hurt anybody is dead."

"We have to take whatever justice we can get," said Carter. "It's damned hard to come by in a world run by greedy violent men."

Ireni gave Carter a nudge on the shoulder.

"Focus, Ms Marxist Cheerleader. This is not the moment for your political speculations."

"Speculations? This has nothing to do with Marxism. And how about all the millions of murdered civilians from resource wars all over the planet? Who do you think did that? Greedy violent men."

Minoa raised her head and gave Carter a look. Carter straightened.

"Okay okay. The important thing is no one will associate you with some white dude falling off a cliff near Tewake Pueblo. It's on him for wandering away from the tourist zone."

"Amilcar saw me."

Carter jumped up and faced Minoa.

"He ... he knows you went up there?"

Her voice whined upwards.

"He followed me to where I scaled a cliff to the top of the plateau. I don't think he climbed up but he could have seen me push Brereton over the edge."

Ireni tapped Minoa's leg.

"Wording, Minoa. The man fell."

Carter shook Minoa's shoulders.

"Listen to me. From below he could only have seen a man falling off the cliff. An accidental fall. Period."

"I looked over the edge."

"He would have had to look up at the right instant to see you."

Carter glanced up to demonstrate.

"He was drunk."

"Perfect. No one will believe what he says anyway."

Ireni switched to patting Minoa's leg.

"Maybe Minoa should report it to police, just to be safe. Once they determine it was self-defense, she'll be clear of all problems."

Carter flashed Ireni an expression of horror.

"Are you kidding me, Miss-head-buried-in-a-calculus-text-book-since-you-were-twelve? I'm the one who's been arrested multiple times. You do not want to trust police to come up with the right explanation. They might need Minoa to fill the private prison company's detention quota."

Ireni ignored her.

"How did the fight with Brereton start?"

"He said he would give me a ride back but instead he led me to some rattlers."

"Rattlesnakes?"

"This has to stay between us. Promise."

Carter nodded at Ireni.

"Got it. You want us to promise we won't tell anyone you saw one or more rattlesnakes on Pajarito Plateau? Top secret information. Makes sense."

She rolled her eyes at Ireni to signal 'crazy.' Ireni responded with a tiny 'who knows' gesture.

"Yeah, perfect sense." Carter continued with a sarcastic tone. "Los Alamos is a top secret lab, right? Those reptiles could have spied some classified research. Probably planning to sell it to a Russian or Chinese operative."

"I was trespassing on Tewake land, intruding on their customs and beliefs. I didn't have any right to see those rattlers."

"Not that I understand why we're promising to keep rattlesnakes secret, but isn't that what anthropologists do? Observe other people's customs?"

"I don't know anymore what they do. But if I were to reveal where I saw those snakes, it would bring unwanted publicity to the pueblo."

"Does this have something to do with that article you were going to write?" said Ireni.

"I'm not in academia anymore. I can't pretend to be a disinterested observer. There would be real consequences if this were revealed."

"What about revealing that bastard murdered his own daughter with a rattlesnake? Shouldn't you reveal that? Otherwise he got away with it."

Ireni hit a fist on her thigh.

"Rain-rain, the man's dead. So what'd he get away with?"

Carter clicked her tongue.

"People should know. Truth matters."

"I'll tell Dreema's mom. Nobody else cares at this point."

Minoa's voice trailed so low it was hard to hear.

"Minoa needs to recover. We'll talk about it all later." Carter sounded like a kindergarten teacher. "Let's get her a nice meal and home to bed."

"Upsy daisy."

Ireni sing-songed as if calming a mental patient. She and Carter made little encouraging noises as they pulled Minoa to her feet.

"I need to see Georgia."

"Sure you do."

"Later."

They herded her up the slope to Carter's car.

Chapter Thirty-Six

When Minoa drove down the winding county road south of Santa Fe, she missed the turn for Tierra Feliz. Somebody had forgotten to turn on the floodlights illuminating the adobe wings and Kokopelli statue at the neighborhood entry. Pulled a U and drove back, squinting into darkness out the side window. Stars above, stars below. The words flashed across her mind as she spotted what looked like a small constellation of stars, maybe the Pleiades, fallen out of the sky onto the desert floor. She turned and drove toward it, busting the cluster apart into a scattering of house lights.

Georgia let her in the door without meeting her gaze and shuffled back into the living room in those same fuzzy slippers. She sat down in an armchair and clicked off the TV.

"How is Aracely doing?"

"She's fine. Would you like a soda?"

She stood up.

"No, please sit down. I have something to tell you."

Georgia sat back down and waited, palms on thighs, face bland.

"I have some bad news. Brereton died."

The only change was a widening of the eyes.

"I have to tell you something else. It's important that you know. Brereton tried to kill me. And he killed Dreema. And another woman as well."

She smoothed the stretchy pants across her thighs.

"He did?"

Minoa suppressed the urge to grab her by the shoulders and shake.

"He used rattlesnakes to kill people. He must have loosed a rattler into Dreema's bedroom. Did you have any idea he was comfortable handling snakes?"

Georgia's eyes veered to the side and stuck. She moved her lips as if gearing up to speak but nothing came out.

"I'm sorry, Georgia, but this ruins the basis for a wrongful death suit. Still, the lawyer could bring a class action suit on behalf of Tierra Feliz residents for substandard construction. You might get some kind of settlement."

Georgia continued to stare at a vase of roses wilting beside the huge TV screen.

"Georgia, I realize this is an awful shock, another death in the family on the heels of ..."

"It's my fault."

Her posture turned mushy as if someone had taken hold of the spine and deboned her with one pull. When she looked at Minoa the sagging lower lids revealed pinkish inner rims.

"In no way is any of this your fault, Georgia. I'm telling you so that you don't pity Brereton."

"Maybe I should have told you."

She dropped her gaze to where her fingertips were pinching folds of pink stretchy fabric on her pants, pinch, pinch, pinch.

"Told me what?"

"Back in Tennessee where we grew up, Brereton's dad was a pastor in one of those snake handling churches. When we got married and moved out west he made me promise never to tell anybody. He said people out here would think he was a stupid hillbilly if they found out."

"What? When Dreema died of snakebite you never suspected him?"

"Of course not. She was his daughter. He loved her ..."

Her voice drifted off. She stood and walked over to the sliding glass door. To Minoa it reflected the scene in the living room, sliced through with shards of blackness, minus Georgia's blanked-out silhouette.

"It's my fault my precious Dreema had to die."

She hit a fist on the glass, hit again and again. The blows grew heavier and turned to pounding. With each blow the glass quaked with a muted 'humph' like someone punched in the gut. Minoa stood.

"Georgia, please."

"Noooo ..."

The word dragged out into a keening wail. Her fist slid down the glass and she dropped her forehead against it like a weight. Then pulled back and slammed her head against the door. Over and over. Minoa took long strides to her, grasped her shoulders, hauled. But a crazy power surged up Georgia's body. She broke free, flinging her arms, shot back to the glass door and hammered her skull against it as if trying to crack open the cranium and pulverize the brains.

"I want to join my precious baby! I want to join my Dreema!"

Minoa wrapped her arms around Georgia's waist and leaned back hard, but Georgia kept screaming and beating her head.

"Please take me, Jesus! Please take my soul!"

She smashed her forehead into the glass and left it there, then slid down to hang from Minoa's arms. After a moment Minoa released her and she crumpled onto the carpet. A couple hopeless dry sobs convulsed her before she went quiet. Minoa stood there, waves of feelings coursing up and down her body to crash into each other in a hollowed abdomen. She shoved her balled-up hands into her still damp pockets and stared out the glass door at darkened desert vanishing into deep space behind a faint overlay of her own face. She couldn't feel the soles of her feet. Her voice, when it came out, scraped her throat.

"You've got Aracely to take care of, Georgia."

Georgia twitched all over like someone was poking her with an electric shock cattle prod, then dribbled out some words on either side of 'Amilcar.'

"He can't have her. He's violent. He attacked me. He pulled a knife on Berry."

Tiny choked protests filtered up like bubbles through water.

"Georgia, you're going to have to cope. There's nobody else."

Minoa grasped her arms and pulled her most of the way to her feet. Her body felt like a burlap bag full of old vegetables. She stood there with knees half-bent, back humped, neck crooked, eyes splayed. Blood smudged her hairline. Contradictory impulses wracked Minoa, one part panicked concern, another part so furious she had to use willpower to keep from slapping those sagging cheeks. After a moment Georgia's eyes focused and then spasmed as if she were falling backwards into a bottomless pit. Minoa clamped arms around her, held on tight. Georgia rigidified, went limp, laid her cheek on Minoa's shoulder and stayed there so long, unmoving, weight dragging, that Minoa wondered if she'd gone to sleep. She finally backed off, padded over to the couch and lay down, closing her eyes. Minoa pulled a folded crocheted quilt off the arm of a chair and spread it across her.

She walked down the hallway to an open doorway and stepped inside. Spotted a lamp on a chest of drawers and turned it on. Aracely was sleeping on a twin bed with an ocean-themed quilt, cute little colored fish with long eyelashes smiling like a fashion shoot. She glanced in the closet, pulled open a drawer. Clothes neat and ordered. Aracely's twining locks splayed across the pillow. Her cheeks puffed with the endearing fleshiness of childhood. Through her parted lips came puffs of air that Minoa could just hear if she held her breath. Apart from a few memories—running into a rattler in the bathroom, getting hit by her dad, losing her mom—she'd probably grow up okay. It was possible to lose your mom and have a dad with problems and still grow up okay, right? Right. She walked out, glanced at Georgia lying on the couch. Saw the eyelids tremble. She wasn't asleep, just hiding. She'd face up to her fate soon, she'd be forced to no matter how she tried to avoid it and bewail it. Everybody had to.

THE END

About the author

EA Mayes grew up in New Mexico hiking mesas and mountains, avoiding rattlesnakes and sunburn. After college she bounced around Latin America, then had jobs building solar greenhouses, bonding people out of jail and court interpreting. She obtained a doctorate in Comparative Literature and taught at several colleges. She's ghost written books for clients like a mafioso in witness protection and an indicted spy. Now she writes murder mysteries and a Substack newsletter on crime fiction.

Check out http://eamayes.com for information on New Mexico Noir titles and loads of related New Mexico curiosities.

Subscribe to Mysteriousities https://eamayes.substackto read in-depth original articles exploring crime fiction in today's world. and find out what's coming next from New Mexico Noir.

About the Author

Excerpt from Gavilan Mesa, the second New Mexico Noir novel

"... first-degree murder, a capital felony punishable by up to life imprisonment without parole."

Valeria's head swung around to scan the gallery. Her pageboy hung in clumps, her cheery smile fractured. Reporters outnumbered spectators in the courtroom. Looked like the local news media viewed the alleged murder of a multimillionaire by his undocumented nanny as prime headline fodder.

Catching Minoa's eyes Valeria injected a transfusion of terror and agony into her soul before a deputy forced her to turn back to the judge. The public defender sat beside her, bald head as shiny as the polished wood defense table. At the other table sat two District Attorneys, combined ages about the same as Valeria's lawyer. The judge, a fierce-faced suburban dad, did the arraignment without looking at the paperwork.

Valeria threw one more visual SOS to Minoa before being led out a door in the back of the courtroom. Minoa staggered into the hallway, collapsed against the wainscotting, choking on emotion. Footsteps across the marble floor roused her.

The PD was walking down the hall. She hurried over and stepped in front of him.

"Look." She put up a hand like a stop sign. "I'm Valeria's friend and I want to know what's going on with her case."

His eyelids puffed. He handed her a card.

"You can call my office to make an appointment."

He continued walking, scuffed Oxfords slapping the floor. She took a few long steps, positioned herself in front of him again. They both stared. He motioned at a door.

"Alright, we can talk in there."

Once inside the client conference room he shut the door, folded into a chair and squinted at her from the far side of a bony sternum.

"What is it you'd like to know?"

She glanced at his card.

"Here's the first thing I'd like to know, Mr. BieglerL does she have a choice as to which Public Defender she gets?"

He leaned back his head, bald but for a ring of steely survivors, and roared, revealing a mouthful of browning teeth. By the time the head came back down the expression was clamped tight and calculating, the defense attorney poised to begin arguments before an unpredictable jury.

"Listen Ms.?"

"Diamond."

"Ms. Diamond, I've defended hundreds of people accused of homicide and, given the fact that the majority were indubitably guilty, my record is incomparable. I may be able to get a deal for your friend that lowers the charge to second degree homicide or, with some mitigating factors, maybe even manslaughter."

"Deal?" She smothered a scream. "She doesn't need a deal. She's innocent!"

He gave her a world-weary look.

"Maybe she is. Nevertheless she's facing a first-degree murder charge."

"But how can they possibly think she did it? She just started working for Brent Harrison as a nanny. It makes no sense."

"The discovery process is revving up but here's what we know so far. That bottle of mescal that killed her investor boss was saturated with rat poison and had her fingerprints all over it."

"Rat poison?"

"Opened sack of that rat-killer was found in the garage and is now in state's evidence along with a pair of her panties."

"Her panties?"

"Yes, her panties that are being analyzed for residues of her boss' semen. She mentioned a sexual encounter to the cops. But don't get your hopes up they're going to write this off as one of those abuse victim self-defense cases. The DA sees 'unwanted sex' as an excellent motive for premeditated murder. And everybody knows poison is a woman's murder weapon of choice."

She tried to breathe and failed. A fog of panic engulfed her senses as her toe seemed to touch empty space at the edge of a promontory.

"But ... even if he raped her that doesn't mean she poisoned him. Brent Harrison was a rich and powerful man who must have had enemies. If they look into his affairs, they'll find loads of possible suspects."

"Any suggestions?"

"Well, he was contemplating the purchase of a large tract of land that many people don't want developed."

Biegler's Marx Brothers eyebrows twitched as if he was suppressing a chuckle.

"So some historic preservation aficionado found out and sent him poisoned liquor?"

He stood. Minoa struggled to speak.

"Wait. Valeria has immigration problems. She's out on bail after being detained by ICE."

"Most people south of Airport Road have similar problems."

"So even if she gets released, she may be deported."

"She'd probably rather be sent home on a jetliner than sit around here in jail. Maybe I can use that in the negotiation process."

He picked up his briefcase.

"I think something terrible happened to her in El Salvador. That's why she fled."

"Are you suggesting mental impairment?"

"Maybe PTSD?"

"We'll request a mental health evaluation."

He walked to the door. She gathered herself, shot up out of her chair.

"Stop talking about negotiations and evaluations. She didn't do it and you have to get her off."

A touch of sympathy mellowed his wizened expression.

"I'm simply trying to convey to you, Ms. Desmond, that I can try to bargain down the charge. Manslaughter carries a six-year max. That's a lot less frightening than life without parole, isn't it?"

"It's Diamond, Mr. Bugler. Why don't you focus on defending her innocence instead of selling her out from the get-go? I'll be in touch, you can count on that."

She swirled past him, jerked open the door of the conference room and hurtled down the hall and stairs. Outside, confronting the razor-edged sunshine, she squeezed her eyes shut to ward off a burning sensation as if acid were squeezing out of her tear ducts. Within the spinning hurricane of emotion she felt herself slipping down down down into a dark hole. What was already terrible had just gotten worse. Rape as Valeria's motive to murder Brent? For a millisecond she wondered if it could be true, if Valeria had felt so enraged by Brent's assault yet gagged by her circumstances that she filtered poison into his booze as an act of revenge. Maybe she'd only wanted to make him sick. Maybe ... Stop, she screamed at her thoughts. Valeria didn't poison Brent. But who did?